DEMITRI

SMALL-TOWN ROMANTIC SUSPENSE

ROCK HILL
BOOK ONE

CM SMITH

Publisher: Lots of Pages, LLC

Cover Design: CM Smith

Editing: Brandi Zelenka, My Notes in the Margin

Proofreader: Linda Pichler

ISBN: 9798308607328

 Created with Vellum

CONTENTS

Dear Reader ix
Russian Words xiii

Prologue 1
Chapter 1 5
Mia
Chapter 2 13
Demitri
Chapter 3 21
Mia
Chapter 4 29
Demitri
Chapter 5 39
Mia
Chapter 6 47
Demitri
Chapter 7 53
Mia
Chapter 8 63
Demitri
Chapter 9 71
Mia
Chapter 10 79
Demitri
Chapter 11 89
Mia
Chapter 12 95
Aunt Linda Texts
Chapter 13 99
Demitri
Chapter 14 107
Mia

Chapter 15   115
Demitri

Chapter 16   123
Mia

Chapter 17   131
Demitri

Chapter 18   139
Fom the Text Messages of Demitri and Joker

Chapter 19   143
Mia

Chapter 20   151
Demitri

Chapter 21   161
Mia

Chapter 22   171
Demitri

Chapter 23   179
Mia

Chapter 24   189
Demitri

Chapter 25   197
Mia

Chapter 26   203
Demitri

Chapter 27   213
Text Messages From Everyone

Chapter 28   219
Mia

Chapter 29   229
Demitri

Chapter 30   237
Mia

Chapter 31   245
Text Messages from the guys

Chapter 32   249
Demitri

Chapter 33   257
Mia

Chapter 34   265
Demitri
Chapter 35   275
Mia
Chapter 36   283
Demitri
Chapter 37   291
Mia
Epilogue   301
Bonus Epilogue   309
Bonus Bonus Epilogue   315
Mia's Drink Recipes   321

Aiden   323
Also by CM Smith   325
Acknowledgments   327
About the Author   329

My name is Demitri Pavlov. My father was the head of the Bratva for the east coast. He ruled the area with an iron fist, bringing in drugs, women, and murder. I wanted nothing to do with it. When he died, the family fell apart. I had freedom for the first time in my life.

I've learned not to trust anyone. Finding someone who shares that philosophy? Who wants no strings and no commitment? And a desire that matches mine? Perfect.

Mia Alexander fit the bill for all of my fantasies. She wanted the same things I did. Her own past creating invisible chains around her heart.

After breaking my own rules and falling for Mia, she's in danger because of me. I'm being pulled back into the life I fought so hard to leave behind. And they will use Mia against me if they have to. Because I'm never going to be truly free. My name ensures that.

But I'll be damned if Mia is hurt because of me.

I'll make sure the world burns before that happens.

My name is Demitri Pavlov. And I will protect what is mine.

DEAR READER

Thank you for joining me on our journey to Rock Hill, the little town on the range of Briar Mountain. If you read the Briar Mountain series, you've met the women of Rock Hill and might have some idea of what I'm going to warn you about here. If you haven't, just know I come at it with humility, humanity, healing, and some humor.

Our heroines have been through some things, and while I don't dwell on their past, it's part of their story and will be talked about. Prepare yourself for their stories of SA, toxic relationships, abuse—both mental and physical, as well as their journey of healing. I was also told I need to warn you there might be some torture of our poor hero, like broken bones torture. I hope their stories can give those of you who are going through something similar hope for a better future.

I've included information on how to contact a number of different services on the next page for those who need help or want to learn how to help others.

Stay well and healthy, my friends.

—CM

Resources

For those that need help or want to learn how to help others, please see the information below:

Domestic Abuse Hotline: National Domestic Violence Hotline -- 800-799-7233

Sexual Assault: Rape, Abuse, Incest, National Network (RAINN) -- 1-800-656-HOPE (1-800-656-4673)

Suicide Prevention Hotlines:

988 - Suicide and Crisis Lifeline (The old number will work indefinitely; it is 1-800-273-TALK [8255])

1-800-784-2433 (1-800-SUICIDE) - National Hopeline Network

1-866-488-7386 (1-866-4.U.TREVOR aimed at gay and questioning youth)

Substance Abuse:

National Council on Alcoholism and Drug Dependence (NCADD)-- 1-800-622-2255

Partnership for Drug-Free Kids -- 1-855-DRUGFREE or text your message to 55753

Substance Abuse and Mental Health Services Administration (SAMHSA) -- 1-800-662-4357

Mental Health: National Alliance on Mental Illness (NAMI) 1-800-950-NAMI (6264) www.nami.org

DEDICATION

This one is for Dr. Jen Greenberg.
Woman, you did the damn thing and I am so fucking proud of
you, Dr. PhD! Brava!
I also want to dedicate this to the survivors. The ones who have
fought every day to become strong—mentally and physically.
The ones who are still going.
And the ones who might need a shoulder to lean on to get
through the day. Know that I will be your shoulder.
You are worth it.
You deserve the wins.
You are perfect just the way you are.
And may you one day also have perfect orgasms—multiple and
squirty.

RUSSIAN WORDS

Babushka—Grandmother
Bratt—Brother
Dedushka—Grandfather
Da—Yes
Dyadya—Uncle
Krasotka—Beauty, Gorgeous
Malenkaya Sestrichka—Little Sister
Moya Lyubov—My Love
Ledi—Lady
Malenkyi—Little One
Otetz (Formal)—Father
Plemiannik—Nephew
Plemiannica—Niece
Poshyol te Nakhuy—Fuck You
Printz—Prince
Sestra—Sister
Suka—Bitch
Tupaya Suka—Dumb Bitch
Za Tvoyo Zdorovye—To Your Health

PROLOGUE
MIA

LEFT FOOT.
  Right foot.
  Deep breath.
  Pace yourself.
  The goal is five miles today.
  You can do five miles.
  Left foot.
  Right foot.
  Deep breath.
  Feel the burn, embrace it.

"Fuck!" I yell, stumbling over a stick in the path. "Fuck you stick!"

Running is supposed to make me happy. Supposed to release some endorphins or shit like that. I've been running for five years. Still waiting to be happy about it. But the gym doesn't work on bar-owner schedules, and as my mom's voice continues to reminds me when I have feelings of inadequacy,

I'm not getting any younger and my figure isn't going to last forever.

That would be one of many reasons I don't talk to her anymore.

Left foot.

Right foot.

BAM!

"Oof!" a male voice grunts as I make contact with a hard chest.

"Fuck," I grunt in return, because I don't bounce off the hard chest. His arms are bound around me, holding me up.

"You alright?" the man asks.

I don't respond, instead I try to get away. I pull at his arms, but they don't move. I try to take a step back, but there's nowhere to go.

"Let me go," I demand.

"Hey, it's alright. Just making sure you're okay."

"I'm fine. Let me go."

But it's too late. It's not this man holding on to me, but another. He's a man I've been afraid of coming after me for over ten years. The eyes staring at me? They aren't the crystal blue of this man. They are cold, brown, and want to hurt me.

"Get off of me! I won't let you hurt me again!" I yell, pushing at his chest.

"I'm not—"

"Shut up! I'm sick of your lies! I know you want to hurt me. It's all you ever do!"

"Mia!" he yells back. "Mia, it's me, Demitri!"

"No. No, you're lying. Why are you lying to me? Get away! Stop touching me! You'll never touch me again!"

I hit his chest with my fists, trying to push him away, but he doesn't move.

"Mia," he says in a low voice. "I'm not touching you."

"But…" I trail off as I realize he's right. His arms have dropped from around me. He's standing still as a statue, but he's not coming for me. I'm the one who's clinging to him.

"I'm sorry, Mia. I'm sorry someone hurt you, but that wasn't me."

"Demitri?" I whisper, finally focusing on the man in front of me. "I know you."

He nods, his face a mask of worry and pain. "You know me."

"I thought—"

"It's alright. I know what you thought. And it's okay. I swear I'm not going to hurt you."

I take in the man in front of me, with his piercing blue eyes and tall frame. His body that's strong without looking like a meathead. And while he's gorgeous, it's always his face that makes me *feel*. And right now, after attacking him for being someone from my past, I just have to get away.

"I'm sorry, I have to go."

Without another word, I turn, but he reaches out and grips my hand—gently. Always gently. In all the ways I need him to be, at least.

"This isn't over, Mia. You know that."

"I don't know what you want from me."

"I want your friendship." He moves closer, leaving space between us. "I want your body." His free hand rises to my face, where he lifts my chin to look at me. "I want you to see me when I give you pleasure and make your body quiver."

"Dem…I don't…"

"Doesn't matter. You know I'm right. You know we aren't done. You know you still want me. We can do it on your terms. But we will do it again."

I shake my head, but even I know I'm full of shit. I do want him again. And that terrifies me.

"Tomorrow night." He grins, knowing I won't turn him down. "I'll meet you at closing."

With that, he lets me go. What am I getting myself into?

CHAPTER ONE

MIA

TUESDAY NIGHTS at the bar are usually quiet, but tonight we have a group. They're taking up like three tables in the corner of the room, and they are serious about their drinks. They are also serious about their business.

One thing people forget about is the helpers—bartenders and owners—hear everything. We know so much about what's going on in the towns we live in that we could write a book on broken promises, sins, and even the happy moments. These guys have been coming in for a few years now. I know they run a security company together and that they also plan and execute rescues of people needing out of bad situations. As someone who could have used their help once upon a time, I usually give them a discount. It's something I can quietly do to let them know I appreciate it. I know Daniel, who runs the thing, and his wife Victoria, but I don't know the others' names. Just their drinks. Beer.

I only know Victoria and her husband because of my own personal past. I have a shared history with her sister Lizzy.

"Hey, Boss," Brodie calls from the window between the bar and kitchen. "Food's coming up. Want me to take it out?"

"Nah, I got it."

Brodie has been with me for a little over six months. College kid, hard worker. He's adorable in an annoying little brother kind of way, but I know he's going to break some poor girl's heart one day. He's reaping the rewards of working at a bar next to a large college campus. He gets action more than I do—or did. I haven't been taking anyone new home with me lately. Thinking about the why makes my stomach flip.

Demitri Pavlov. Well, he goes by John Smith now, has been hiding in plain sight for over a year, working in a garage that restores custom cars and bikes. He goes up to Boulder Canyon quite a bit working with some guys up there who run a garage, trading parts and talking shop. I've been with him a few times, but only because no one forty minutes up the mountain range will have any idea who I am. I'm nobody. And whatever this thing between Demitri—or John—and me is, it's not for public consumption. It's a secret. And something about that makes it even more exciting.

I carry the food to the table. "Here you are, round one of food." I smile, placing the appetizer plates on the table. "Will there be more joining you tonight, or is it just you six? Also, you're new?" I point to a good-looking man sitting with the regulars.

"I'm Sam Carmichael, ma'am." He dips his head in greeting.

"Well, I'm Mia, not ma'am," I sass to the laughter of the guys. "This is my place, so let me formally welcome you to City Brews."

"Thanks, it's a nice place."

"Sammy here is PD over in Briar Mountain." Victoria smiles. "And we have a few more meeting us here tonight."

"Yeah? Other women? These guys look like they could use the company." I hitch my thumb at the other three guys. "Sam, I don't know you well enough to know if you need company yet, but I know they're always here alone. Unless it's some odd relationship where you're all with her?"

The comment gets the reaction I'm hoping for, the new guy, Sam, laughing until there are tears in his eyes, the other three guys unconsciously covering their dicks, and Daniel looking like he's ready to go scorched earth if someone even looks at his woman too long.

"Oh, that's funny," she laughs. "But honestly, they couldn't handle me. Even if they tried at the same time."

I fist bump Victoria while the guys get their shit together. The door opens, and a woman comes in. Daniel stands from the table, walking over to her. They share a very platonic hug and he brings her to the table, where everyone seems to know her. So, not a naked partner for the lonely boys.

"Welcome to City Brews," I greet her. "What can I get you?"

"Just a beer. I'll share their pitcher." She looks at everyone, daring them to argue.

"I'll grab a mug and an extra plate." I wink at her and make my way back to the bar.

Not twenty minutes later, the door opens again and two more people walk in, sharing a very indecent kiss at the entrance. Makes me sad that I'll never have that, but I get over it quickly. I don't *want* that. Never will. That's not what my life has in store for me. And I know the line. If I keep telling myself the lie, maybe one day even I'll believe it.

I keep an eye on the group, giving them time to say their hellos before I take the new pair's order, and smile to myself when they start congratulating the couple and passing hugs around.

I make my way back to the table, smiling when I genuinely welcome them. "Couldn't help but overhear. Congratulations, lovebirds. I'm Mia, this is my place. Welcome. What can I get you to drink?"

"Thank you." The new woman smiles in return. "How about something fruity and frozen?"

"Oh, that sounds good," Victoria adds. "Make it two."

"Beer's good," the man says.

"And more food," another adds. "Whatever we can all share."

"That would be amazing," the first guy replies. "Need to keep my strength up, you know."

I laugh, leaving the table to put in the orders to their groans and laughter. I get to work mixing up a pineapple concoction I know Victoria likes, hoping the new girl likes it too, and tell Brodie the food order. They look deep in conversation, so I give them a few minutes before I carry the tray their way. When I get closer, I can't help but overhear the conversation, and it makes my blood run cold.

"Ivan Pavlov. Katya Sokolova is his illegitimate daughter. And chatter on the street is she's looking to take her place as heir and ruler of the Pavlov Family. She wants to revive the Bratva."

All the men sit in silence, Victoria looking like she wants to throw up. Another looks like she wants to rip apart the building. What I don't plan for is my own body freezing up, the tray slipping from my hands as the glass, liquid, and ice all land on the floor. Nine sets of eyes turn to me with various degrees of shock. I stare back, knowing I look like a deer in headlights, willing my brain to work.

The first thing I think is what comes out of my mouth. "You have to tell Demitri."

"How do you know Demitri?" Daniel asks.

"He's a customer," I reply quickly. Too quickly.

"I'm going to call bullshit on that," the new guy says.

"I'm sorry, but who the fuck are you? You're sitting in my bar and accusing me of lying?" *Shut up, Mia! Now they all know you're full of shit!*

"Official introductions." Victoria stands, making her way around the table. "My husband, who you know, Daniel." She pats the top of his head, and he gives her an indulgent smile. "He owns ANON, a security company with these smartasses —Aiden, Grady, and Nate." She pats each head respectively as she moves around the table. "This is Sammy, who you met earlier, a cop over in Briar Mountain. This is Mary, an old friend of ours who works in an agency I'm not sure you're supposed to know about, so I'll leave that up to her to tell you. This is Joker, who works with those yahoos, and this is his new wife, Ginny, who plays the cello like you wouldn't believe. Guys, this is Mia. Now, how do you know Dem?"

"Maybe I should be asking you how you know him?" I fire back, defense always my best offense.

"He's a friend of mine," she assures. "And these guys, they just want to make sure he's safe. Do you know where he is?"

It hits me then that they don't know how to get in touch with him, or that he's living here under a different name. I have the power here, which makes me both happy and worried.

Daniel comes to stand next to me, putting his hand on my shoulder. When I flinch, he immediately drops it, and I can see in his eyes that he understands why he shouldn't touch me. Victoria whispers something in his ear, and he grimaces before giving me a knowing look. Victoria knows, and now it seems Daniel does, too. Maybe I should get a fucking shirt that announces '*Hi, I'm Mia, and I was in a horrible abusive relationship where he beat me and raped me for two years before I could get away when he almost killed me'* and make it easier for everyone to know my trauma.

"You're family, Mia," Victoria quietly says, squeezing my fingers, somehow knowing that touch is okay. "Lizzy is my sister."

I nod, the memory of the trial coming back. "You've always known it was me."

She winks in response and takes her seat again.

"We need to find Demitri," Daniel tells me again. "He might be in danger and not know."

"So call him," I hedge.

"We would if we knew his number," Aiden replies. "He disappeared after the last mess he had to get involved in, and we've lost all contact."

"What you say next will determine if you ever get a drink in here again," I tell them, my voice stronger than I feel. "What kind of danger is he in?"

"The kind that involves his family," Aiden replies. "And I'm not trying to be vague or obtuse or anything. We don't know the danger, we just know there *is* danger."

I stare at the man, deciding he's being completely honest with me. His face is wide open, his eyes shining with an earnestness you don't see often, and I nod.

"You don't even have to give us the number," Daniel offers. "Can you get ahold of him and see if he can meet us here tonight? And if he can't tonight, sometime soon?"

"I can do that. I'll be back."

I turn away before I lose it, grabbing my phone from under the bar and sending a text.

Mia: There's a group of men here who need to talk to you. Claim to be friends.

Demitri: They give you a name?

Mia: Daniel, Aiden, Grady, Nate, and
Daniel's wife, Victoria.

Demitri: What the fuck do they want
with me?

Mia: They think you're in danger.

Demitri: And how are you wrapped up in
the middle of this?

Mia: I heard your family name and dropped
the drinks. I didn't mean to. I'm sorry.

Demitri: Don't apologize. They were talking
about me?

Mia: Yes.

Demitri: Did you get a little protective over
me, Mia?

Mia: Not talking about that. What do you
want me to tell them?

Demitri: We're going to talk about it,
eventually. You know this. Tell them I'll be
there soon.

Mia: Come in through the back.

Demitri: Yes, ma'am.

I put the phone down and raise my head to find all the
eyes on me.

"Give it twenty," I tell them as quietly as I can. I scan the bar, taking note of the handful of other patrons, but they're all sitting too far away to hear anything that might have been said.

Daniel mouths a 'thank you' and we go back to acting like the last ten minutes never happened.

And we wait.

CHAPTER TWO
DEMITRI

I TOSS the phone onto the couch beside me and run my hands through my hair. What the fuck could the ANON guys want with me and what danger could I be in? I've been living under the radar for years now and have stayed out of the way. The shit with my family? Doesn't involve me. The day I walked away and turned on everything I always knew was the last day I had anything to do with them.

"Fuck!" I yell into the empty room.

I stalk to the bedroom and drag on a pair of jeans, an old t-shirt, and grab my leather jacket before shoving my feet into my work boots and heading out of the front door. Plus side of having to leave? I'll get to see Mia tonight. Wasn't supposed to, but I'll take it. I hop in my old work truck and make my way to the bar.

After parking at the back of the building, I slide in through the back door and pull a ball cap low on my head. Just because I haven't been spotted before now, doesn't mean I shouldn't be careful. I check the place before stepping from the back hallway, taking note of everyone in the place. I pause to appreciate Mia standing behind the bar, looking like her jeans have been painted on, her long, dark hair pulled back, showing the perfection of her face. Wonder if I could talk her into a non-scheduled night of fun?

Shaking my head, knowing I'm a fool, I slip onto a barstool. I smile at Mia.

"*Krasotka*." *Gorgeous.*

"Hey." She eyes me warily. "They're over there." She tips her chin in the direction of the group.

"Big crowd."

"Yep."

Without a word she sits a shot of vodka in front of me and makes me a water. I slam the shot and pick up the water. "Thanks. I needed that."

"Yell if you need anything," she whispers, a smile playing on her lips as she eyes me up and down.

"I'll do that." Standing, I tap my knuckles on the bar and turn to face the music.

I slowly walk to the table and pull out the empty chair obviously waiting for me. No one speaks as I sit down and put my glass on the table. I finally look up at everyone, clocking the faces and names I know and the ones I don't.

"What's up? Wanna tell me why you dragged me out at ten at night on a Tuesday?" I might only be thirty-three years old, but six a.m. happens early.

"We got some news," Daniel starts, and I notice he's trying not to be his usual asshole self towards me. That's new. Ever since he found out I knew his wife, he's been about a fraction of a second from trying to kick my ass. The guy might be jacked, but I'm scrappy. Had to be in the life I grew up in.

"Okay."

I sit and wait for them, not offering anything of my own until I know it's needed.

"It appears you've got a sister."

"Yeah, she's in jail. Where I'm guessing she still is, since no one has notified me differently."

"She's still in jail," he confirms. "But it looks like you have another sister."

"What?"

"Do you remember a maid by the name of Polina? Would have been about twenty-five or thirty years ago."

I close my eyes and think back. We had a lot of staff in and out of the house growing up, women from Russia moving through. Polina? That one rings a bell. She was my father's personal maid. Beautiful. She was there one day and gone the next, and my father was on the warpath for months after. Yeah, that tracks.

"I remember a Polina."

"She was more than a maid," Grady speaks.

"She was one of my father's whores."

Aiden nods gravely, confirming what we all know already. My father was not a good man.

"And when she found herself in the unfortunate situation of being knocked up by my father, she had to disappear. What happened to her? And since I'm sure she's not the only spawn running around, why is this one so important?"

"Because we think she's trying to revive the Bratva."

My stomach drops at the idea. "No." The word is out before I realize it, and I'm not sure who I'm talking to—them or myself. I can't help but look to the bar and Mia. I look at the people around the table. "She can't do that."

"Whether she can or can't doesn't really matter, does it? The fact is, she's trying. And has some support," Grady points out.

"Fuck."

"We're still looking into it," Mary, who I know is DEA,

offers. "We know she was involved in a rash of high school overdoses recently."

"Wait, that was her?" I ask, astonished. Everyone in the state has heard about the high school athletes overdosing during games or going crazy at school.

"Partially." I turn to a man I haven't met before. "I'm Joker," he offers. "This is my wife, Ginny. She was working with someone, and now she's gone rogue and solo."

I look at the woman sitting next to him. She's quite beautiful, and I've seen her face before. "The music teacher?"

She smiles. "That's me. And I'd really rather not talk about it, if you already know what happened?"

"Works for me." I shrug. "You're amazing with a cello, by the way."

"Fuck yeah, she is," Joker mutters under his breath, and if I'm not mistaken, it's Ginny who kicks him in the shin under the table.

"So, why are you telling me all of this? How do I fit in?"

"You got the inheritance?" Daniel asks.

"I got the legal money, sure. But even more was taken by some alphabet office."

"Not mine," Mary offers, smirking at my choice of words.

"That legal money is still more than most will see in their entire lives. And we think she wants it. She needs the capital now that her partner is no longer involved. She needs money to get the support from others that might be waiting for just this moment to come back from hiding." Nate, who's been quiet this whole time, finally speaks, looking directly at me.

"And she needs the name to make that happen. More than money, she needs the name," I mutter.

"Which means she needs you to prove it."

"As long as you're alive, you're a threat to what she wants. Which means you aren't safe," Daniel adds.

I rub my hands over my face, trying to clear my head and think.

"Does Aunt Linda know?" I finally ask. Aunt Linda, who knows all, who has a direct line to the President of the United States, who knows how to use every firearm ever made with exact precision, and who is a fucking vault when it comes to secrets, is who met with me when I gave up my family to the feds. Also, don't ask how I know she has the direct line to the President. I can keep secrets, too.

"Figure that's our next stop," Daniel says. "I'll set it up and let you know."

"What are you going to do?" Aiden asks.

"I'm not gonna do anything until we know more. I can't put my life on hold for a possible threat that we don't know more about."

"Stay safe out there."

Out of everyone sitting at this table, Aiden understands the most. He knows what it's like to have family ties and loyalties you don't want but can't get rid of.

"Yeah, I'll try."

"Maybe you should think about not staying home for a few days? At least until we can get something set up to keep you safe?" Grady offers.

Unconsciously, I flick my eyes at the bar. Mia's standing there, talking to another customer, making a drink, completely oblivious about the possible trouble she could get into just for knowing my name.

"I'll work on that. Let me know what you find out."

"We would if we had your number." Aiden smirks.

"You aren't smart enough to get it on your own?"

"Guess we could always ask our favorite bartender for it," Nate challenges.

"Fuck you," I growl at him. "She stays the fuck out of this, understand?"

Nate looks at me, not offended at all, and shrugs his shoulders. We both know they will all come back here if needed to get in touch with me, now that they know Mia has my number.

"Give me a fucking phone." I hold out my hand. Aiden, trying to hide his smirk, pulls his out and hands it over. I put my contact in and text myself. "There. Now one of you has my number."

"I'll talk to Aunt Linda in the morning and call you," Daniel promises.

"Perfect," I reply, unable to hide the sarcasm in my voice.

I stand from the table, leaving my untouched water behind, and sit on a stool at the bar.

"What's going on?" Mia quietly asks when she's standing in front of me.

"Seems like I have family drama."

Her eyes widen, and she takes an unconscious step back.

"Are you in danger?"

"I don't know, but until we can talk to someone tomorrow, they think I need to find a place to stay for a few days."

"Is it that bad?" She chews on her bottom lip—her tell that she's nervous, or afraid.

I shrug, not wanting to lie to her. Anything with my family is usually bad news. I watch Mia as she works something out in her head. She makes her decision, then reaches under the bar and pulls out a keychain.

"Go to my house."

I've been working for a year to get an invitation to her house. It only takes my life being under threat to get that invite. Huh.

"Are you sure?"

"Yeah, go to my house. I'll close up here as soon as I can and meet you there."

"Need to swing by my place and pack some things."

"Whatever you need for a few days. It'll be fine."

Not sure who she's trying to convince, but I'm not going to give her the opportunity to change her mind. I rap my knuckles on the bar and leave the way I came in—through the back.

This is gonna be interesting.

CHAPTER THREE
MIA

I WATCH Demitri walk down the back hall to leave the bar, and all I can think is I've just fucked up in the worst way possible. He's never stayed the night at my house. Hell, he's never been past the living room. That's not the kind of relationship we have.

"You look like you either just made the biggest mistake or the best decision of your life," Victoria quietly says from across the bar.

"What? Oh, no, I'm fine."

She rolls her eyes at me, a small smile on her lips. "You can tell yourself that all you want, but you can't hide what others see. You care for him."

"Of course I do. He's a friend."

"Mia, that man is more than your friend."

I'm shaking my head before she's finished. She puts her hands up in surrender.

"You know it's alright to have feelings for someone. In fact, it can be quite liberating to give over to those feelings."

"I don't have feelings. Not anymore."

She nods, an understanding in her eye I don't see very often. "It might feel like that, but you do. I know you do."

I stare at her, not willing to say anything else and give myself away. I refuse to admit the truth, even to myself most days. She finally gives me a sad smile and taps the bar, turning back to her boys, as I've heard her call them before. Daniel stands and pulls her into his body for a quick hug and kisses her forehead before they both sit down.

Demitri. Tall, strong, and all man has invaded my thoughts since the first time I met him, right here in this bar with most of the same people.

FOUR YEARS AGO

"Looks like you all were serious over there." I smile at the man standing in front of me.

"Yeah, you could say that. But they're done with me for the night."

"Get you a drink?"

"Shot of Beluga Gold Line if you have it."

I raise my brows at him. "Well, aren't we fancy? Afraid the best I can do is Beluga Noble."

"It'll have to do."

I look at the man in front of me. He's hot, I'll give him that. Tall, lean but solid, blond hair that just begs to be grabbed, lips that are just a little too plump, blue eyes that look like they can see into my soul. But he doesn't look like he's comfortable in his own clothes, even if those are a pair of faded jeans and a t-shirt with what looks like a burn hole in the hem.

He also doesn't look like someone who could afford the expensive top-shelf drink he just requested.

"So, you from these parts?" I ask as I pull out a shot glass and find the bottle of liquor.

"Isn't that my line?" he quietly returns.

"Touché." I grin, pouring his drink and sliding it across the bar.

I watch him as he checks out my bar. It's nothing spectacular, but it's clean, spacious, and mine.

"So, I'm guessing you named the bar after you? Mia's?"

"Yeah, I'm thinking about changing it, though. Bars are supposed to have *'manly'* names like Pat's Place or Jim's Juice, or something like that."

"What are you thinking about changing it to?"

"I'm not sure yet, but something that screams alcohol, you know?"

"How about Rock Brews, so you have the city and the beer?" he asks.

I scrunch up my nose. "Eh…"

"Maybe not?" He smiles, and my knees damn near give out.

I can't speak, but I shake my head.

"City Brews?" he offers, an almost shy and hopeful look on his face.

"Huh. City Brews. You know, I don't hate it," I smile at him. "That's going on the list, for sure." I pull out one of the many pens I end up wearing in my hair every night and write it on the notepad next to the register. 'City Brews' has possibilities, that's for sure.

"Does it earn me a Beluga Gold Line next time?"

"Next time? Is there going to be a next time?

"If there's good Russian vodka, there will be."

I give him another shot and move to take care of a customer. I make eyes at my friends who have been sitting at the end of the bar staring, openmouthed, at me since I served the man. I don't even know his name, and I can't figure out if that's a good thing or not.

When I'm finished with my customer, I check on the table mystery man was sitting at, and they are ready to close out their tabs. They slowly trickle out after paying, but Mr. Vodka stays.

"Who is that man?" Grace asks when I finally make it back to the corner they are sitting in.

"I don't know," I whisper. "Didn't give me his name."

"You had a really long conversation to not get his name," Sofie points out.

"Guess it's Beluga. Or Gold Line. That's what he ordered."

"I'd go with Vodka if those are your options," Nola snorts.

I roll my eyes. "Alright, white wine spritzer," I point first to Sofie, "and Sex on the Beach," I point to Nola. "Want to tell me about those guys you were making eyes at earlier?"

Sofie's cheeks go red as Nola looks away, avoiding all eye contact.

"Didn't think so."

"She has to flirt with the customers to get the tips. We know this," Grace tries to save me.

"Okay, yeah, but she was really flirting with Beluga boy. The woman was almost drooling over him." Nola smirks. "Think she'll take this one home?"

"Alright, ladies. I'm cutting you off for the night. I let you sit here and drink my booze and ogle men all night and this is the thanks I get? You calling me out? Doesn't work that way, sisters."

They know I'm bullshitting them, and their dramatic sighs and eye rolls are all part of the act. I'd love to say this is the first time we've done this, but it's not. As a matter of fact, this is pretty much an every time they are in here occurrence. They also have no idea who I've taken home with me.

They all wave on their way out the door, and I turn back to the man of interest tonight.

"Another?" I ask, wiping down the bar in front of him.

"Depends."

"On?"

"If you're going to keep calling me Beluga."

I smirk, pulling out the bottle and pouring him another shot. "Depends."

"On?" he asks when I slide the shot his way.

Our hands brush as he reaches for the glass, and I know I'm in trouble when I physically react to his touch. I pull my hand back quickly, and he notices but gives me a pass.

"On if you tell me your name."

"Do you need my name?"

"I do if I'm taking you home tonight."

I know it's a challenge. A dare. Will he take the bait or not?

He throws back the shot and closes his eyes, savoring the afterburn. When he opens them again, there's a fire within the blue, and I know I've won. *Act unaffected,* I tell myself as I wait him out.

"Demitri. Demitri Pavlov at your service."

"Mia Alexander."

I stick out my hand. Another challenge, and he doesn't fail. He pulls my knuckles to his mouth and brushes his lips over them, an electric tingle racing through my entire body.

"Nice to officially meet you."

"It'll be even nicer with no clothes." I smile before walking away to make more drinks. His low laughter hits between my legs and I know he's leaving with me tonight.

PRESENT DAY

"Hey, Boss. Not sure how long it's healthy to stand there and not blink."

I'm brought back to the present by Brodie waving his hand in front of my face, a dopey grin on his.

"Shut up," I chuckle.

"Let's go. It's been a long night, and I gotta go see a girl, if you know what I mean." He waggles his brows dramatically.

"Yeah," I laugh. "I know what you mean. Get on out of here. I'll lock up. Thanks for your help tonight."

"See you tomorrow!"

He's gone before I can reply, and I can't help but smile after the kid. Kid? When did I become the old lady? Fuck, I'm only thirty-one years old.

I look at the engraving on the bar top, running my fingers over the words '*City Brews*' and close my eyes, taking a deep breath. It's because of my Beluga Boy that I leveled up. It's because of him that I'm in the black every month and not worrying about keeping the lights on. Everything good in my life is because I met him one random weeknight. And I can't tell him. I can never tell him how thankful I am to have him in my life. How big of an impact he has on everything around me.

I pull out the bottle of Beluga Gold Line and pour myself a shot. Letting the liquid slide down my throat, the afterburn smooth and a little sweet. There's vanilla in this, which is why I had the cheaper bottle four years ago. I purchased this one the day after I met Demitri, and the only people who have ever tasted this bottle are him and me. And that's how it will stay until the last drop.

After putting the bottle away, I clean the shot glass and wipe down the bar one more time. I pull the cash out of the register along with the card receipts and head back to my office. After a quick count, I bag the cash and put it in the safe for the night. The receipts I put into a file to deal with in the morning, and I turn off the lights. I double check the doors and walk through the now dark room and down the hallway. I step into my office long enough to grab my jacket, purse, and keys before locking up the back door and walking to my car.

It's time to go home. Time to go to Demitri.

CHAPTER FOUR
DEMITRI

WILL I ever tell Mia that I've now searched her entire house and learned all her secrets? No chance in hell. I want her to tell me her secrets. I want her to fucking *want* to tell me her secrets. And, more importantly, there weren't any to learn. Her house is fucking spotless—and impersonal, just like she wants the world to think she is. It's a small two-story, and until I snuck up there tonight, I've never been upstairs. I wonder if she's got cameras in the house? There are no pictures on the walls, no photo albums, no notebooks or journals, nothing on the fridge. Even her bookshelf is weird, with all the books facing in, so it's just blank pages shown. She might be a little psycho for that, and I should probably be worried about staying here.

Not going to change how I feel about her, though. That ship has sailed, and yeah, I know that makes me pathetic, okay? Deal with it. I never wanted to scale her walls—just her body. But then I started talking to her. And not only is she stunning and beautiful and has an ass that can make a man fall to his knees, she's so fucking smart, and funny, and sarcastic. She deals out shit better than anyone I've ever known. When she comes home after a long night at the bar and puts her hair up and those librarian glasses on? I'm a teenager trying not to jizz in his pants. She is what fantasies are made of. All the fantasies.

So, I've let her string me along for four fucking years. I've taken her drips and scraps and lapped up every little bit of her she's let me, and I'm addicted. When she forgets that her walls are steel covered in concrete covered in brick and shows me the cracks? I live for those moments. They don't happen often, and they never last long, but they are worth every agonizing hour of waiting.

I've pulled a faceless book off the shelf and discovered it's a paranormal romance about the four horsemen of the apocalypse and settle in to read. Yeah, I read romance books. Knowledge is knowledge, people, and I've learned some of the coolest shit from these books. I've also picked up a few moves, not that Mia would ever let me try them. At least not yet.

I don't know how long I've been reading when I hear Mia pull into the driveway. But I don't put the book away. I might be completely under her spell, but I have some self-respect—and the book is getting really good.

"Evening, dear." I grin, looking up at her when she comes through the door. "How was your day?"

"Smartass." She huffs out a laugh, dropping her oversized bag on the floor by the couch before falling into the cushions. She rolls her head, looking at me. She's exhausted but fighting it. "Finish all your snooping already?"

"Unfortunately. No salacious diaries or naked photos in the bedside table. I'm really disappointed."

"You didn't look hard enough."

"You weren't going to be gone long enough for me to test the floorboards."

"What're you reading?"

"*Obsession.*" I hold up the book for her to see.

"Ahh, that's a good one." She winks at me and sits straight up on the couch. "Well, come on Beluga Boy, let's go to bed. You have to be up in the morning, and this wasn't a scheduled evening."

I jolt at her words. And completely glitch. Bed? Like, a bedroom? Upstairs?

She looks at me, her forehead crinkling in confusion. "You alright?"

"To bed? I figured…" I trail off. She sighs and closes her eyes. Not in an irritated way, but in a lost the war kind of way. Her shoulders drop, her fingers fidget with the edge of her shirt. I stand, moving until I'm standing just outside her personal bubble. "Mia," I say quietly. "I can sleep on the couch. You offering to let me stay the night is more than I thought you'd do, so the couch is fine, okay?"

Without opening her eyes, she raises her head. "I don't want you to sleep on the couch, Dem."

"What do you want, Mia?" I inch closer.

"I want you to tell me what happened tonight, but I can't stay vertical while you do. So, you're going to go upstairs with me and we are going to slip into bed and you're going to tell me a nighttime story."

"I'll come back downstairs when I'm finished if that would make you feel better?" I offer.

"It wouldn't matter," she mutters to herself.

"What wouldn't?"

"If I scream, you'll hear it no matter where you are."

The statement is like a gut punch. Nightmares. The woman has nightmares and is afraid of screaming in the middle of the night.

"My only question is what do I do if you start throwing punches?"

Her lips quirk up on one side. She's trying to hide her smile but failing miserably.

"Guess it's a good thing I don't do that, isn't it?"

"Yet to be determined."

"So you coming or not?" she asks, opening her eyes and finally looking at me. I don't know what I see in them, but I'm not capable of saying no.

"Lead the way, *Krasotka*."

Without another word, Mia turns and walks to the stairs, not pausing before ascending them to the master bedroom at the top. I follow silently, grabbing my overnight bag from beside the couch. She points to the hallway bathroom before turning into her room. I guess that's my sign to stop there first. I hear the water in her en suite turn on through the wall and take my time changing into a pair of flannel pajama bottoms and a clean t-shirt. The thing with Mia is to always prepare, but never assume. If something happened between me leaving the bar and her getting home, her anxiety would have been triggered. But then she would have come through the door ready to swing at someone. I have no expectation, but I brush my teeth and put some fresh deodorant on before leaving the bathroom.

Mia is already sitting up in bed when I hit the door. She's wearing one of my old t-shirts and has her hair piled high on her head, all of her makeup washed off and those fucking glasses on her face. She's beautiful. She also has a no bullshit look on her face. No sex. Got it.

"Do you have a side?" she asks as I walk into the room. "Of the bed?"

"Not particularly. The middle?" I smile, going to the empty side.

"Ready to talk about it?"

"No. But I don't know that I'll ever really be ready to talk about it."

"But you will? With me?"

"For you, I'd do anything."

It's not until the words are out there that I realize how true they are. I love this woman. And if I could ever rid myself of the shackles of my last name, I'd throw all pretense out the window and swear my life to her. But I can't do that, and I guess she finally needs to know the full story why.

She's staring at me, not talking, chewing her bottom lip. I reach over and pull it free. "Don't hurt yourself because of me, *Krasotka*. I'm not worth it."

"Fuck that, Demitri."

"Mia, you don't understand. All my life, I was a tool. A pawn. A chess piece in a game I never wanted to play. People treated me special because of my last name, because of my dad. They didn't understand why I had issues with what I saw going on around me. And then they tried to destroy me to keep me in my place."

"What happened?"

Closing my eyes to try to shield myself from the pain, I blow out a breath and begin. "I don't know how much you know about my family, but my father was Ivan Pavlov, the leader of the Russian Bratva on the east coast. He was not a good man. Drugs, guns, women. That was his life, and he bought and sold everything with the blood of others. One of my first memories is my father hitting my mother because she told him no. She had just given birth to my sister and ended up with a c-section. The woman couldn't even stand up straight and he thought he owned her and could use her as he wanted."

"Oh."

One word, said with so much meaning behind it, I can feel her pain.

"If this becomes too much for you, tell me to stop. Please."

"No. Keep going."

"After that, they lived as a married couple only. I know my dad regretted what he did, but not enough to do the right thing. Mom stayed because she knew he'd never let her take me with her. I was a boy. My dick guaranteed I'd never do anything of my own free will." I can't help the bitterness in my voice, but I continue. If I don't get it out now, I don't know if I'll ever be able to. "Mom died a little every day. He slowly killed her by flaunting whatever side piece he was fucking that week in front of her. By the end, she was a shell of the mother I knew when I was little."

"How old were you?" Mia asks, whispering. Like speaking loudly would change the way this tragedy ends.

"I was fourteen. My sister was eleven. But where I wanted nothing more than to run away from that place and that life, she craved the attention my father didn't initially give her. She paid attention and soon became his right hand. If it were up to my father, he would have found somewhere to hide my body, but some of my uncles didn't believe in women running the show. And none of the other men working in the *business* did anything more than treat women as their property."

"I'm sorry."

I give her a small smile before continuing. "I tried to run away when I turned fifteen. I thought I was a man then. Ivan beat me to the point of hospitalization when they found me. It was while I was healing that I met Mika and fell in love. With her and cars."

I pause to take a breather. This is the hard part, the part that reminds me why I'm okay with the parts of Mia that she's willing to share with me and don't push her for more. More would put her in danger. More would put a timeline on her life, and I can't do that to her. Or me. Because I know I'd never survive.

"Tell me," she quietly demands.

"Mika's dad was on the payroll. Vasili worked on all the cars the family owned. Turns out, the garage he worked out of was a front for my father. All he ever wanted to do was work on cars and not get sent back to Russia. His wife was born here, and he was afraid, as were some of the others who had been here a long time. Anyway, he started taking me to the garage and showing me how to do some basic stuff. Mainly, I handed him tools while he did the work. But I started picking up things, and before too long I was doing oil changes and basic mechanical tasks. I started learning about custom rebuilds and my first car was a sixty-nine Dodge Dart Custom. It was this hideous baby poop brown, but that thing was a fucking tank Ivan had lying around the property, so Vasili helped me restore it and paint it."

"Sounds like he really cared about you, Dem."

"Yeah, he did."

"What happened?"

"I was working with Vasili one day in the garage and this girl came in wearing a school uniform. You know the one—plaid skirt and white button up blouse. Her socks went to her knees, and she had brown penny loafers on. Her hair was dark, dark brown, long and straight, and that day she had it pulled up in a ponytail that bounced when she talked. She stopped by to tell her dad about a test she aced that day, and I was hooked. After that, she would stop by almost every day, and eventually I gathered up the balls to ask her out."

"That's sweet." Mia has a wistful smile on her face, like she's reliving her own first love story. Only I know how that one ends, and it's almost as tragic as mine.

"It was. Until my father got wind of it. Her 'Russian stock' wasn't Russian enough for the heir of the Pavlov family. He demanded I break it off with her before I did something stupid like 'fall for the girl.' He threatened me, he threatened Vasili. He beat the maids to let me know how serious he was, but I didn't care. I loved her. We were going to get out and never come back. Until she didn't."

Mia reaches over and silently grabs my hand. She knows the sweet is about to become scary.

"We had plans to go to the movies one Friday night, and she never showed up. Vasili disappeared from the garage and some other guy, one of Ivan's stooges, started coming in and keeping an eye on me. I had more guards around me at all times. Fuck, I couldn't even piss in peace. But I found ways around them. I had lived in that house and hidden from my father more than they knew, and I snuck out every night trying to find Mika."

"Did you find her?"

I shake my head slowly, the pain resurfacing in my stomach. "No. And it wasn't until my father started making these passive comments about my future and any future women I would be with that I knew he had done something to her. As punishment."

"What did he do, Demitri?"

"He sold her."

My voice is raw, barely audible, but I know she heard me when I hear her intake of breath. I can't look at her, not with the guilt I carry with me every fucking day.

"Dem, it's not your fault."

"Yes. It is."

"No. It's your father's fault, and you had no control over him or what he did. You were just a fucking kid, for God's sake. Fuck. I'm so sorry."

"That's not all of it, Mia. She's dead. And it's all my fault. Because I loved her, she's dead."

"No." She shakes her head almost violently, cupping my face and turning it to her. "No."

I close my eyes and all I see is Mika's body, beaten, used. Too thin.

"They knew I was close to finding her. He fucking killed her because I almost found her. And he sealed my fate and made sure I'd never try to leave again."

"But you did."

"It took years, Mia. Years of watching and waiting. Knowing things that he did to other people. How can I not be just as dirty as he was? I...I did things, too."

"You did what you had to do to survive."

We sit in silence for a few minutes, neither of us knowing what to say now that my pain and shame have been unleashed into the room. She finally looks at me, but I don't see pity. I see determination.

"What happened tonight?"

I tell her about the theory that I have a sister and how I think I probably have more than one. When I'm finished, she nods her head.

"Then it's settled. Until you can talk to this Aunt Linda, who I'm going to need to meet, by the way, you're staying with me. Here."

"I can't put you in that kind of danger, Mia. I just told you what those people are capable of. If this is real, and they are looking for me, you'll be in their way. I can't have you be collateral damage."

"So you'll just disappear again like you did four years ago? Ghost and leave me in the dark? For how long this time?"

"I—"

"No. I'm a fucking adult, Demitri Pavlov, and I make the decisions about my life. Not you. Not your family, who may or may not be a threat. Me. And my decision is to help you. To fight with you. *For* you. Do you understand?"

CHAPTER FIVE
MIA

SHUT UP! Shut up! Shut up! What the fuck are you doing, woman?

"Mia." The way he says my name snaps me to attention. "No."

"Yes. No one knows you're here. You're safe until we can figure shit out. Deal with it."

He chuckles, his shoulders vibrating with the motion, and he shakes his head.

"Stubborn woman."

"Yeah." I'm not going to argue with that.

"What a fucked-up pair we make."

"I don't think we're that bad. Trauma bonding at its finest, right?"

"Why do you always do that?"

"What?"

"Make a joke about it. You went through hell, Mia, and nothing about it is funny."

"If I don't laugh, I cry. If I joke about it, I own it. If I own it, nobody can hurt me with it."

He jolts on the bed like I just struck him, his eyes reflecting the pain that is always in mine. He opens his arms to me, a physical touch I only allow a select few to offer, and I willingly settle on his chest while those strong arms wrap around me. Comforting me. Holding me. Keeping me together.

"One day, Mia Alexander, I'm going to get you to tell me your story. More than the jokes. More than the broad brush strokes."

"Maybe one day I'll be ready to do just that, but this isn't that night."

He knows the basics. What was in the news. He knows someone who was supposed to love me abused me. He knows I finally broke out and got free. Physically, anyway. But part of me also knows that he's aware I'm still a prisoner mentally.

He kisses the top of my head and holds me tighter, only letting go to pull the covers over both of us. "Sleep, *Krasotka*. I'll watch over you tonight and make sure the bogeyman stays away."

His strong heartbeat and even breathing lulls me into a deep sleep. One free of screams and memories.

I'm not sure how long the sun has been up, but it's way too bright when I open my eyes, and I realize I forgot to close the blinds last night. Demitri is still curled around me and I wonder if he has to be at work today. If he does, he's late, I know that much. But I guess that's what happens when you're up until almost dawn, unleashing all the pain in your soul. This beautiful, damaged man has been through so much, and I don't know how to help him. I don't know if I'm capable of helping him.

He's right, I have my own trauma. And the only place I

talk about it is with my therapist and the group of women I've surrounded myself with who all experienced some version of the same thing I did—with the same fucked-up asshole. He's also right that one day, I need to tell him all about it. He deserves to know—he's earned it. But I'm afraid. I'm afraid if he knows, he'll walk away. And for as much as I keep him at arm's length because I have to, the thought of him walking away forever crumbles my already shattered pieces. He's the first man I've allowed myself to be with more than once since, well, since the fucked-up asshole.

I feel his arm tighten around me, and I'd be an idiot to not feel the erection along my ass. Demitri's awake.

"Your entire body is primed to flee," he mumbles.

"It's getting late, I think. Don't you need to go to work?"

I try to pull away, but his arm is a vise grip around my waist. I check in with my body to see if I mind the closeness, and find I don't. Huh.

"I texted them last night after you fell asleep. No rush today. You needed the sleep."

"We can't just stay in bed all day. I have shit to do."

"You know, you can only bullshit a bullshitter so many times, Mia. I know you're running. I'm pushing my luck right now because I don't want to move away from your body. But I've learned your limits, *Krasotka*."

I open my mouth to argue, but I don't want to. I'm tired of arguing. Of fighting.

"I don't know what you want," I finally tell him.

"What I want and what I need and what I'll take are all different things. What I should do is get up and walk out of this house and never come back."

I jolt at his words but feel him shaking his head on my shoulder. He's not done.

"What I want to do is roll you over and touch you, but I know you can't let me. What I need is for you to realize that this thing? The thing between us? It's more than fucking, and it always has been. What I'll take is whatever parts of you that you can give me."

"I think it's too early for this conversation, Dem."

He chuckles, his body lighting mine up where he moves against it. If only he knew he was the only man to make me *want*.

"I know. But we're still going to have it. And you need to know the only reason I'd walk away is to keep you safe."

"What if walking away broke me more than any physical harm could?"

He finally removes his hand from my waist, but only to lift it to my face and tilt my chin until I'm looking at him. The vulnerability I see in his eyes reflects my own, and I know whatever happens this morning is going to change things.

"I'd never willingly walk away from you, Mia. Please know that."

"But you might have to," I whisper.

"If this shit starts to go sideways, yeah, I'll have to walk away. For a while, anyway."

"Like last time."

"Just like last time. I came back, came back to *you*. As soon as I knew it was safe." He takes a deep breath and continues. "I couldn't stay away."

"Demitri," I breathe out his name. It's a prayer, a request.

"We aren't getting out of bed today, are we?" He kisses my shoulder, his finger running along my jawline.

"Not until we have to," I confirm.

"Good."

I close my eyes as he continues to explore my body. His fingers, rough and worn with hard work, still feel like silk gliding over my skin. I let them wander until I can't take it anymore.

"Dem, I...I can't." I squeeze my eyes shut, knowing I'm hurting him, too.

"I know, *Krasotka*. Thank you for allowing me what you did."

I roll over, facing him. "Why?"

That question. So many whys to ask. Why does he let me treat him this way? Why does he keep coming back? Why does he put up with me and my...hangups? Why does he look at me like I'm the only woman in the world? Why does he make me feel like maybe one day everything will be alright?

"Wrong question," he replies. No anger or disappointment in his voice. "Maybe you should be asking why we still have so many clothes on."

I huff out a laugh and shake my head. "What am I going to do with you?"

"I have ideas. Should I assume the position?"

And what does that say about me that he asks that knowing there is only one position? Without a single word, Demitri rolls onto his back, shimmies his pajama pants off, and sits up enough to remove his shirt. He's gloriously naked in front of me. I unconsciously lick my lips before leaning over and kissing his chest right over his heart.

"Thank you," I whisper. It's a phrase of gratitude and praise all in one.

I stand from the bed, remove my shirt, and slide my panties down my legs. I hear his intake of breath, but I can't look at him when I'm naked. I know what he sees, what I try to hide, and while he's never said anything, I know he knows. I'm damaged. Broken. That I have scars on the inside and outside. Forever touched by evil.

"Come here," he rasps. "Are you good?"

I nod and walk to the edge of the bed on his side. "I'm ready."

Without asking, he raises his arms over his head and grabs

the headboard. He gives me an expectant look, silently asking where the ties are. I shake my head.

"Not this time. Just..."

"I'll keep my hands right here, Mia. I promise."

Stretched out on the bed, hands above his head, creating his own restraint, willingly giving me control over everything is what turns me on. It's the only thing that turns me on. Without it, I can't have sex. Demitri knows this, yet he keeps coming back. Again, why?

"Are you ready?" I ask, crawling onto the bed and straddling his thighs. His cock stands hard, twitching, like it's trying to reach for me.

"Yes."

I motion to the bedside table and Demitri reaches into the drawer, pulling out a small bottle. Opening the lid, he drops some of the lube on his cock, fisting it and pumping twice. He smirks at me, raising a brow. "Need to make sure."

The unspoken words are because he can't make sure I'm primed and ready for himself.

I nod, giving him that one, and raise up on my knees. His fist grips himself, nudging the head at my entrance, and I slide down, the brush of his hand on my pussy almost making me pull back, but I resist. I *want* him to touch me. But I can't *let* him. I feel everything too much. He feels so good until it's more than I can handle.

But I want to make him feel good. The look on his face as I ride his cock. The way his muscles flex as he tries to thrust up from beneath me—the very little I let him. The way his chest heaves when I place my hands on it to give myself better leverage.

"*Krasotka*. You feel so good."

I feel a small smile as I adjust my body over his again, rising up and down on my knees, my pussy squeezing his cock in quick, shallow dips. I circle my waist, fluctuating my movements to allow him the most friction.

I watch his hands grip the bed frame and then flex out. I know he wants to touch me. I know he wants nothing more than to take over. To grab my hips and guide me exactly where he wants me. But he holds back. For me.

His body tenses under mine, and I know he's close. I increase my speed and allow my dips to take more of him inside of me. My eyes water watching the mixture of pleasure and pain on his face, knowing this is all I can give him. My pleasure comes from watching him come undone under me.

"I'm almost there," he growls. "Yes. Like that."

I grind down on his cock, rocking back and forth, and when I've almost had enough, I feel him unleash his orgasm. His body shudders, and his hands relax. He lowers his eyes to my body, stopping to admire my tits, heaving with my own exertion.

"Are you alright?" he asks, an expectant look on his face.

What he really wants to know is if I got off or if I'm in pain.

"I'm great." I smile, knowing that neither of us believe it.

I swing my leg over his body and stand up. As much as he's trying to hide it, I see the disappointment in his eyes, and it hurts. Not the way he fears I do, but in my soul. When I get to the bathroom door, I turn around and look at him.

"I need you to know that if I could be different, I would. For you. But also for myself."

"Mia, I don't want you to do anything for me. I only wish that you could see the barrier and break through it. If I could help you, I would, but this is a battle I can't be a part of."

A tear breaks free as I nod. I silently step into the bathroom and close the door behind me. After starting the shower and letting the water warm up, I step under the stream and let the tears flow. I'm not crying because I had sex, I'm crying because I want to have better sex. I want to be able to let go in a way that allows the intimate moments 'normal' people have. I want to be able to orgasm without fear of losing myself. I want to love and be loved in return. But I can't. That was taken away from me, and it doesn't seem to matter how much time has passed, I haven't been able to take it back.

This is my life. It's the only way I know how to live it.

CHAPTER SIX
DEMITRI

I watch Mia slip into the bathroom before I move off the bed. Her pain kills any afterglow I might have, but I feel like this is a new development. She's never shown her vulnerability before. Never let it slip that what we are doing is slowly killing her. I wish she knew that I'm not here because of the sex. Not anymore. Might have started that way, but it's become something else. Something more. In all honesty, if Mia told me she didn't think she could ever have sex again, I would still be here. I crave her presence in my life. When she asked if I would ghost her again, it took everything in me not to confess that I'd never left her, she just couldn't see me.

I finally drag myself out of bed and go into the hall bathroom to clean up. There're a lot of things to do today, and they won't get started until I can wash off the shame of what just happened. The guilt. I never want to make her feel that way again, but God help me, I don't know how to stop.

Stepping under the hot water, I place my hand on the wall that I know connects to Mia's bathroom. She might not let me be there for her post-sex breakdown she thinks I don't know

47

she's having, but I do know, and I am here, as much as she'll allow it.

Should I walk away? Probably. I know that what's going on here isn't healthy—for either one of us. But I don't know how. I don't know how to look at the woman who means more to me than anyone else in this world and tell her I'm done. Because I think we both know it would be a fucking lie. I'll never be done. She's my endgame, even if that game is never finished. I'll die knowing that I was here as much as I could be.

But for now, I have to put those feelings on the back burner. I need information. I need to know what's going on with this mystery woman the guys claimed was my sister. Does it surprise me the old man had an illegitimate kid? Nope. Not at all. There're probably a dozen more running around out there who don't know where they come from. If their moms were smart, that's exactly how it would stay. The Pavlov name brings nothing but pain, one I wouldn't wish on my worst enemy. Too fucking bad that enemy's name is already Pavlov, isn't it?

I get out of the shower and dry myself off, pulling clean clothes from my overnight bag and getting dressed. When I walk by the open door to the bedroom, I see the bed has already been stripped and I hear water running from somewhere in the house. Laundry. Can't have any reminders that we just did what we did. Not in her personal space. If I were a stronger man, I would have told her no. I would have stopped her. But I've tried that before, and it backfired in a horrible way. That was the night I learned if I'm in this at all, I'm in this under Mia's rules.

I make my way down the stairs, following the sounds to find Mia in the kitchen making coffee and toast. She's already dressed, her still wet hair pulled back into one of those clip things. Also, little known fact—Mia doesn't eat breakfast.

Unless it's five a.m. at the diner and it's because she allowed herself to drink the night before and she needs the grease. When I see her pull out the grape jelly and butter, I know the toast is for me. Just like my favorite vodka at the bar, she surrounds herself with things that I like, things that will make me happy. I only wish I knew why.

"Coffee's ready. Take a seat."

She isn't looking at me, concentrating hard on spreading the jelly on the toast. I give her a few minutes before I can't take it anymore.

"Mia, is this going to be too much? Me staying here?"

She jerks her head up, finally meeting my eyes. "What? Why would you ask that?"

"Because what just happened, what we just did? That wasn't healthy. For either one of us."

"What do you mean?" she asks, avoiding my gaze.

"You know damn good and well what I mean. Doing something that brings tears to your eyes and makes you cry in the shower afterwards isn't healthy."

"I did it for you!" she tries to defend.

"I didn't ask you to do anything for me. Don't you get it? I like you, Mia. I like your brain, and your wit, and your smartass comments. Yeah, I like your body, too, but when you see it as a weapon…" I trail off, knowing there's no way to say this without laying all my cards on the table. "I appreciate you asking me to stay here. I really do. But I don't expect for you to ever offer yourself to me, nor do I want you to if that is the aftermath."

"So you don't want me." It's a statement. In her mind, it's her truth.

"That is not what I said, and you need to hear me. I want you. I always want you, even when you're being your stubborn self. But—and this is the but I need you to listen to, Mia—I will not touch you or let you touch me from here on out if the aftermath is you having a breakdown and crying in the shower."

"And if I say that's the only way intimacy happens for me? That it always ends that way?"

"Then we have a lot more trust to build up and a lot more talking to do before the clothes come off. And one day, we'll talk about your missing orgasm, too. But I've probably already pushed you too far today for that."

"All before coffee. What an ass."

I stand up and slowly walk toward her. I make it very clear that I'm going to touch her face and make sure all my motions are at Mia speed—slow. I cup her cheek, lean in, and kiss her forehead.

"I'll let you use the jokes now. I'll let you have this one, but I'll keep working. I'll keep waiting. I'll show you that you can trust me. That you can let yourself be free with me. And I think we do that by slowing everything way down."

"Are you saying you want to date me?"

I chuckle. This woman. "Mia, I've been trying to *date* you for four fucking years."

"I don't know."

"No need to decide right now. I'm just telling you what my plan is. When you're ready to get on board, I'll be here."

She doesn't reply. Typical for her when faced with choice. She will want to think about it, agonize over it, turn it inside out and upside down, and then decide. It's the reason she's so successful owning a bar in a small town like Rock Hill. I keep my hand on her face, gently rubbing my thumb back and forth over her cheek, until I can tell she's at her limit. Other people touching her is hard. Knowing what I do, I understand why, but I hate it all the same.

I pull back and grab the coffee cup on the counter behind her and the plate with toast. I nod my thanks and take it back to the table, sitting down and eating. Mia leans against the counter, drinking her own coffee, watching me. She jumps a little when my phone rings, and when I see the name on the screen, the toast I just ate threatens to make a reappearance. But the time has come. I can't avoid reality any longer.

"Morning, Aunt Linda," I answer.

"Boy, I don't know what time-zone you're in, but it's after noon."

"The time-zone where I didn't go to sleep until almost dawn. Spill it. What do you know?"

"More than I can say over the phone. When will you be here?"

I look at Mia, gauging her response. "I think we can be there in about thirty?" I say while asking Mia. She shrugs her okay.

"We?"

"I'm bringing someone. A friend."

I fix my gaze on Mia as I say friend. She's not just a friend, and she knows it.

"A woman kind of friend?" Aunt Linda asks.

"Yes, a woman friend. We'll see you then." I disconnect the call before Aunt Linda can say anything more, and Mia grins at me. "What?" I ask her.

"Nothing." She shakes her head. "Nothing at all."

"Smartass," I reply, standing up and taking my cup and plate to the sink. "Let's get this over with."

We head toward the front door, Mia picking up her over-sized bag and slinging it over her shoulder, following me outside and locking up. When we've settled in the truck, she turns to me.

"Who are we going to see?"

"Her name is Linda. Everyone refers to her as Aunt Linda. She's a...contact for various organizations. A handler of sorts. She knows things. She knows all the things."

"Including your secrets?"

"All of my secrets."

"Oh."

I know what she's asking. Does she know about her?

"Yes, she knows who you are, *Krasotka*. I told her about you a long time ago."

"You did?"

Without taking my eyes from the road, I let her in on a secret. "I never left Rock Hill when all the shit with my family went down. I just disappeared from public. But I never left."

"Why not? And if you never left, how come I never saw you?"

"I couldn't leave you," I admit. "But I knew it wasn't safe to be around you, either. People were trying to find me, and if I was with you, they might have hurt you to get to me."

"What's changed?" she quietly asks. "How is that not any different than what's going on now?"

"We don't know for sure what's going on now, for one. And I don't know that I could find it in myself to walk away from you no matter what's going on."

"Why?"

"I'm not strong enough. That's why."

She doesn't ask any more questions, and I offer no more answers. When we pull into the parking lot behind The Center, the local community space in Briar Mountain, the air in the cab is thick with unsaid words. Maybe one day we'll be able to really talk about things, but right now there's other shit to worry about.

"Are you ready?" I ask, turning off the truck.

"Since I'm not really sure what to expect, sure!" She gives me a fake smile and wide eyes, and I laugh at her reply.

"Same. I feel exactly the same. Let's go see how much my life is fucked, shall we?"

CHAPTER SEVEN

MIA

I follow Demitri into what looks like apartment buildings, my anxiety spiking. I knew there were some housing units behind the community center, I volunteered here when I was in college, but I thought they were all for recovery and rehab. We pass three little kids playing in the lobby and a woman who, if I had to guess, is their mom. She looks haunted and has a full arm cast, along with some bruising on her face. I look at Demitri, who just shakes his head and keeps walking, quietly saying hello to the woman, who shrinks back from him. Well, that's familiar.

Only when we are in the elevator does he speak again. "This is a place for people trying to get away from bad situations. Families, women, men. The guys in the bar last night? That's what they do."

"I knew they helped people. I just didn't know they brought them here."

"Not all of them, but Daniel's parents own this place, and they restructured the housing spaces back here a few years back. One building has space dedicated to some of the older residents of town who need a little assistance and don't have family to turn to. The other units in the building are reserved for the families that need help. Some end up staying while others go to a safe member of their family or start brand new lives with the help of the friends here."

We step off the elevator and make our way down the hall where Demitri knocks on a door with a gold four on it. The lady who answers is not exactly what I'm expecting. She's on the shorter side, maybe five-two, five-three, with the bob haircut of all women who aren't quite ready to go full pixie. It's brown with gray woven into the color. She could be fifty or seventy, I'm not sure, but it's her eyes that take me aback. They are piercing. Like they can see right into the center of my soul and they know all my secrets without me ever opening my mouth. I want to think she's a friend, but the self-preservation side of me fears she could easily be my foe.

"Dem." She smiles, leaning in so he can kiss her cheek. "This her?" She shrewdly eyes me up and down.

"This is Mia," he answers, and I can tell he's rolling his eyes without looking at him.

"Ah, Mia Alexander. Aged thirty-one, owner of City Brews, formerly Mia's Place. From Hamilton, Montana, daughter of Lee and Mary Alexander. Sister of Caleb and Lena, aunt to—"

"Aunt Linda," Demitri cuts her off harshly. "That's plenty of showing off. Want to invite us in so we can get this show on the road?"

I'm staring at the two of them, and a large part of me wants to run. Who the hell is this lady and why does she know so much about me? And my family?

"Killjoy." The older woman rolls her eyes. "Come on in. I have some food set up for us. I figure you haven't eaten much and you," she looks at me, "look like you could use a good meal."

Demitri steps aside and lets me enter first, sighing as I stare at him when I pass. Yeah, buddy, we have some talking to do later on. First question? Why the fuck does this lady who I have never met know so much about me? And did he know all of that as well? And for how long? The questions keep coming as I follow her to the table, where she has a lasagna sitting. It does smell amazing, but I don't know if I trust this lady enough to eat anything she's cooked.

"Don't worry," she answers my unasked question. "I didn't make it. Or poison it. It's from Danielle's. Safe as can be."

"That's super reassuring," I mutter as I sit.

"Will you put her out of her misery? Please?" Demitri asks.

Finally, she grins, and it's like seeing a whole new person. "Why do you always have to kill my fun?"

"Because your fun is terrifying my girl."

I snap my head to look at him, wondering if he even realizes what he just said. His girl? Am I his girl? Do I want to be his girl? Yes. Yes, I do.

"Fine." She smiles, completely changing her looks. Now she looks like the fun aunt or the young grandma. "Mia, my name is Linda. Everyone calls me Aunt Linda and I work for a few different organizations, and my job is to know things. It's to have people tell me things that I can then get into the hands of the other people who also need to know things."

"That's not cryptic at all," I say.

"Sorry, honey, that's all I can give you. My job is to keep the secrets I'm told until the information can help the greater good."

Demitri turns his body to me, his hand on the back of my chair, not touching me, but letting me know he's there. "When I knew I had to get out, that I had to make it permanent, I was sent here to tell her everything. She sent my information to the FBI, DEA, and probably a couple of other alphabet places."

"Why does she know so much about me?"

"Oh, honey, that's easy. When our boy here met you, it was my job to make sure you were safe for him to be around. One-night stands are one thing, but, well, you've never quite been a one-nighter, have you?"

I feel my cheeks burning, unable to say anything.

"Come on, we're all adults here. Sex happens."

"You know everything about me? My past?"

She becomes somber, slowly nodding her head. "I do."

"Did you tell?"

"Not my story to tell, sweetheart. I might know more than what's been put out there publicly, but your secrets are safe with me. Promise."

I nod, the lump in my throat making it hard to swallow.

"How about we move on to whatever the fuck is going on right now?" Demitri offers, grazing his fingers along my shoulder before turning back to the table.

Aunt Linda dishes out the food, and we pass around a water pitcher. Once we've all got our meals in front of us, she begins.

"Your father's genes are obviously taking root in his offspring. Your half-sister is trying to take over the power and control of this area using his name."

"How?" Demitri asks.

"Remember a couple of years ago when all the high school kids were overdosing?"

"Yeah."

"That was her. Well, her and some crazy man. She's laid low for a while and is trying to make a comeback. She has some inside help."

"Who?" Demitri barks, putting down his fork.

"Andrey Novikov."

The color in Demitri's face drains. He pushes his plate away, and his eyes dart from the door to the windows and back. "No," he whispers, more to himself than to us, I think.

"That's why we think you're in danger, son. He's starting to make waves asking around for you. And I'm afraid if he finds you..."

"What?" I ask before I can stop myself. "If he finds him, what?"

"I'm dead. And anyone suspected to be attached to me is dead, too."

I see the fear in his eyes, the sweat breaking out on his forehead, the bob of his throat when he swallows.

"Who is Andrey Novikov?"

"He was Ivan's *Kurkhan*."

"What's that?"

"His hunter. Or enforcer. He's the one who dealt with those deemed disloyal. The last time I saw him, he promised he'd get me back for bringing down the family. For telling the secrets. For selling all of them out."

"Why is he not in jail?" I ask.

"Because he's never been caught. There's no proof that he's the one doing the things other than me. I'm the only one who's seen him in action."

"What do we do?" I ask.

"We keep our boy safe, and we let all those agencies who get their rocks off taking down the bad guys do their jobs."

"How does my 'sister' play into this?" he asks, adding finger quotes around sister.

"She plans to legally claim a portion of the inheritance. Your father's will stated his legitimate offspring inherited. But what's legitimacy mean these days? One DNA test and, BAM! you're legit. But she can only do so much through the courts without you being there. Without you, she doesn't have much to claim."

"This is all because she wants money?" Demitri asks. "Fuck, she can have the money. I don't need it."

"Bullshit. You give her the money and then what? She can only do so much without a dick, and you know it. She'll reel you back in, put you as the head of the family, and do all the dirty work in your name. And when it all comes down again, you'll be the one to take the fall. Come on, kid, you know how this plays out."

"How do we keep that from happening?" I look at both of them, hoping one of them has an answer.

"Technically, Demitri Pavlov doesn't really exist anymore. John Smith does."

"But there are enough people who know who I really am, that it doesn't really matter, does it?"

"I know, which is why I tried to get you to leave. But did you listen? No. Couldn't leave your girl, here, could you? I mean, it's just your life."

"I don't need a fucking lecture, Aunt Linda. I'm not leaving. So what do we do?"

"You lie low. You stay hidden. No one knows about your connection to Mia, right?"

She looks at both of us, but I avoid her stare. This isn't good.

"Who else knows his name, Mia?" Aunt Linda asks.

"My friends do."

"That would be the other three that you meet with regularly?"

"Yes. And a couple others who also have some, umm, experience."

"Who? I need their names."

"Umm, Charity Rhodes and Lizzy Thorpe. I'm pretty sure her sister, Victoria, knows as well."

"How does Vic know?"

"The woman is super observant, Demitri. I have a feeling

she just knows."

Aunt Linda laughs, picking up her fork to start eating again. "Yeah, she knows. She's almost as good as me."

"I'm sorry," I whisper to Demitri. "I really fucked up, didn't I?"

"No, *Krasotka*, you haven't fucked up. I'm not worried that your friends are going to turn into spies for the Bratva."

"Are they in danger, too?"

"Not if I can help it."

"I'm still confused," I confess louder so Aunt Linda can hear. "What does Demi—err—John need to do to stay safe? What can I do to help?"

"You can keep him hidden. Stop talking about him to your friends. You never know who might be listening."

"You know this means she's going to start calling me Beluga Boy again, right?" Demitri smirks.

"Might want to change that to Vodka Boy. Hate to tell you this, but that Beluga stuff is only popular to Russians." She chuckles.

"Watch your mouth." Demitri narrows his eyes.

"Hate to say it, but she's right. All my years, I've never had someone ask for Beluga other than you."

"But you still had it," he points out.

"Not the kind you wanted. And that bottle I had was five years old, and you were the first person to take a shot from it."

"Alright, we're getting off topic. What's the real plan for this woman you claim is my sister?"

Aunt Linda holds up her finger and stands from the table. We watch her walk into a bedroom or office, and when she comes back, she's got files stacked up in her arms.

"Demitri, it's not just one you need to worry about. It's many. And if any of these other spawns of Ivan find out who they are, they could try the same thing."

"Fuck me," he gasps, looking at the stack in Aunt Linda's arms. "How? Why?"

She stares at him with a look that even I understand.

"Right. Because '*Aunt Linda knows all.*'"

"Exactly." She smiles. "We've been keeping our eye on all the descendants of Ivan for a while." She pauses, her face becoming serious. "Demitri, some of them are no longer with us."

"Did he kill them?"

"They didn't die of natural causes, that's for sure."

"How many?"

"Total? We've located about fifteen so far. Eight of them are still alive."

"Your father killed seven of his own children?" I ask in horror. What kind of man was Ivan Pavlov?

"Why?" Demitri asks.

"The sons he found, well, they aren't exactly breathing any longer."

"What about the daughters?" Demitri demands to know.

"Two of them."

"How many of the eight are boys?" His voice is gruff from holding in his emotion.

"Two."

"I have two brothers out there somewhere? How were they able to hide?"

"I hate to point out the obvious, but there's not a big Russian population in this area, Demitri. The smart ones? The moms who were able to keep their babies safe gave their children American names. Jackson and Travis. They are safe. Their moms are married to men who adopted their children with the help of a friend. We've known where they were their whole lives."

"How old are they?"

"Jackson is twenty-three and Travis is nineteen."

"And you've known this? For how long?"

"Honey, I've been keeping track of your family for forty years. Since your grandfather was in charge."

Demitri stares at her, his mouth open, in pure shock. I need to rescue him.

"Demitri," I quietly speak his name. No response. But when I reach my hand out and lay it on his arm, his face snaps to the side, his eyes silently begging me to save him. "Why don't we continue this another time? You've just had a lot of information dumped on you, and I'm sure Aunt Linda will answer your questions once you've been able to process it?"

While I'm looking at Demitri, my question is more for her. Numbly, Demitri nods, glancing at my hand where I'm touching his arm. And believe me, I get it. I've never initiated any kind of physical touch outside of sex with him before. This is new territory and all that.

"I'll come to your house tomorrow, Mia," Aunt Linda announces, standing and packing up some of the mostly untouched lasagna. "This is his favorite. Please take it with you."

I nod, accepting the offering. "Do you know where I live?"

"Of course. I might bring Daniel with me, if that's alright with you?"

"Daniel can help? I thought he was more of a search and rescue operation."

"Have to be honest, he's probably going to bring someone with him. Someone who isn't as worried about the law as others might be. But it will be someone safe. Someone trusted, okay?"

"Yeah, okay I guess."

I nod my thanks and stand up, holding the food in one hand. Demitri still hasn't moved. I reach out and grasp his hand in my free one, the need to make sure he's alright overriding my usual aversion.

"Are you okay?" he looks at me, almost like he's coming out of a trance.

"I'm good. You?"

"I think I've been better."

"Give me your keys. I'm driving."

"I'm fine."

"Fuck that. Give me your keys."

"No. I can drive."

"I said no. I won't get in the fucking truck unless I'm the one driving. You going to leave me here all alone?"

He scowls at me but hands over the keys. I notice Aunt Linda smirking at me and tilting her head in approval. I lead Demitri out and make sure he heads to the passenger seat before I haul myself up behind the wheel.

"Have you ever driven a truck before? A classic truck?"

"You heard where I'm from. You don't get out of Montana without driving a truck, Demitri."

He smiles. It's small, but it's there. Like he's pleased I just willingly gave him a little piece of me. Maybe one day I'll tell him why I left Montana. Maybe.

CHAPTER EIGHT
DEMITRI

"I'm going to work with you tonight."

Mia looks up from the table where she's going through her bag. "What? No. It's not safe."

"Fuck that. I'm going with you. If it's not safe for me, it's not safe for you. So you're either calling in or I'm going with you."

"Who the fuck do you think you are?"

Her anger takes me by surprise, but it really shouldn't. She stares at me, waiting for an answer.

"I'm only trying—"

"To control me? To tell me what to do? To take charge? Fuck you. How about that? You do not control me. No one will ever fucking control me again, do you understand? I am going to work and your ass is staying in this fucking house."

"So I can't tell you what to do, but you can tell me what to do? How's that fair?" I challenge.

She deflates in front of me, all the fight leaving her body. Her mouth snaps closed, the argument she was getting ready to make gone. I walk as close to her as I feel like I safely can before I speak again.

"I don't want to fight with you. But I want you safe, same as you want me. Now that I know Andrey is out there looking for me, the thought of you being out of my sight makes my skin crawl. I don't want to control you. I don't even want to be in charge. But the thought that there is even a possibility that you could end up like Mika fills me with a dread I can't fully express."

"And I don't want you to leave the house for the same reason. If something happened to you, would I even know? Or would you just disappear and I'd never know? If you're home, I know where you are. I would know if someone was trying to get in. I would know if they took you. I would know."

"Can we compromise?" I ask in a last-ditch effort.

"How?" The look on her face is priceless. The lack of trust would hurt if it were anyone else.

"What if I stay in the office all night? I'll do some work, you do your thing, no one will see me, and I'll know you're safe, you'll know I'm safe. Everyone is happy, right?"

She squints at me, pursing her lips. "I don't hate it," she finally replies.

"Please?"

She lets out the sigh of someone weary. "Fine. I still don't like it, but if you'll stay in the office, we can compromise."

I smile, feeling like I've just won something, when she sticks her finger up and narrows her eyes at me.

"You will not turn the microphones on and listen to me all night. You will not get mad or jealous because you think I'm flirting with someone. You will accept that this is my job and what I do during my work hours is separate from whatever this is."

I clench my jaw to keep from laughing at her. "Yes, ma'am."

"Okay then. And I'll send Brodie in every once in a while to check on you."

"Brodie? You sure about that?"

"What's wrong with Brodie?"

"Nothing. But if no one is supposed to know I'm there, Brodie would be a someone, right?"

"He doesn't count. I know too many of his secrets. Come on then, let's go."

She stands from the table and slings her bag over her shoulder, whatever's inside it clunking around. I swear she actually does have a kitchen sink in there. I asked her once what she carts around in the bag and she completely shut down on me. But it's never very far from where she is.

She locks the door as we exit the house and starts walking toward her car.

"Where are you going?" I ask, looking between her and my truck.

"I'm driving. You're in hiding, remember? People aren't supposed to see you with me or I'll be in danger?" She smiles sweetly and rapidly blinks her eyes.

"Smartass. Fine. You drive."

I match her sweet smile with my own, and she scowls. I know she's trying to make everything uncomfortable so I'll give up and stay home. But as stubborn as she is, I can match it.

She grumbles while getting in her car, and I let my smile spread before sobering up and getting in beside her. Can't let her know how much I'm actually enjoying this. When she gets feisty, I get turned on. And it has nothing to do with sex. The woman has no idea how she makes my life light up when she's being the real her. And the best part? I don't even think she realizes how much her mask has slipped with me over the years. The Mia I met four years ago never would have let me see her angry. Or worried. She would lash out proactively, protecting herself first and foremost. Remember those drips and scraps? This is me living it up with them.

"Do you need anything before you're shut in for the night?" Mia asks when we get to her office.

"You going to lock the door?" I joke, but the look on her face tells me she's thinking about it. "Mia. Don't even."

She gives me an evil grin and shrugs. "It would have kept you where I want you."

"Go to work. Make the big bucks. And flirt just enough for the tips, but not so much that I have to watch the men walk away with rods in their pants, okay?"

"We'll see. I mean, I guess I'll try. But momma's got bills to pay."

She turns and flounces to the door. Fucking flounces, her ass swaying just so. This woman. Just as she walks through the door, she turns back, her face suddenly serious. Doubt—and is that fear?—etched on her face. "My friends are coming in tonight. It's our weekly meeting. I would really appreciate it if you tried not to listen to our conversation. What we talk about? It's private. For all of us."

"Mia, I'll never purposely pry into your secrets. You have my word."

She stares at me, chewing on her bottom lip, before nodding and walking away, pulling the door shut behind her. I stare at the closed door, trying to read her thoughts through it. I know the friends she's talking about. A group of women who call themselves *Brett's Girls* that came together over their history of trauma with the man. I hate that name. Survivors. That should be their name.

Not going to lie, the urge to call Aunt Linda and ask her for the history on all of them is there, but much like I don't want anyone looking into my past and asking questions, I won't do that to these women. I know enough to know the basics, and that's already enough to make me want to throw up.

I look around the office, trying to take my mind off of Mia's past, noticing the camera angles on the wall of monitors. One behind the bar facing out to the room, one facing the front door, one for the back door, and one focusing on the area Mia usually holds as hers. There's also one in the kitchen and the hallway with the bathrooms. She's got the whole place covered, which makes me feel a little better about things here.

I turn to the desk and pull my laptop from the bag I brought with me. I boot her up and get to work. Even if I can't be in the garage, it doesn't mean I can't do something to stay productive. After a few minutes of quietly working, I pick up my phone and make a call.

"John?" the man answers.

"Hey, Sarge. What's going on?"

"Nothing, man. You're the one who called me. What's going on with you?"

"I won't be able to make it up there next week. Might need to make arrangements for one of my guys to do the pickup."

"What's wrong?"

"Why do you think something's wrong?"

"Because you don't just come up here to pick up parts. You come up here to bullshit with me and the other guys. If you can't do that, something's happened. What?"

"Sometimes I really hate that you know shit the way you do."

He laughs, and I have a feeling this isn't the first time he's heard this. "Doesn't change the fact you're facing something."

"Yeah, well, I'm not really supposed to talk about it. So, just trying to stay out of sight for a little while."

"Family?"

I never told Sarge my real name, but the man knows everything. He can get a grown man to spill his guts with just a look. And obviously a phone call.

"Yeah. Can we leave it at that?"

"How bad?"

"I don't know, man. Could be really bad. Right now, trying to mitigate that."

"Your girl safe?"

"And stubborn."

"Good. Someone has to keep an eye on you."

I lower my voice, not wanting anyone to hear me. "What if keeping an eye on me puts her in danger? How do I live with that if something happens to her?"

"You can't live your life like that. Unless you know there's a credible threat, one that you need to call the authorities in on, all you can do is stay aware of your surroundings and keep those close to you safe."

The way he speaks with authority almost makes me believe it's really that simple. But I come from a world where nothing is that easy.

"I'll keep that in mind."

"I know you don't believe me, and trust me, I've seen some shit, but it's all we have. And you call me if you need help, alright? I can make a few calls to some friends of mine."

If anyone else had told me this, I wouldn't put any faith in it, but Sarge does know people. I happen to know one of them pretty well, he helped me get through everything with the family last time. He's a former FBI guy who found me when he was undercover. He blew his cover when things went to shit, just to protect me. He's the reason Daniel and his crew tolerate me now. Before that, I'm pretty sure they were ready to take me out for the good of mankind.

"Thanks. I'll remember that. But I'm still sending one of the guys to you for the parts."

He laughs. It's rough, but you can feel the heart the man has for those he deems worthy. "I'll talk to you soon."

We disconnect the call and I finish a few other things, including the work schedule for the garage to cover my absence. As I'm sending all that out, I happen to look up at the camera and see that Mia's friends have arrived. It's only then that I realize it's already after eight. They are all crowded around the end of the bar. Their unofficial seats, honestly. I've never seen them sit anywhere else. It allows Mia to keep working, and for them to have a conversation.

I try not to pay too much attention to what's happening, but one of her friends, the one who looks like she's a porcelain doll, looks right at the camera and mouths 'not okay.' Then I pay all the attention.

CHAPTER NINE

MIA

"Wʜᴀᴛ ᴅᴏ you mean you don't want to talk about your secret man meat?" Sofie asks, taking a sip of her drink.

"That is not okay," Grace agrees.

"Did you just look at the camera?" I ask, turning around to look at the red light over my head.

"Yes. Because when you watch this back later, which we all know you will, we want you to really listen to what we're saying."

"That's kind of fucked up, you know that, right?" I frown at the women in front of me.

"It's only because we care," Nola calmly states. "We don't want to see you fall into another bad situation. One a lifetime is plenty."

"It's not a bad situation," I quickly tell them. "Just something I can't talk about right now, okay?"

Grace sits up straighter, her eyes boring into me, trying to break me. Out of all of them, she's the only one who can. "Mia," she quietly says. "Are you in trouble?"

I look at the room of patrons, all out enjoying their night. Carefree, having fun, just living their lives. The couple in the corner who have been playing footsie under their table all night while making goo-goo eyes at each other. The brothers ribbing each other at the pool table over who sucks more while they bitch about their fantasy teams and who's going to win the season. A few other people dot the tall tables and booths. And the woman Brodie called as his the moment she walked in the door, sitting alone with a glass of wine, reading something on her phone. At least, that's what she was doing the last time I looked at her. Now she's staring directly at me. Her eyes. Crystal blue. Just like Demitri's.

"Grace." I smile like nothing is wrong. "I'm going to ask you to do something for me, and I need you to do it without any question. Nola, Sofie, I need for you to really try not to act like anything could possibly be wrong. Talk about your latest book or the gossip from the hair salon. Please."

"Okay," Grace quietly responds while the other two do exactly as I request. "What do you need?"

"I need for you to go into the office and tell the person that we aren't talking about that's sitting in there that he needs to look at the cameras and the single patron on the right wall, please."

"I have to go to the bathroom," Grace announces, almost too loudly, as she stands from her stool. "Be right back."

One of the dude-bros comes up to order another round of drinks and I get to work making their beers. I look toward the woman every few seconds, unable to keep my eyes off of her. She hasn't moved. She's still staring at me, her blue eyes telling me she knows. She knows I know Demitri.

Grace comes back to the front and takes her seat at the bar again, her face pinched with a hint of fear. Once the dude-bro goes back to the pool table, I go back to the corner with my friends, wiping down the bar like it owes a debt.

"He's calling someone," Grace quietly tells us. "He said to not do anything stupid, and he's watching." Surprisingly, she grins. "He also said to tell you he's got the volume up, so you shouldn't talk about how hot he is."

"Jackass." I can't help but laugh. "He didn't say who he was calling?"

She shakes her head. "No. Just to maintain the status quo."

"Well, this just got hard, didn't it?" I ask.

"Probably. And you have a lot of talking to do later."

"I'm sticking around for that." Nola raises her hand like she's in class.

"Me, too!" Sofie grins. "This sounds like something exciting. Don't want to miss it!"

"You are all way too happy about this."

She opens her mouth and looks behind me, closing it quickly. I turn around and the woman is standing at the bar.

"What can I get you?" I ask as unaffected as possible.

"I'd love another glass of red, please." She smiles, but it's forced. Practiced. It doesn't reach her eyes, which are fucking with my head. But beneath that, it seems like she's here for a reason that maybe isn't necessarily to kill me? I hope?

"Sure thing, beautiful." I smile and pull a fresh wine glass from overhead.

Equal opportunity flirting. A compliment is a compliment, doesn't matter who it comes from. And let's be honest, women are better tippers as long as you aren't flirting with their man. And I'm trying to act like I normally would in case this isn't her first time in here.

"Are you visiting Rock Hill?" I ask, trying to figure out what her plan is.

"Just driving through," she quietly replies. "Visiting the campus tomorrow in Briar Mountain."

"My alma mater. It's a beautiful campus."

"That's what I hear. Never been there myself. Have some friends who used to be there, though."

I hand her the glass and a napkin, taking her cash. No card. No name. No trace. But I put it in the empty drawer of the register. I've watched enough true crime shows and SVUs to know fingerprints are important.

"Let me know if you need anything else." I turn back to her, but she's already retreating to her booth.

I look at the girls, who all have faces ranging from shock to concern. I shake my head and move down the bar to help someone else, keeping my eyes on the woman as often as I can.

It takes about twenty minutes, but the door opens and two men walk in. Only these aren't two strangers, they are two of the ANON guys. They grab seats at the bar and I make my way to them when I've finished helping the person in front of me.

"What can I get you?" I smile.

"Two drafts," big guy one replies. I wish I could remember their names.

"Coming right up."

I pull their beers from the tap and slide them across the bar.

"You guys getting into trouble tonight?"

"No, but we're always up for some fun," big guy two grins at me.

I swear I hear something break in the back. So do the guys, their eyes flickering to the hallway. Big guy one has a smirk on his face. He makes eyes at the camera above us and sticks out his tongue. Ahh, boys.

"Behave." I point at the man who winks at me. Smartass. "You're nothing but trouble. And those dimples get you away with it, don't they?"

"Absolutely."

I roll my eyes before I retreat to my girls. Grace has her eyes on me, but Nola and Sofie look like they are two breaths away from drooling.

"Who are they?" Sofie asks, her voice all breathy, her face flushing.

"Dunno, just two beers."

I know they've seen them in here before. There have been plenty of nights the ANON guys have stopped in for a drink when they've been here. And this is pretty much the response every time.

"You'd find out their names if you went and talked to them, you know."

"Not going to happen. I'd never have a chance with someone like," Nola waves her hand in their direction, "that."

"Fuck off with that nonsense. You're a beautiful woman. You just need to accept it and grow a pussy," I tell her.

"I thought it was 'grow some balls'?"

"What happens when you hit balls? They go down like a sack of potatoes. What happens when you pound a pussy?"

"What?" Sofie asks, fully invested in the scenario.

"If done right, they orgasm."

"Huh." Grace purses her lips, trying not to laugh at me. "So, you're balls then? Because last I heard, your orgasm was M-I-A."

"Shut up," I grin, slinging my hand towel at her.

"Just pointing out the obvious here."

"I can't believe you don't think they're hot." Nola looks at Grace. I'm amazed that she can even tear her eyes away from big guy one.

"Grace has her eyes stuck on someone else. And he's not in the room with us right now."

We all know I'm talking about her boss, James Covey. She's been head over heels in love with him for years, but she'll never do anything about it. Trauma, am I right?

"True." She doesn't even try to argue. "They are objectively handsome, I guess, but they lack that something that I like."

"Yeah," Nola snorts. "Tom Ford suits."

"Hush." Grace waves her off. "You have no idea what you're talking about. Even if he does look good in his suits."

I've officially lost them all. Two are drooling over the guys at the bar and one is lost in her head, dreaming of things that'll never be if she can't find her way out of the darkness we all still live in. Yes, I realize that makes me a hypocrite. We don't judge around here.

When I turn back for another sweep of the bar, the woman's seat is empty. I look around the room to see if she's moved, but she's nowhere to be found. Her empty wine glass sits on the table.

"Fuck," I whisper to myself. "Did she go to the bathrooms?" I ask the gang, who shrug in response.

My phone vibrates under the counter, and I pull it out.

> Demitri: She's gone. Slipped out the door. Is it time to close up?

I look at the clock on the wall. It's only eleven thirty.

> Mia: Not yet. Thirty more minutes. I'll make it last call in ten.

> Demitri: Need everyone gone.

I pace behind the bar, the clock mocking me with minutes that seem to last hours. At eleven forty on the dot, I call out my favorite words of the night.

"Last call!"

The dude bros groan and rush the bar, as expected. Nothing like sucking down a pitcher of beer twenty minutes before getting in your car to drive home. Idiots.

"Who's your designated driver?" I ask before handing over the pitcher.

"Loser in the corner. He lost the first game tonight. Quit drinking after two," dude bro one says.

"You know he's military and can kick your ass, right?" dude-bro two replies.

"Not a chance. I'm still his big brother."

The two grab their beer and continue bickering on the way back to the table. A few other people come up to either pay their tabs or get one more drink, and thankfully, no one seems too sloshed to make it home safe. At midnight, I walk the last customer out and turn the lock on the door while flipping off the open sign. I turn and face the people still remaining.

"I'll go get our boy," big guy one says, standing from his stool. "He in the office?"

"I'm right here," Demitri answers, appearing from the hallway. "And I think I need a drink."

"And then we all talk," big guy two and Nola say at the same time.

Without a word, I flip over two shot glasses and grab the bottle of Beluga Gold Line and pour. We take our shots and I pour another while filling two cups with ice for water.

"I guess it's time," Demitri says after taking his second shot. "Aunt Linda is going to be so pissed off."

"Boy, I knew you wouldn't be able to keep your trap shut. Guess it's a good thing these are the people you surround yourself with."

Aunt Linda appears from the back hall, and I'm stunned into silence. How the hell did she get in here? When Brodie sticks his head out of the kitchen window, I have my answer. He looks at me with a guilty expression before turning to Aunt Linda.

"Good to see you again, Auntie. Mia, I'm done and gone. I don't need to know what all this is about. See you tomorrow."

I wave to Brodie and wait for the back door to slam closed. That boy can never leave anywhere quietly, but I guess it's good to know he can open things with no sound.

"Well, let's get this shit show on the road," Aunt Linda tells us, sitting on a bar stool. "And make me a beverage, will you?"

CHAPTER TEN
DEMITRI

From not telling anyone to telling everyone, I guess? That's all I can think when I look at the bar full of people. Aiden and Grady are one thing. Even Aunt Linda being here shouldn't freak me too much, but Mia's friends? I don't want them anywhere near this mess. This is my mess. Because no matter what I try, I'll never get away from my family completely.

"What did she say to you?" I ask Mia.

"Nothing. Said she was driving through, but didn't give anything else away."

"How did you know?" Aunt Linda asks.

Mia looks at me, not giving anything away when she replies, "Her eyes. She has the same eyes as Demi—John."

"Ugh, seriously, can we cut the John shit? Everyone here knows—"

"John, dear, watch yourself," Aunt Linda sternly replies.

"Actually, I didn't," the woman sitting at the end of the bar says. She's got brown hair, blue eyes, and pale skin. "I only know you as Beluga Boy." The smirk on her face almost makes me laugh, but Aiden beats me to it.

"Beluga? Like a whale?" he laughs.

"No," Mia deadpans. "Like the vodka. The expensive shit, unlike that draft drivel you two drink when others are paying attention, big guy one. Or should I call you Old Fashioned, Irish boy?"

Aunt Linda snorts into her glass, and Grady chuckles next to him.

"Mia, Mia, I thought we were past all this no-name stuff."

"Yeah, well, good luck with that. I know what you drink, I don't need to know your name and background."

"We need to know names. We can remember them," Mia's other friend says. "I'm Nola. This is Sofie," she points to the first woman, "and this is Grace. That's Mia," she grins as she points to my girl, "and Beluga Boy must be John? Or something. So, who are you?"

Mia leans against the counter behind her and smiles at her friend. Part of me thinks it's because Mia is used to being the one in this group to speak out. Doesn't take a genius to see that if one takes five minutes to watch them interact, but Mia has always taken the step back to let her friends speak and shine.

"I'm Aiden, and this is Grady."

"And why are you here? Who are you?"

"We work for ANON, and we're here because he called us?"

"Are you asking me or telling me?"

"Telling?"

"Alright, enough flirting. That was painful," Aunt Linda interrupts. "I'm Aunt Linda, and I'm here because I am, so just go with it."

"She knows things," Mia whispers to her friends. "She might be the only one I trust to be here."

"Thank you, dear."

"Anytime."

I look between the two women and frown. I don't think I like these two getting this close so fast. Aunt Linda is a powerful woman, one who can fucking kill if she needs to, and I don't want any of this touching Mia.

"Turn that frown upside down, son, and get over yourself. She's involved, and the universe doesn't give a shit what your feelings on the matter are."

"I really hate it when you do that."

"I know. Tough shit."

"Alright, enough. What are we all thinking?" Mia asks, putting an end to my bickering with Aunt Linda.

"I don't think she was here for him," Grace says. She's been quiet since the bar closed.

"Why would you think that?" Aiden asks.

"She showed up after they were already here. She had two drinks and left before closing. The parking lot is empty, correct?"

"Yeah, I watched the video feed when she left. She got in a taxi," I confirm.

"She never went down the back hall, or even tried to look at anyone else in the bar. She sat in the first booth and faced the bar. If she was here for anyone, it was Mia."

"What would she want with Mia?" Grady asks.

"Who knows. But that's my take on things. You have a better idea?"

"I think she knows we've been trailing her for months and that we come here. Maybe she was trying to get intel on what we know. Which is not a lot."

Aunt Linda jumps up from the stool and goes over to the booth where the lady was sitting. I can't think of her as my sister. The only sister I have is rotting in jail after being taken down by the FBI. She sits down and starts doing her Aunt Linda thing. None of us say anything, just watch. She feels on top of the table, under the table, and in the booth.

When she frowns, I know she's found something she doesn't like.

"What is it?" I ask, getting up and joining her at the table.

She shakes her head, giving me a hard look. When she raises her hand and I see what she's holding, my entire body sags. Some type of bug. Or camera. It's a flat disk type thing, but with tech these days, who the fuck knows exactly what it is. I turn to look at Grady, who immediately knows something is up and pulls out his phone. I look at Mia and put my finger to my lips, letting her know to be quiet.

I help Aunt Linda up and we walk back to the bar. She holds up the small disk in her hand and Aiden and Grady immediately start cussing. Mia takes out a notebook from under the bar and hands it to me before plucking a pen out of her hair and holding it out.

It's a listening device or a camera. Be careful what you say.

Mia closes her eyes and takes a deep breath before nodding her head. She turns to the women and shows them the note before placing the notebook on the bar face down.

"So, what's the plan for this weekend? Are we still going over to watch the baseball game at the University?" she asks, a fake smile plastered on her face.

"Can we go to the diner while we're over there?" Nola asks. "Their food is so much better than anything we have here."

"I beg to differ." Grady smiles. "Sandy has some good food, but Danielle's? That place has the best lasagna and cannoli I've ever had."

"I don't disagree with you," Sofie interjects, "but I'm with

Nola on Sandy's after a ballgame. Pretzels and beer go with diner food better than a heavy meal."

Grady thinks about it before nodding. "Fine. I'll give you that one."

"Hard to argue with me. I'm always right."

"I'll take your word for it."

Mia shakes her head, looking at me with an incredulous look on her face. She flips over the notebook and writes:

What are we waiting for?

I reply:

Grady called someone. Hoping they can help.

She quickly writes back:

How long do we have to wait?

Before I can write my reply, Grady gets up and goes to the door and unlocks it, opening it up and letting someone in before closing and locking it again. Joker. The newest ANON member. I hear he's a super hacker and security guy. Also heard he was a sniper in the Army. Not someone I'd want to fuck with, that's for sure.

He tips his chin our direction and looks at Grady expectantly who holds up the unknown object. His brows raise, but he doesn't give anything else away, taking the disk from Grady and walking to the bar. Sitting on a stool and pulling out a laptop, he gets to work.

After about five minutes of clicking around, he finally

looks up. "Okay, it's paused. What do we need to be worried about it recording?"

"It's not a live recording?" Aiden asks.

"Nope. It records for three hours, sends the data, and records for another three. It's also sound activated, so it will shut off and not record anything when there's no one here. Saves battery. Kinda nifty, wonder if Daniel would let me have some. Looks like it last sent at eleven. What kind of conversations do we need to be worried about here?"

"The last hour should be good. There's a fake conversation if you can save that one," Aunt Linda replies for all of us.

"I can do anything," he smirks in return,

"Umm, who are you?" Nola asks.

"He's big guy number three," Mia chuckles, pouring Joker a beer and sliding it across the bar.

"How many big guys are there?" Sofie asks.

"Too fucking many." Grady grins. "Of course, we're the only ones who matter."

"I'm Joker. I work with these assholes. And I break into tech shit. Mostly legal, of course. Now, is someone going to tell me what I need to delete on this recording before it's sent? Easier to manipulate it before that happens than have to try to hack the system receiving it."

"Can you track it to the location getting it?" Aiden asks.

"Yup. But we have about twenty more minutes before that happens, and we need to fill this thing with inconsequential conversation."

"I think the only part that needs deleted is this conversation we are having," I reply.

Joker nods, clicking away on his laptop.

"Well, I guess everyone's helping me clean this place up for closing. Chairs being put on tables and stools on the bar and glasses clinking. That's pretty inconsequential sounding, right?" Mia looks at Joker.

"Sure is." He stands and glares at everyone. "You heard the lady. Let's clean. We can talk movies. Musicals. How hot my wife is."

"But I don't know your wife." Grace gives him a once over. "Or you."

"Well, you should. She's amazing. Her name is Ginny, and she plays cello."

Everyone moves, following the order to clean, but Aunt Linda grabs me and pulls me to the back hallway, away from the recording device.

"We need to play this carefully, son. I agree with Mia's friend, I don't think she was in here for you."

"Then why? I know you don't believe in coincidences, Aunt Linda."

"I don't. I think she was absolutely here for something, I just don't think it was for you."

"What could she want with Mia?"

"Location. Access."

"You think she's what? Going to try to move her drugs through here?"

"It follows her pattern. She moves into a town, finds a place to move product, and then gets out before the heat can get to her, leaving someone else to take the fall. She's done it in Briar Mountain, where there's a connection between your girl's past, in Diamond Cove with the rich kids, in Rock Hill at the high school, and in other schools up and down the range. If she's looking at getting power, she needs money and capital. If she can't find you, the easiest way to do that is with drugs."

"And a bar is an easy place to move that kind of product."

"Bingo."

"You think she wants to use me to help her move drugs?" Mia interrupts us, her face ashen and her lip curled into a snarl. "Not a fucking chance."

"She doesn't know that yet. That's why she left her present. This woman isn't stupid. She's been operating with someone for years and has never gotten caught. Hell, we weren't even sure of her name a year ago. You need to play this carefully. At least until we know what she's playing at," Aunt Linda smiles at Mia. "I have faith in you."

"I don't like this one fucking bit," I growl, turning and walking away.

Aiden, Grady, and Joker all notice and leave their chores to corner me on the other side of the room.

"You need to calm down," Joker says quietly.

"Fuck you."

"Not my type, buddy, and you know I'm right. You won't do anything but push her away if you go all alpha macho on her."

"You have no idea. You don't know what I've seen, what I know."

"You're right, I don't. But each of us has our own burdens, have seen some shit, and we're still here," Joker says, a faraway look in his eyes. "And I'm telling you, from experience, that the best thing you can do right now is let her know you are here, you aren't going anywhere, and that you want to keep her safe. You can't demand shit. Trust me, that will backfire faster than you can fucking say you're an asshole."

"So what do we do?"

"We keep her safe. It's what we're trained to do." Grady smiles. "Kind of our fucking jobs. We take turns, we act normal, we keep an eye on things."

"I can't be seen in public right now, remember?"

"Which is why you have us."

"Enough penis plotting," Mia whispers from behind us, making us all jump. "Time to go." She nods her head to the disk, and Joker goes over to retrieve it off the bar and put it back in the booth where Aunt Linda told him it needed to go.

"She's going to be trouble, you know that, right?" Aiden quietly tells me as we walk toward the bar.

"Yup. But she's my trouble."

"Take your trouble home, man. Keep her safe. And don't smother her." Joker grins. This is where I should point out that when that man grins in any form or fashion, it's actually terrifying, right?

"Let's get out of here," Mia whispers when I'm close enough to her.

"Yes, ma'am."

"And Dem, we're going to talk about whatever plan you and the big guys came up with without me, so I can tell you if it's something I'm willing to go along with."

CHAPTER ELEVEN
MIA

HAS anyone ever looked at their life and wondered how they got here? You know, the place where you're living with the guy you like but can't let touch you while he and his buddies are whispering about you behind your back thinking you won't notice that you're being followed? Yeah, me neither, but here we are.

The funniest part to me is that they think they're being slick, that I don't know they are there. I sure hope they're better at this shit when it's a paid job. Let's take yesterday, for example. On my way to my therapist's office, which I had to tell Demitri he wasn't invited to, I noticed a black Range Rover behind me. Wouldn't usually notice a car or SUV, but a jacked up, shiny, chromed out monster? You notice that kind of shit around here. And I've noticed it every day for two weeks.

Might have given it a pass, but when I came out of my appointment, it was still there, idling across the street and it immediately pulled out behind me. I could see Aiden behind the wheel, but he wasn't with Grady or Joker. I couldn't remember the guy's name, so I guess this is big guy four. All of these guys are huge, overly tall, muscular, and look like they can kill you with their pinky.

On my way to the bar, my phone rings, and I answer it without looking at the caller ID. Driving safe and all.

"Hello?"

"Mia, it's Aunt Linda. How's the brute squad today?"

"Stupid," I laugh. "If I know they're following me, anyone watching would know it as well."

"It's a good thing they are all pretty. And I might know how to put an end to it."

"How? Please, for the love of everything, tell me how."

"Meeting tomorrow at the community center over here in Briar Mountain. Let's pull them all together and tell them what's going to happen from here on out."

"Deal. I'll see you then."

"I'll send you the details. And don't tell lover-boy. I want to meet with you first."

"Sure thing."

I hang up and pull into the bar's parking lot. No one will be here this early, but I have admin shit I have to get through if bills are going to be paid this month, so here I am. Besides, the woman who they think is Demitri's sister hasn't been back, and I haven't seen anything suspicious going on around me, so this should be fine.

I look in the rearview mirror as the Range Rover drives by, not following me into the parking lot, and I pull around to the back of the building. I gather my bag and get out of my car, beep the lock, and make my way to the door. Unlocking it, I feel something is off, but I'm not sure what.

I close the door behind me, making sure it's locked, and go into my office. Nothing looks touched, but there's a scent in the air that's not normal. At least not normal here. It's musky, rich. Like men's cologne, but the super expensive kind. Unless Brodie came in to some mystery money, someone was definitely here who shouldn't have been.

I turn on the monitors, not willing to go into the big room until I check the cameras. I look at the open door and decide to close and lock it before sitting down behind my desk. I scan around the room and don't see anyone, so I play back the overnight recording. It's motion sensor unless you manually turn it on, and at four this morning, they clicked on.

I expect to see a beautiful woman with crystal blue eyes, but there's no way that figure could be her. It's a man. I'd bet my life on it. Yeah, bad pun. I'll see myself out.

I pick up the phone and call Demitri. "You need to call the goons following me and tell them to get their asses back to the bar. You need to come, too. Someone was in here overnight," I blurt out before he can even say hello.

"On my way."

He hangs up on me while I watch the man on the screen go directly to the booth and pick up the bug we found a couple of weeks back. Fuck. This changes things.

It only takes about twenty minutes for everyone to gather in my office. No one said a word until Joker did his thing and determined it was safe to talk. Still, there have been very few words as I pull up the video.

Demitri, Aiden, Grady, and Joker all hover over me while we stare at the screen. Big guy number four, it turns out, is Nate, who I previously met in Briar Mountain. The picture hasn't changed, no matter how much I wish it would. A burly man walks in from the back and goes straight to the booth to collect the disk, then turns to leave. He doesn't show his face directly to any one camera, so he obviously knows where they are, but I don't think that matters. Demitri knows who it is if his sharp inhale of breath means anything.

I turn to look at him, wondering if it's this Andrey guy he talked about the other day, but he shakes his head.

"Worse," he answers the unspoken question. "So much worse. We need to get out of here."

"Community center office in an hour?" Aiden asks. "We'll round everyone up."

"Fuck," Joker blurts loudly, "watch that part again!"

All of us turn back to the screens, Joker taking over the controls and slowing the replay. The man drops some kind of liquid on the floor at the bar opening and keeps walking like nothing happened.

"Do you have outside cameras, too?" Joker asks me.

"Just over the front door. But I have a security system on both doors and no alerts went off last night."

Nate stands, heading to the door. "Okay, we need to get out of here, and I'm going to look up a few more things."

Joker closes the laptop and stands, leaving before we can say anything to him.

"Meet us at the center in an hour," Aiden tells Demitri and I before following behind Joker, Grady trailing after him.

"What the fuck is going on?" I quietly ask, my hands shaking.

"I don't know, *Krasotka*, but we'll figure it out. Call Brodie and tell him you aren't going to be here tonight." When he sees the look I give him, he amends his statement. "At least tell him you're going to be late. Please."

I agree and call Brodie on the way to the parking lot. I lock the door behind us and follow Demitri to his truck. I couldn't drive right now if I tried, and I know this will make him feel better.

On the drive over the mountain to the community center in Briar Mountain, Demitri tries to converse with me, but I'm not in the mood. My mind is on my bar, where I'm worried that this has nothing to do with Demitri and what it means then.

CHAPTER TWELVE
AUNT LINDA TEXTS

Aunt Linda: Our girl is going to be freaking out. Need to calm her down.

Source: Do you blame her?

Aunt Linda: No, but she's going to have to learn to control her reactions.

Source: I think you're underestimating her.

Aunt Linda: Not at all. I need for her to be successful in this. I need for her to understand the importance of hiding all your cards. If she can do that, there's no stopping her.

Source: Are you sure you want her this involved?

Aunt Linda: She's who he wants, so she's involved. I couldn't get him to leave before because of her. No chance in hell he's going now.

Source: If he did go, we'd at least know if the unsub was after her or him.

Aunt Linda: Well, you talk him into leaving her then. I'm old and tired.

Source: And full of shit.

Aunt Linda: There're so many pieces at play right now, so many reasons to be careful, but this is something we have to see through, and you know it.

Source: You need to be honest with her.

Aunt Linda: The plan was to talk with her tomorrow. That's not an option now.

Source: Figure it out.

Aunt Linda: Working on it. What's the idiot doing, anyway?

Source: He wants back what he thinks he lost.

Aunt Linda: It's going to end badly for him. This kind of thing always does.

Source: He thinks he's better than us. He thinks he's better than all of them.

Aunt Linda: What's his endgame?

Source: I think you know. But you also
know he's not working alone. And that's
one tough bitch to bring down.

> Aunt Linda: Do we know where she is right
> now? Has she been in touch?

Source: She's lying low right now. Not
making any moves on her own.

> Aunt Linda: This has to end. How many
> times will this family have to die before they
> stay dead?

Source: I'm afraid to answer that.

> Aunt Linda: Yeah, I know.

Source: Go see your girl. Tell her the truth.
See what happens.

> Aunt Linda: You know your little game today
> is throwing everything off.

Source: Have to have a little fun every now
and then.

> Aunt Linda: By terrifying everyone?

Source: They have to know.

> Aunt Linda: But they don't, and I can't say
> anything.

Source: Sure you can. I'll say it again. Go
see your girl. Make her understand.

Aunt Linda: Is that an order?

Source: Even I know better than to do that.

Aunt Linda: That's what I thought. Talk soon.

CHAPTER THIRTEEN
DEMITRI

THE MEETING ROOM IS FULL. That's the only word for it. And there are some faces I've never seen before. Before the meeting could start Aunt Linda came in and took Mia, saying she needed a word. I don't like when that woman needs a word. It's never good.

I look around at everyone, waiting for someone to say something, but it's like everyone is waiting for Mia to return. She's somehow become the center of everything, and it makes my skin crawl. I don't want her anywhere near this shit, and no matter what I do, she keeps getting drawn in. There is the very real fear that if my family is trying to make a comeback, I know they will hurt her to get to me. It's the entire fucking reason why I've been hiding in the shadows. If they get her anyway, it's all been for nothing. And now there's a new fear after this morning. The man on the screen seen breaking into her bar was one of my father's soldiers—and my uncle. One who dealt in pain and blood. One who relished in the selling of young girls to old men with money. After he broke them.

It feels like forever when Mia and Aunt Linda come back into the room, Mia looking a little green around the edges and

Aunt Linda looking like she's just out for a daily stroll. Mia walks directly over to me, sitting down in the chair reserved for her, and drops her face into her hands, rubbing them up and down before sighing in exasperation.

"What's wrong? What did she say to you?" I whisper as I watch the woman in question claim her seat across the table from us.

"Nothing I hadn't already thought about. Just drop it for now, okay? Let's figure out what's happening and we can deal with everything else later."

"As long as you're sure you're okay."

"I'm fine." She gives me a closed-lipped smile, but we both know she's full of shit.

"Okay," Daniel Allen says from the front of the room. "We have new and old faces, so let's do a quick introduction so we know we're all friends here. Daniel Allen, the A in ANON. I run logistics and operations. Nate? You're next. Name and what you do."

"Feels like fucking kindergarten all over again," the man in question replies, rolling his eyes. "Hey, I'm Nate."

"Hi, Nate," a few of the guys answer with big ass grins on their faces.

"Oh, not kindergarten, AA, or a support meeting. Anyway, I'm tech for ANON. I'm also one of the Ns in ANON." He turns to look at Joker sitting next to him.

"Joker. ANON. Not part of the letters, just one of the peons. Tech and hacking." He turns to the man next to him.

"Mostly legal, right Joker?" Joker laughs before the man goes on. "Sam Carmichael. I'm with BMPD."

"Why's the police here?" Mia asks.

"Because I asked him to be here," Daniel replies. "We need to make sure any plans we come up with are legal, and we know he's clean."

Mia nods, and Daniel points to the next man.

"Grady, but you all knew that, right?" He grins. "I'm backup support and run the personal security arm of ANON. Oh, and I'm the other N. The first one, of course."

"Fucker," Nate mumbles as he throws a waded-up paper ball at him.

"Enough," Daniel barks.

"Aiden. The O in ANON. I coordinate the teams and their schedules. Maintain the database. Shit like that."

"I'm Mary with the DEA. Those are the only letters I know."

It's my turn, and I'm not sure what to tell them. "So, I'm Demitri Pavlov." A few people gasp, but most know who I am. "I have no clue what's going on, but I'm pretty sure it involves my family."

I reach over and squeeze Mia's hand, giving her my strength.

"I'm Mia. I own City Brews over in Rock Hill. I'm with him. Have no idea what's going on."

She turns to look at the woman beside her. I've never seen her before, so I have no idea who she is or where she came from.

"I'm Kat Decker. I work at the University. I'm here because if it's drug related and my campus is a threat, I need to know."

"I'm Vic Allen. Kat's sister. Daniel's wife. I've had the unfortunate privilege of meeting your uncle Stanislav." She looks at me. "He was stealing money from the community center. He was also working with my ex-husband. Who enjoyed beating me."

Mia looks at her, a knowing look on her face. "He was an Ashby, wasn't he?"

"He was."

"All of them were fucked in the head. Every single one."

The two women share a knowing look before Daniel clears his throat. "I'd prefer we don't talk about him. Ever. Please."

Victoria blows him a kiss before the next person speaks.

"I'm Davis Mills. Former FBI and current bar owner in Boulder Canyon." He tips his head to Mia. "I brought down the Pavlov family the first time."

"Only FBI agent I've ever liked." I grin at him.

"I'm Aunt Linda." Linda smiles at the group.

"Is that all we get?" Mary asks, a grin on her face.

"Yup."

"Alright. We all know who you are. Let's get down to business. Joker, what did you find?"

Joker pulls up a video on the screen behind Daniel, showing the outside of Mia's bar taken from across the street.

"The hardware store next to the bar has external cameras I was able to access. The perp zapped the security system on his way in. High-tech stuff. Don't know who these people are working with, but they have money. Something like this isn't cheap."

"Illegal stuff usually isn't," Aiden says.

"He went in, did what we all saw him do on the inside cameras, and left."

"Any idea what he's driving or who he is?"

"I know who he is," I speak up. "His name is Sasha Pavlov. My uncle."

"You said he's worse than Andrey?" Mia asks.

"Yeah," I say with a laugh. "He was one of Ivan's spies. He kept an eye on the others, reported who was doing what, and made unilateral decisions on when it was time to kill one of our own."

"He wasn't brought down with the others?"

"No," Davis answers for me. "He went underground when the heat started ramping up. No one's seen him in over five years."

"Until today."

Joker types a few keystrokes and pictures of my uncle pop up on the screen. He was bigger than Ivan, but not as commanding. He used brute strength to get his point across, whereas my father used cunning manipulation to get what he desired.

"It's thought he's killed or had a hand in the killing of over a hundred people—men, women, and children."

"So what angle is he playing?" Daniel asks.

"Could he want the power for himself?" Aiden asks.

"Then why help Demitri's sister?"

"Not my sister," I say before I can stop myself. "She's not my family."

Mia places her hand on my leg and squeezes, calming me.

"We need prison records. Who's visited your family, what names they used, what their backgrounds are." Grady writes notes, not looking up.

"What is this woman's name?" Mia asks out of the blue. "The one who was in the bar?"

"She's been known to have a few names," Nate offers. "Kara, Karina, Katya. Her legal name is Katya Sokolova. After her mother."

"And this Andrey guy? What's his story?" She turns to look at me.

"I can answer that one," Davis offers. "We couldn't connect him to anything big when we took the family down, but he had a few possession and theft charges levied on him, and he did a short stint behind bars."

"And now he's teamed up with Katya and Sasha," I say, trying to wrap my head around it.

"And they want me for some reason," Mia whispers, more to herself than anyone.

"Until we know more, we can only be proactive in keeping everyone safe." Daniel stands. "So with that in mind, we're putting a detail on you Mia. Full-time, twenty-four-seven."

"Will they be better than this one?" She looks at Grady, who grins at her. "His skills of following people without being noticed are kind of lacking."

Everyone at the table laughs while Grady flips off my girl. "I wasn't trying to hide, Princess."

"Yeah, but we know these people are after me, so it would reason that they would follow me at some point, right? And if you're being so flashy with the following me and shit, then how can we catch them doing the same?"

Joker grins at Mia, nodding his approval. Grady looks like he's been caught with his hand in the cookie jar.

"That will change." Daniel side-eyes Grady. "But you need to know that there will be someone on your tail."

"And you'll wear this." Joker stands and brings a watch over to her. "It records, has a tracker, and can send an SOS with just the push of a button."

"Is this all really necessary?" She looks around the room.

"Yes!" everyone, myself included, responds.

"Okay, fine. I'll wear the fucking watch."

"Oh, she needs to meet my sister." Davis grins at her.

"That's my wife you're talking about," Joker growls.

"Still my sister, asshole."

"Enough," Daniel says.

"Demitri, we need you to be seen. But not too seen. Go to work, live your life. As far as anyone needs to know, your name is John Smith. You own the custom garage in town, and you just moved in with your girlfriend."

"Okay."

"We'll be following you, too."

"You'll make sure he stays safe?" Mia asks.

"Yes."

"What are we doing about the woman?" Mary wants to know.

"Nothing we can do until she makes a move, right?"

"Right. But we can't sit back and watch it happen. That's how people end up dead or missing. This family follows a pattern. And if she's working with two ranking members of what was, we should be able to track their progress. The drugs are next."

"And then the women disappearing," Davis adds.

"Mia isn't going to be one of them." I stand quickly, my hands on the table. "I need you all to know that if something happens to her, if one hair on her head is harmed, I will burn the fucking world to the ground. And I'll take out anyone who gets in my way."

The threat is there. If any of these people take a wrong step and Mia gets hurt, I'll kill them with my bare fucking hands.

Daniel quickly ends the meeting before all the alpha personalities in the room start showing off and we all end up in the hospital. Do I know anything that I didn't when I walked into that room? Nope. My family is back. And they want Mia. To what end doesn't matter. All I know is they'll never fucking touch her without going through me first. They might share my blood. They might have been loyal to my father. But they stopped being family the night Mika died.

CHAPTER FOURTEEN

MIA

I STARE at Demitri on the way back home. He says nothing, and eventually I can't stand it.

"Why were there so many people there? Why did they need to be there? I still don't know what the plan is. What about the stuff on the floor of the bar? What. The. Fuck. Demitri?"

It all comes pouring out, all the questions I had through the entire meeting. I stare at the watch on my wrist. Big Brother is watching, and all that shit.

"Also," I add before he has time to respond, "do you think Joker is listening to this conversation now?"

That gets a grin out of him. "He doesn't give a shit unless you need him, *Krasotka*."

"How do you know? How well do you know him? And why was there a cop there?"

"If what Daniel told me earlier is true, the cop was there because Joker needs someone to smack him on the back of the head when he goes too far over the 'mostly' legal line. They are friends from Boulder Canyon."

"Okay, that's one. How about everyone else? The ones not actually employed by ANON?"

"So, Vic is married to Daniel, and she pretty much makes the rules. If she wants to be somewhere, she is, and he never stops her."

"True love." I roll my eyes.

"They called Davis because he's the one who brought me in and hooked me up with Aunt Linda. He knows my family almost as well as I do. He blew his cover *for me*."

He's silent for a few minutes, lost in his own memories. I let him have them before going in again, trying to get more answers.

"What about the other woman, Kat? She said she was Vic's sister?"

"Yeah, I guess she was already in the building talking to Vic, but she went through some stuff at the University surrounding my family, so I guess she just wanted to be there."

"Or she's nosy."

"That, too." He chuckles. "And Mary is DEA. She's going to be the point person for the alphabet crew, I guess."

"I guess she makes sense. But no one said anything about the stuff on the floor of the bar. Is it poison? Pee? Do I need to tell Brodie not to walk behind the bar until I can get a professional in there to clean it up?"

"It's water. Plain, basic water. It's a Sasha thing. And, yes, we need to clean it up. He would put it out to see if someone would slip in it and fall. If they hurt themselves, all the better. In some cases, it was guaranteed to cause an injury."

"That's kind of boring, Demitri."

"I didn't say the man was smart."

We sit in silence for a few while Demitri rides the curves along the mountain range separating Rock Hill from Briar Mountain. This area is always dangerous, so I appreciate his care.

"What time will the bar open tonight?" he finally asks.

"Brodie will open at four. He can handle it until about six. That's when the after-work and dinner crowd start coming in. And before you say it, this is my livelihood, and Brodie can't make much more than a draft beer. I need to go to work."

"I know." He sighs. "I hate it, but I know. What do you do if you get sick? Or want a vacation?"

I laugh. "I don't get sick. And when I do, I call Pat from Barlowe's in Briar Mountain and he sends one of his guys over to help for the night. I haven't taken a vacation since I opened the bar."

"You haven't been back home to see your parents?" He glances at me in surprise.

"Why would I? My mother would just tell me I'm getting old and fat, my father would try to get his friends to hit on me, and my siblings would tell me how perfect their lives are."

"Your mother thinks you're fat?"

"I'm exactly two sizes bigger than I was when I graduated high school. Until I start pushing out babies, she thinks you should stay the same size. Anything other than that is fat in her eyes and unacceptable."

"She sounds...fun."

"You have no idea."

"And your dad does what?" he asks in a 'if I ever see him, I'm going to kick his ass' tone.

"Exactly what I said. Why do you think I moved here for college? There are schools in Montana with business and culinary programs."

"Did he do that with your sister, too?"

"Yup. And she married one of them. Made daddy so happy. Found out later his friend paid him for the privilege of deflowering my sister."

"That's seriously fucked up."

"Sure is. I left the day I turned eighteen and I haven't been back."

"And you moved here and—"

"And met Brett Ashby, local cop. Thought he'd be safe. He wasn't."

I think he knows not to push any more than that. And isn't that just the bitch of the matter? He's been the perfect man. Patient, kind, too fucking understanding. It's been weeks. He's been sleeping at my house, playing protector to me day and night. But he hasn't been back in my room since that first night. He's held strong, keeping me where I usually have to be—at arm's length.

But I don't like it. Not at all. Today when he grabbed my hand, that was the first time he'd touched me. He still understands my safe zones, and he didn't break them. But it made me realize I miss his touch. I miss him holding me like he did that night. The night I slept through and didn't wake in a cold sweat, screaming. The night I woke up rested for the first time in a long time.

And then I went and ruined it by having a breakdown in the bathroom. Talking about these things is always hard. If I could forget them, I would. But the memories are never far away, triggered by so many things.

"What are you thinking about, *Krasotka*?"

I feel my face heat in embarrassment. "Nothing."

"Bullshit."

"Yup," I agree.

"You still don't feel like you can tell me things, do you?"

I hear the disappointment in his voice. The sadness that I'm keeping things from him. That I'm keeping *everything* from him.

"I want to tell you," I quietly confess. "But I don't know how."

"The beginning is usually the best place to start."

"I'm afraid you'll walk away. Decide I'm too much work and tell me to fuck off."

He laughs. A hard, almost choking sound. "You think you're easy?" He finally wheezes. "Mia, you are the most controlling person I've ever met. And that's saying a lot, considering my father was Ivan Pavlov."

"So you're already tired of me, then?"

"Did I say that?" He turns his head, giving me a cutting look. "No. I did not say that. I also don't care that you're controlling. It's what you need to stay sane in this world. I'd never hold that against you, and when you're controlling other people, it's a fucking turn on. What I'm saying is, if I haven't walked away yet, there isn't anything you could tell me that would make me do it now."

I stare out the window, watching the scenery go by. How do I tell him everything? How do I get through telling him all the dark parts of myself? I blow out a hard breath and close my eyes.

"My parents didn't want me. I was the third child that made their perfect family off-balance. I was also a number of years younger than my siblings, who were the perfect eighteen months apart. My father started grooming me when I got my first training bra. I wasn't supposed to go to college. I wasn't supposed to want things for myself. I was supposed to get married young, have grandchildren they could ignore, and he didn't care how old the man was, as long as he took me out of their house and off their budget."

"Fuck," he murmurs. "He sucks."

"Yeah," I laugh humorlessly. "And I knew from the age of ten that's all I should be. I also knew there was no way in hell I was going to do that. I worked hard. I entered cooking competitions. After all, a proper wife knows how to cook, right? This was acceptable, but they didn't know why I wanted it so badly. Every competition I entered came with a scholarship prize, not cash. Because if it had been cash, they would have kept it for themselves."

"Smart girl." He gives me a small grin.

"By the time I was a junior in high school, I had enough money to pay for college. To move out and away. I applied for every college that was more than one state away. One in Louisville, Kentucky, one in New York, Florida, and Virginia."

"And Briar Mountain," he finishes the list for me.

"Yeah, and Briar Mountain. I thought the small-town college would be better. Not as many people. I think I was wrong about that."

"What happened, Mia?"

The way he asks when he already knows the answer is going to be painful. The gentleness of his voice, prompting me to go on, but still making it sound okay if I stop. Not sure when it happened, but we are sitting in my driveway. The truck is still running, and neither of us seems to be in a hurry to get out of the cab. Maybe this is what I need. The safety of an enclosed space with an easy exit. And let's face it, sitting in a truck isn't a facing each other activity, so the fact that I don't have to look at him while I talk put me at ease. If I can't see his eyes—the same eyes that are so expressive when he looks at me —maybe, just maybe, I can get through this.

"I met Brett my second week on campus. My roommate talked me into going to some party at a frat house. There was booze and other substances flowing freely. A guy tried to give me a drink, but I'm not stupid. I knew what roofies were, and I wasn't going to take that chance. I slipped away and made my own drink while dumping the first one. That same guy kept watching me, waiting. When whatever he gave me didn't take effect like he wanted, he got aggressive." I pause to take a breath. "Other people there pulled him away. A big fight broke out, and the cops were called. Brett was the officer who showed up."

"Was he the only one?" Demitri asks, nothing but curiosity in his voice.

"Yeah, and looking back, I know I missed everything that night, but he was a cop. They're supposed to be safe, right? I ran to him for help. He was nice, Demitri. Really nice. He calmed me down, talked to me. Asked me about home, about my majors, my schedule. I told him everything. Even about not talking to my parents since I left."

"You were alone and vulnerable."

"That's exactly what I was. And he took every opportunity to remind me of that for the next two years."

"What did he do, Mia?"

"He made me fall in love with him," I admit. "Only then did his true colors come out. But by then I was so dependent on him, I couldn't get away. He started with his 'lessons' whenever he perceived I did something wrong. Don't ask what I did wrong. According to him, if it was a day ending in Y, everything was wrong. The bar was constantly moving, and no matter what I did, it wasn't good enough."

"Tell me. Please."

"It started small. Reprimanding me and telling me how worthless I was. Then he would demand I do whatever it was over again with him supervising. If the toast was too brown, do it again. If I missed a spot on the floor, do it again. The pictures on the walls were never dusted good enough. The spines on his books. Eventually, it graduated to physical things. He'd smack me if he didn't like what I said. He'd grab my arms hard enough to leave bruises if he felt like I wasn't paying enough attention. And then, it moved into raping me when I would say no, and after I tried to get away the first time, he tied me up and used me as a punching bag and a plaything."

"I'm sorry." Two simple words, no pity in his voice, just acceptance that this is what I went through.

"I was weak. I couldn't leave. I needed him, and he needed

me. If I could just be better, it would stop and he'd love me again."

A tear slides down my face, quickly followed by another. And now that they've started, I'm not sure I'll be able to get them to stop. I can't talk anymore, and Demitri must know it, because he turns the truck off and gets out of the driver's side door. When he opens my door, I jump at the sound.

"Can I help you to the house?" he quietly asks, his voice strong and sure. "Can I touch you?"

I nod, tears still streaming, and don't flinch when Demitri picks me up from my seat and cradles me on the way to the door. I put my head on his chest, his heartbeat strong and steady. Calming. A sound of safety amongst the chaos.

I watch him through the watery haze of my vision and realize I'm not panicking. This man is touching me, and much like the night we slept with him holding me, I feel nothing but cherished and safe.

When Demitri opens the door and walks inside, I cling to him, willing him to not put me down. He hears my silent prayer and sits on the couch, holding me tight to his body, whispering words in Russian.

When I can speak again, I lift my head and look at him.

"Thank you."

"Don't." He shakes his head. "There's no need to thank me for taking care of you. Thank you for sharing with me."

"Demitri?" I ask, my tongue darting out to lick my lips.

He raises his brows, his eyes watching the movement, but doesn't say anything.

"I would like to try something. If it's okay with you."

"Anything."

"I'd really like to kiss you."

"Yes."

CHAPTER FIFTEEN
DEMITRI

MIA DOESN'T THINK before cupping my face with her fingers. Long and strong, callused from the hard work she puts in every day. Her thumbs rub my cheeks, almost like she's making sure I'm real. When her lips touch mine, I know I'll never be the same. Kissing has always been a no-go. It was too intimate. She told me it was her *Pretty Woman* rule, and I didn't know what the fuck she was talking about until I found the movie.

Her lips are soft, plump, and firm under my own. I know I have to let her lead this kiss, and it takes all of my willpower not to take over, to demand more. When her tongue darts out and tastes my lips, my heart stutters, and I'm a little worried about the situation in my pants. I don't know how long she's going to allow me to feel her body against mine and her lips doing wicked things, but I'll take every gloriously agonizing second she allows.

"I want you," she finally whispers against my lips. "I want..."

"Tell me," I demand when her voice fades.

Her lips are still on mine, our breath mingling together. "I want you to touch me, but I'm afraid."

"What are you afraid of?"

"I'm afraid you'll walk away if I...can't."

"Mia, look at me," I say, pulling back enough that she can. When our eyes lock, I continue. "I'm not going anywhere. There is nothing you can do to make me walk away from you. You run this show. You know how much you can handle, and when it becomes too much, we adjust and figure it out together, okay?"

"Are you sure?"

"Abso-fuckin-lutley, *Krasotka*. You tell me what to do, and you tell me when to stop."

"Kiss me again?"

This time I do what I've wanted to for four years. I adjust her so she's straddling my thighs, put her palms on my chest, and cup her face gently. I pull her lips to me, applying pressure, silently begging for her to open up to me. When she does, our tongues intertwine, a seductive dance as old as time, but we are still learning each other. This is our real first. It's sloppy, hungry, and the best fucking kiss I've ever had.

She pulls back, panting, her eyes hooded with a fire in them that could warm me for the rest of my days.

"Help me stand up?" she asks, pushing against my chest.

I do as she asks and I'm rewarded with Mia's shirt flying through the air behind her. Her bra quickly follows, then her jeans and panties. I have no idea when she took off her shoes, but thank God for small miracles. I roam her body from head to toes, taking in every inch of her. She's beautiful, even if she disagrees when I tell her. She has scars, and while I want to know, she never has to tell me if she doesn't want to or can't. My imagination is quite enough where that is concerned.

"Dem, you have on too many clothes." She smiles at me.

Not wanting to give her any time to question why she

wants this today, I quickly pull off my shirt and fling it in the direction hers went. I undo my jeans and pull them down to my ankles. "If you want the pants all the way off, we have a work boot situation to take care of first."

She laughs, and the sound is so carefree, she's like a completely different person. "I think we can work with this. Keeps you restrained a little, right?"

"Mia." I wait for her to look at me. "If you need to do what we usually do, if you really want to have sex, this is all your call."

She's shaking her head before I even finished the words. "I want to know if I can. No, I *need* to know that I can. I want to give in. I want to feel you while you feel me."

"I'm here for you. Whatever you need."

She stands in front of me in all her naked glory, assessing. There's still heat in her eyes, but now they contain a calculated look, like she's figuring out mental gymnastics. She finally meets my eyes and nods her head. She steps closer, her knees bumping mine, so close I can smell her arousal.

"I want you to touch me."

"Where?" I sound like a man starved.

"Here." She points to the apex of her thighs. She closes her eyes and swallows before opening them back up and looking at me. "I want you to touch my pussy, Demitri."

My hand lifts from my thighs without thought, seeking out the promise of feeling what heaven must be like. I maintain eye contact with Mia, gauging every expression and breath. My fingers brush along her mound, and her whole body shivers.

"Still with me?" I ask, making sure she meets my eyes again. When she nods, I lift one finger, showing her what I'm going to use. She follows the finger until it disappears between her thighs, and for the first time since this began four agonizingly long years ago, I touch perfection. Soft, silky skin with neatly trimmed pubic hair, slick lips, already wet from her arousal. Running my finger through her slit, dipping just the tip into her body, I pull it out and circle her clit before repeating the motion. Each breach of her opening, she's wetter, her breathing more erratic, eyes locked on me, trying to remain with me in the moment.

"Demitri," she breathes, her voice husky. "I can't, I don't..."

I pull my finger back and put it in my mouth, tasting her flavor on my tongue.

"Mia, one day, you're going to let me lick you with my tongue. And I'm going to make sure it feels good for you."

"I'm sorry."

"Nope." I shake my head. "That was more than I hoped for. You're amazing."

"Your turn." She gives me a timid smile.

"Whatever you need, Mia. This is about you. Always."

She crawls over my legs, situating herself on my upper thighs. My hands hang limp at my sides, waiting for her to tell me what she needs.

"Please don't leave me if I can't, or if I cry."

"Your tears are beautiful. Every part of you is, *Krasotka*. And I want all the parts."

Her eyes shine at my words, but I mean every one of them.

She sits up on her knees, gripping my cock and lining it up with her opening. This I'm used to. This is the in-control Mia who takes what she can and feeds off my pleasure. As she slides her slick pussy down my shaft until it's buried in her body to the hilt, I grit my teeth. She always feels so good, but this time is different. This time it's *more*.

"Will you touch me?" she whispers.

"Where?"

"Here." She holds her tits—almost as an offering.

"Can I suck them, Mia? Flick them with my tongue?"

"Yes."

I slowly raise my head and pull one of her nipples into my mouth, gently laving my tongue over the hardened nub and sucking just enough that she feels it. She gasps but doesn't stop me. I pop her nipple out and move to the other, giving it the same attention. When I've thoroughly had my taste, I pull my head back and look at her. She hasn't moved, her pussy still gripping my cock.

"More?" I ask.

"No. Not...not right now, anyway. Can you do something else for me?"

"Of course."

"Will you hold my hips? Help me?"

I place my hands on each side of her body and give a squeeze. "I got you, Mia."

She starts to move, and I give her the illusion I'm doing something, but really, I'm just enjoying the bliss of being with her again. At some point, I do take over, gripping her hips and grinding her on my cock before helping her bounce up and down.

"This isn't going to take long," I warn her.

"Whatever you need."

I know not to push, I know not to try to force an orgasm on her, not right now. This moment was big enough for both of us, that I have no doubt it could throw her over an edge she's not ready for. Hell, I don't know if I could handle her orgasm right now. But one day soon, I have no doubt.

She places her hands on my shoulders, gripping me with the same force I have on her hips, as she starts to move faster, helping me chase my release.

"*Krasotka*." I sigh as the orgasm races down my spine, the force of it so hard I see stars.

When I open my eyes, she's staring at me, her lips quivering, her eyes filling with tears.

"Come here," I tell her, rubbing my hands up and down her back. "Let me hold you. You cry with me from now on."

She falls into my chest, wrapping her arms around my back while I do the same to her. Her sobs break my heart, yet at the same time, I think they might be healing hers.

I don't know how long we sit there, my dick still half hard inside of her. I know we need to move and get cleaned up, but I don't have the heart to be logical right now. We will stay right here until she's ready.

An hour later, we're both showered, cleaned up, and headed to the bar. I knew she wouldn't change her mind on that, and I'm firmly in camp 'pick your battles.'

"Can I ask you something?" I turn my head to look at her before facing the road again.

"Sure. Doesn't mean I'll answer but ask away." She grins.

I don't know what happened in her living room this afternoon, or if it was the confession in the truck earlier, but something has changed our dynamic. Mia has changed. It's like something that was weighing her down is no longer there.

"This has been on my mind, but that day I ran into you last year. In the park?"

"You mean where I ran into you?" She laughs. "What about it?"

"You weren't really there. I have a good idea where your head was at, but why was it such a visceral reaction that day?"

"I just found out that Brett was dead. But I didn't really believe it," she confesses. "That day, I didn't see faces other than his. He was everywhere, haunting me from beyond, I guess."

"That's not where my mind went."

"What did you think?"

"I thought someone had hurt you recently. And I wasn't there to protect you. I figured it was a combination of memories and something new that triggered it all."

"I don't need new triggers to find old ones. I just close my eyes and there they are."

"You've been having nightmares."

"I always have nightmares. The first night in ten years I didn't wake up screaming was the night you held me all night."

"I'm so sorry, *Krasotka*. I'm sorry this has been what you live with every day. I wish I knew you then, I would have protected you."

"Silly boy." She reaches over and pats my leg. "No one could have protected me from myself. Not even you."

At the stop sign before the bar, I turn to face her. "I would have fought all your demons, Mia. All your dark days."

"Or I would have destroyed you right along with me. We can't change the past, and sometimes that means we have nightmares. But I grew stronger because of what happened to me. I grew fierce. Loyal to those I love. I found my passion. Do I have issues? Of course. Don't we all? But I also know who I am. And what I want."

"What do you want, Mia?"

"I want to be able to love without fear. To fully give myself to someone without worrying I'll break again. Without losing myself. To be with you, free from the ties to that past."

Once I park, I reach over and undo her seatbelt and look at her. "I'm going to pull you across this seat and kiss the fuck out of you, Mia Alexander."

"Yes, please."

CHAPTER SIXTEEN
MIA

THE BAR IS BUSY TONIGHT, but that's not unusual for a Thursday. All the college kids from the University show up and hook up Thursday nights. Because let's face it, once you're old enough to drink, you're old enough to know you never schedule a Friday class before noon.

Demitri is in the office doing some work for his garage, Brodie is in the kitchen, and my mind is everywhere but in this bar. I want to tell my friends what happened today, but I can't. Not right now, anyway. I want to talk to my therapist, but her office hours are over. I want to close the bar for the night and go back to Demitri holding me on the couch while I cry. But I don't want to cry anymore.

My phone dings with a message, and when there's a break in customers, I pull it out from under the bar and read the message, smiling.

Demitri: Will you let me kiss you later tonight?

I look at the camera I know he's watching and wink. I haven't been playful or flirty in so long, I was afraid I forgot how.

"Boss, order up!" Brodie interrupts my daydreaming.

I turn around and grab the tray, carrying it out from behind the bar to a table of girls giggling over the new Vivian Briar book. I so want to tell them I know who she is, but I know to keep the secret. We don't spill on pen names around here.

"Here you go, girls." I smile, putting their food on the table.

"Thanks, Mia!" A cute blonde grins at me. She's one of my favorite regulars, and a pretty good tipper on top of it. It takes me a minute, but I remember her name is Lacy.

On my way back to the bar, I slow my steps when I hear a group of guys talking.

"Seriously, dude, one of these and the girl will do anything you want her to. *Anything*."

"I don't know, isn't that, like, illegal and shit?"

"Who gives a fuck if you get your rocks off and she feels good doing it? You just drop it into her drink and she'll never know. Sometimes bitches need a little push. That's all this is."

"But what is it? Where'd it come from?"

"I know someone who's selling it. Some hot chick. And you're going to miss your opportunity. Those girls aren't going to stick around for long after they eat. You need to go over and talk to them, slip this in her drink, and then be the good guy who offers to drive her home when she can't fucking walk straight."

At those words, I stop completely. Brodie always watches from the window when I'm on the floor to make sure nothing happens to me, and I look up, making eye contact with him. Part of being a bartender is listening to the patrons. And when what they are talking about doing in your bar is all kinds of illegal, icky, or just plain wrong, you call for muscle.

I see Brodie leave the kitchen and head toward me on the floor, and somehow I'm not surprised at all that Demitri is behind him. When they're close enough to be effective, I step up to the table. The conversation ends immediately, because while they might be fucking terrible humans, I guess they aren't stupid.

"You need to leave," I firmly tell them. "Now."

"Why?"

"Because I don't allow drugs in here. And I won't let you drug anyone while you're here. How's that?"

"We didn't do nothing, lady. Why don't you go back to being a good little bar wench and leave us men to our night out?"

Well, I know which one was calling girls bitches now, don't I?

I smile, showing just a little too much teeth and lean in close, so he can hear every word of what I'm going to say.

"See those guys over there? The big ones who look like they'd kill for fun? They're with me. And would have no problem removing your head from your body and shitting down your neck. Understand?"

"I want to see the owner. Does he know his employees are talking to customers like this?"

"I bet you would. Let me go get *him*." I tilt my head, smile, and spin fully around, then stick out my hand. "Hi, I'm the owner, Mia. Get. The. Fuck. Out. Now."

"Fuck you. There's no reason to kick me out."

"Isn't there? We can do this the easy way, or the hard way. I guess it's the hard way. I feel for your mother." I turn away from their table and yell above the noise and music of the bar. "ATTENTION! These two gentlemen are discussing drugging some woman here! Cause according to him 'bitches need a little push' so it's okay to drug them! Free replacement drinks for every female in the place, and if you start to feel off, come to me!"

"What the fuck, lady?" the guy says behind me, trying to hide his face from the now curious crowd.

"I gave you the choice—hard way is what you picked by not leaving. Now get the fuck out and never come back. And know I'll be calling Pat at Barlowe's and giving him a description of both of you, along with photos."

"What?" the quiet guy cries. "You can't do that. It's illegal!"

I laugh. "You really want to talk about legalities? Besides, I can. See the signs posted on all four walls?"

I watch them look around to find the 'this room is under camera surveillance' signs. Their attitude drops quickly after that as they slide out of their booth and practically run to the door.

"You aren't going to call the cops?" Demitri asks when I turn to him.

"No need. Brodie already did. They will be stopped right about," I tilt my head and look at the door. Five seconds later I hear the sirens, "now."

Demitri leans in close. "I am so turned on right now."

"Save it for later. We're too busy to leave." I grin at him as I walk back to the bar.

As the women come up for a remake of their drinks, I notice the girls I delivered food to still sitting in their booth, one of the girls crying.

"Brodie," I call over my shoulder. "Can you come help for a minute?"

"Yeah, but if it's more complicated than a simple beer or screwdriver, you're waiting! And hello ladies!" Brodie swaggers behind the bar, putting on all the charm. I'm sure he'll have a pocket full of numbers before he leaves tonight.

Demitri watches me as I head back to the girls.

"You all okay?"

"We will be," Lacy grins. "That guy that just left? He was dating my friend."

Said friend is currently looking like a bad mascara ad.

"If it makes you feel any better at all, the quiet one didn't have the drugs. It was the other one."

"Thanks," Lacy answers. "Still sucks. Who keeps allowing this shit to come to campus?"

"This has happened before?"

"Yeah, a few weeks ago, at a frat party. Girl was out of her mind, but she doesn't drink. Ever. Someone spiked her soda. The cops came and caught the guy trying to do something to her."

My heart hurts for these girls. Some things never change, but the cops showing up now are actually interested in punishing the bad guy.

"Yeah," Lacy's friend adds. "The cop was a hottie, too. Shew, I never knew they made police like that."

"Remember his name?" I ask, already knowing the answer.

"Hottie Carmichael. I was hoping he'd bust the seams on his uniform, but it held on. Disappointing, if you ask me."

I chuckle before looking at each girl, assessing.

"I want you to do me a favor." I pull business cards from my back pocket. "If you hear anything about drugs at parties, or girls being hurt, or if you're in trouble, you call me. Think of me as a neutral, safe space, okay?"

"Sure," Lacy replies. "Can we tell all the guys that come over here to drool over you that we have your number?"

At that, I laugh, shaking my head. "You do whatever you need to. But also tell the guys they can call me, too."

"You're like an awesomely cool aunt, you know that?"

I start at her words, but shrug. "I know a thing or two about what happens on campus. I know you probably think I'm ancient, but it hasn't been too long ago that I was where you are now. And I mean it, if you're ever in trouble, or if some guy is an asshole, or if he hurts you, you call me. If you hear about girls being roofied at parties, let me know."

"Yeah, sure." Lacy stands up, putting cash on the table before helping her friend out of the booth.

"And you keep your head up. You don't need to waste your time trying to make a fuck face that would even *think* about drugging you a priority in your life. Better to know now before you're dependent on him and feel lost, okay?"

"Thanks, Mia." The girl gives me a sad smile and I watch them leave before going back behind the bar.

Brodie is in heaven with options lining up, and I pull out my phone.

Demitri: Saving girls one at a time. You're fucking amazing, you know that?

Mia: Just been there.

Demitri: It's more than that. You give a fuck about them.

Mia: They might not have anyone else that does, you know?

Demitri: Fucking. Amazing.

I put the phone down and make some drinks for Brodie. Next time I look up, I notice one of the ANON guys in the corner nursing a beer. Nate, maybe? When did he get here? He tilts his chin my way and I return the gesture. At least he can have a beer while watching nothing happen.

The rest of the night passes relatively quick, and before I know it, Demitri is helping me in the truck.

On the way home, I ask the question I've wanted an

answer to all night. "Will you sleep in the bed with me tonight?"

His mouth tilts in a small grin. "Depends. Do I get to hold you?"

"All night long."

"Let's go to bed then, *Krasotka*."

CHAPTER SEVENTEEN
DEMITRI

IT SEEMS we've fallen into this alternate life pattern. I'm living with Mia. Sleeping in her bed every night. We've had sex. Not frequently, and not always with an ending we'd both like, but she's becoming more comfortable with me every day. She's opening up to me, letting me see the side of her she doesn't let out very often. What we haven't done? Addressed I'm still here. Or what she and Aunt Linda are up to with their hushed phone calls and secret texts. Oh, I didn't forget that she pulled Mia aside at the last meeting in Briar Mountain. Haven't forgotten at all. Was hopeful that Mia would bring it up on her own, but she's been quiet about it.

We also haven't talked about how long this is supposed to go on. How long are we going to play pretend? Is it even still pretend? I don't know anymore. And as much as I try to see past all of this, I think there's only two ways this ends, and both of them are bad. Either my mystery sister finds me and kills me to take my money and take over, or Mia wakes up and realizes she can't be with someone who has my history.

One thing that's happened in the last couple of weeks of this waiting game we're calling life? The friendship between

Aiden and me has grown stronger. Out of everyone around me, he's the only one who really knows what it feels like to walk away from The Family. Mine might have been Russian and his Irish, but the demands are the same. He's on duty tonight, sitting in the corner of the bar, which we've dubbed the Anonymous Booth, and I've joined him. The downside is he's facing the room and I'm facing away. Being seen, but not too much, just as requested.

"How did you do it?" I ask once we've settled in. "How did you walk away?"

"I didn't give them a choice." He shrugs. "I signed up for the Army. Even my family isn't stupid enough to piss off Uncle Sam and the federal government."

"They didn't try to influence you to stay or make it difficult once you were in?"

"Nah. I mean, they treated me like shit after I swore in. It was too late to talk me out of it when I had to report to MEPS and ship out to boot camp pretty much immediately, but when I came home on leave, I almost think my father was proud of me for following my own road. Doesn't mean he hasn't tried to get me back a time or two." He laughs, a smirk on his face. "Of course, I left the family that kills for fun and joined a team of elite weapons experts."

"Killers with formal training?" I grin back at him.

"That's when he really wanted me back. When he could use my skills to train the other men. I made sure I stayed in until I couldn't anymore. And then I wasn't worth shit to my father. I was just old, damaged goods."

"Injured?"

"Yeah, took out my right side. At the time, I could barely lift a spoon to my mouth. Dear Old *Daid* declared me officially out. Guess it's a good thing he never paid enough attention to know I was a better shot with my left."

"Daid?"

"Da? Dad? Whatever the English word is."

"You stay in touch?"

"I have a cousin who lets me know if what they're doing is going to impact what I'm doing here. He calls with weddings, babies, and deaths. We don't talk about the job. He's next in line since I stepped away. *Daid* had six kids. I'm the oldest, and a son. Have a brother, but he's basically useless."

"I bet he hates that."

"So much. What about you? What else have you learned?"

"I know Uncle Stanislav and my sister, Sonya, are both still in jail. No one has gone to visit them, everyone lying low. We know my uncle is back and working with my mystery half-sister, Katya. According to Aunt Linda, there're more kids out there, but I haven't started looking into them. Is it wrong that I don't want to?"

"No. But I think you have to ask yourself why."

"I don't want anything to do with this name and family. I never did."

"Demitri, did you take the money when your father died?"

His question takes me aback, but I nod.

"Then you're still a part of it. You think there isn't anyone in your family or in The Family that hasn't already had an accountant look into you? To see if you've spent the money and where? They probably have alerts set up to notify them when a quarter goes out of the accounts."

"Is that why they can't find me and kill me? Because I haven't touched the money?"

"Probably. Easier to follow what they really want than it is to have a manhunt in the hopes you'll hand it over without a fight."

I stare at him, my thoughts running wild. It's been weeks of waiting for something to happen. Is this how to kick-start it? So I can finally put it all behind me and move on?

"What are you thinking?" he asks.

"I'm thinking we need to run this by Aunt Linda and hopefully put an end to all of it."

"You ready to do that?"

"I can't move forward until I do. I can't know if this thing between Mia and me is real until the choice for me to be somewhere else is there."

"You that hung up on her, huh?"

"More than you know. I've been a doomed man for four years." I grin as I say the words, knowing Aiden will understand.

"Don't sound so chipper about it." He grins back.

"I don't see you with a girl on your arm."

"Don't push it, friend. I might not be in his favor right now, but my father is still alive and still seeking some type of retribution for what I did, even if he's slow to act on it. I feel like he's got something up his sleeve. I can't put anyone in that path."

"But there is a person?"

"Let's say there's the idea of a person. One that I know my family would never approve of, which makes it even more difficult."

"So her last name isn't O'Connell or O'Driscoll or O'Malley?"

"Nope. It's not Murphy, Kelly, or Walsh either."

"Fuck. That sucks."

"Almost as much as a mysterious half-sibling out to kill me for the family money."

Both of us laugh at that, knowing full well that Aiden could be right here in my shoes at any time.

"Call Aunt Linda. Tell her what you're thinking with the accounts. We've got your back." He smiles, a genuine smile of camaraderie. In our former lives, we would have been on opposite sides of the battle lines. In this life, we can share a beer and laugh together. I'll take this life, always.

"You want to do what?" Aunt Linda asks two days later.

"I want to use the money in the trust accounts."

"Are you insane? Have you seriously lost your mind since I talked to you last?"

"No. But I will if this limbo we're all living in continues much longer."

"What are you bitching about? You're stuck with your girl. How hard can that be?"

I roll my eyes. "Linda, did you ever stop and think that maybe I don't want to be 'stuck' with my girl like this? This isn't exactly the makings of a solid relationship, you know. I can't take her out, I can't woo her."

"Woo? What century are you living in? And it's Aunt Linda."

Every single time I talk to this woman, I end the call with a headache from rolling my eyes. "*Aunt* Linda, this isn't the way I wanted to be with Mia. It's not right. She needs her space to figure out things, and I feel like I'm doing nothing but interfering with her life, not becoming part of it."

And it's true, since I've been staying at Mia's, I've noticed as much as she's been opening up to me, she's also closing herself off in other ways. I always feel like I'm underfoot, always in the way. I'm interrupting her life, and not for the better. And she's been nothing but wonderful about it, but I can tell. The bags under her eyes, even with the solid sleep, have been getting darker. The stress lines on her forehead are standing out more, and I swear she's had more headaches recently than I have.

"Demitri, are you using protection with Mia?" Aunt Linda's sudden question throws me off.

"Am I what?"

"Are you using protection? Now would not be a good time to have an accident."

"Have you been peeking at our shopping lists?" I demand.

"Don't have to. I'm asking."

"Mia's on birth control, a conversation I had with her years ago."

"Hmm."

"Woman, you don't get to interfere with that side of our lives. Understand? I love you for what you've done for me, but that's crossing a line."

"Fine. Just be safe."

"We've both been tested. Clean bills of health for both of us, and Mia has an IUD. Like I said, we had this conversation when we needed to and established what was what in our own lives."

"Okay, okay, back to the topic. I don't like it, but I understand it."

"You don't have to like it. I just need your support to do it."

"And you think this will work? This will bring them out?"

"If anything, it will tell us one way or the other, right?"

"Let's get together with Joker and Nate tomorrow and figure it all out so they can track everything as well."

"Sounds good."

"Demitri, I'm sorry if you thought I was overstepping. I think of you as one of my kids, and I just want you to stay safe until the danger is gone, okay?"

"Thanks, Aunt Linda."

I hang up the phone and look over to see Mia standing at the door, sucking her lips in, trying not to laugh.

"What?" I groan, already knowing.

"Was she really asking you about our birth control?" She giggles.

"Have you met the woman?" I ask in exasperation, throwing my hands up. "What are you going to do?"

"She cares about you."

"I know. And I her. But I wouldn't have had that conversation with my mom, either."

"Still funny." She shrugs.

"I'll show you funny," I growl as I jump from the couch and chase her through the living room and into the kitchen.

These glimpses of Mia are what I crave, what I need to survive. I only hope if I do this with the money, if I pull out the rats, we get to have more.

CHAPTER EIGHTEEN
FOM THE TEXT MESSAGES OF DEMITRI AND JOKER

Joker: Money moved into secondary
account.

Demitri: Any suspicious activity yet?

Joker: Are you kidding? Of course there is.

Demitri: I knew it.

Joker: Want to know what's going on?

Demitri: Of course.

Joker: The minute the money disappeared
from the account, tracing started running.
Looks like it was set up a while back. They
traced it to the new account.

Demitri: Did they get any of it?

Joker: Fuck you. I set that puppy up tighter than Ft. Knox. There're more firewalls and alarms than the CIA has.

Demitri: Sorry. Didn't mean to hurt your feelings.

Joker: ...

Demitri: I know you aren't typing, dude. The three dots aren't gonna get me. Again.

Joker: *gif of Chris Evans smirking*

Demitri: Oh, the guy's got jokes.

Joker: I don't joke.

Demitri: *gif of Chris Evans laughing*

Joker: Enough funny business, I'm going to let them in so I can trace them back.

Demitri: And how much money are you letting me take?

Joker: A million. Did you know you're fucking loaded?

Demitri: That's not my money. I haven't touched it.

Joker: The man's dead. He was a horrible human. You can't get revenge, but you can spend his money like you don't care.

Demitri: Doesn't feel right.

Joker: When you find the right thing to
spend it on, it will.

Demitri: Noted.

Joker: I'll let you know what I find.

Demitri: Thanks. Glad you're on my side.

Joker: You should be. Talk later.

CHAPTER NINETEEN
MIA

"I know, I'll be fine, Demitri," I say into the phone. "Seriously, I'll be home in a little over an hour, okay?"

"Will you let me know when you leave?"

"Yes, dear."

"Fine, sorry. Just worried."

"I know." I sigh. "I'll let you know when I leave, okay?"

We disconnect the call, and I sit in my car, shaking my head and laughing to myself. Sometimes I'm not sure who the worrywart of this, whatever we're calling it, is. I stare up at my therapist's office, not wanting to go in, but knowing I need to. There are things we need to talk about, things I'm ready to talk about, but that doesn't mean I don't dread it.

"Get your shit together, Mia. Pull up your big girl panties and go tell the professional that you want to know how to have a fucking orgasm," I say to myself in the mirror.

I take a breath and open the car door, stepping out into the warm fall day. Walking into Dr. Malcome's office every week is like a homecoming in a way. When I found the courage and strength to get away from Brett, this was my first stop. I knew I couldn't go back home, and as much as I loved the little town of Briar Mountain, there was no way I could continue to live there with *him*, knowing at any time he could pull me over or knock on my door. The Briar Mountain PD is smaller than Rock Hill's, and he would have no reason to be on this side of the mountain. I found Dr. Malcome my first week here.

"Mia," Sally, the lady who is really in charge, smiles as I walk through the door. "She's ready for you."

"Thanks," I reply, walking through the lobby and into the inner office.

"Mia," Dr. Malcome nods.

"Doc."

I take my seat in the big, oversized chair and bring my legs up. Putting the pillow in front of me and holding it, I look at the doctor. "Okay, ready."

She chuckles. This is our way. We don't talk until I'm situated, and this has been my situation for over ten years.

"What's going on?" she asks, eyeing me with that head shrinker look I think all therapists have.

I inhale and blow out the air in my lungs before speaking. "I want to know if I'll ever be able to have an orgasm."

She does a double take, her eyes blinking rapidly. "You *want* to orgasm?"

"I know, right?"

"Well, I guess that's going to be up to you. I know we've worked on your feelings surrounding your past, but not the physicality of it. Bottom line is, having an orgasm during sex when you didn't want to doesn't mean you enjoyed the act going on. It means you had a physical response to what was happening, Not being able to have an orgasm now is an emotional response to the trauma you faced. It's why finding a partner you trust is just as important as how good he might look."

That's right, folks, I, Mia Alexander, had an orgasm while Brett did what he did to me. I understand that it wasn't in my control, and that I didn't do anything wrong. Well, I understand it now. Took a few years.

"I don't understand if I could do it during *that* why I can't do it when I want to."

"It's all a mental game, Mia. Because of what you went through, sex in and of itself is hard. Intimacy, which most women and some men need to orgasm, is a whole other level that you have to be ready for."

"I am ready," I assure her.

"What's changed?"

"I think I'm in lo—serious like with someone."

"Tell me about him."

"He's put up with me for four years? He was a one-night stand who didn't freak out and run away like the ones before him did. He came back. He became my friend. He's been fighting for me and with me since day one, and down in his soul, he's a good man."

"You trust him?"

"I do."

"You feel safe with him?"

"Yes."

"You feel like your foundation is strong enough that you can put your mind and body in his hands and he will take care of you?"

I hesitate before answering, searching both my mind and body for the answer. "I have some anxiety over it," I tell her. "But not fear."

"Being anxious and stumbling into an anxiety attack because you feel threatened are two different things."

I know what she's saying, we've had this discussion before. When I opened the bar and threw up because of my nerves, it wasn't panic induced anxiety. She's helped me see the difference when my heart rate increases because I feel a threat and when I feel excited about something. I nod for her to continue.

"I have homework for both of us." She grins at me while I groan. "You are going to talk to this fella. If you truly trust him and feel safe, you have to be able to talk about things, good and bad."

"How did I know you were going to say that?" I curl my lip in mock disgust.

"Because you're a smart, capable, logical human."

"What's your homework?"

"I'm going to call a colleague of mine and talk to her about ways to help you. We went to school together and her focus was on sexual health and post trauma healing. I think she might be the expert. She's close, just over in Briar Mountain."

"Oh?" I can't hide the surprise in my voice.

"You might know her? Dr. Thorpe?"

"Thorpe?" I gasp as recognition hits. "The Prof?"

"So you do know who she is. I think she might be willing to help us. It might be worth going and seeing her—as long as you don't forget about me and my plain old general psych degree."

"I don't think you have much to worry about, Doc."

"Shew." She wipes her brow. "I'll let you know when I talk to her, and we can figure out our best approach going forward."

"Thanks."

"And Mia, I want you to know that I've seen the work you've put in. I know you get frustrated that you aren't where you'd like to be on all fronts, but after what you went through, the fact that we're even having this conversation means you're healing. Be proud of yourself."

I stare at the woman who I credit with basically saving my

life all those years ago, the tears welling up and falling. "Damnit, Doc. I was almost all the way through without tears today."

"If you don't cry, were you really even here?" She smiles at me and winks.

"I'm going to tell Sally on you," I warn her.

She laughs and shakes her head. "Get on out of here. I have a call to make and you've got a man to talk to."

"Yes, ma'am." I roll my eyes.

"Mia," she calls my name when I get to the door. "You know if you ever want him to come along, he's welcome, right? He might have his own questions. If he's that great, those questions will be about how to best support you."

"Thanks, Dr. Malcome. I'll let him know."

I leave the office and say goodbye to Sally before escaping back to my car. Emotionally drained, I send Demitri a text letting him know I'm finished and will be home shortly. Then I call Grace.

"Mia? Everything alright?" she asks on the first ring.

"Yeah, fine. Just left Dr. Malcome's office."

"Ahh."

This isn't new. All four of us attend her practice and usually need to debrief after with someone we can really unload on. Someone who can understand because they lived through it, too.

"I asked her how to have an orgasm."

"I'm sorry, what?"

"I want to know how to have an orgasm. I know it's mental. Tied to my anxiety and fear, and I want to know how to move beyond it."

"Did she give you any advice?"

"She's going to call and talk to another therapist. She wants me to talk to Demitri."

"And how do you feel about that?" I can hear the smile in her voice.

"Well, doctor, I feel a little fucked up in the head about it all."

"So... normal."

"Yeah," I laugh. "Basically."

"I agree with her on this one. That man is in love with you and just wants to protect you and ensure your happiness. If anyone is going to bring your orgasm back, it's him."

"I know," I whisper. "That doesn't make it any easier."

"Nothing worth it is ever easy. You need to talk to him."

"You need to talk to your boss."

"Ahh, yes, the deflection part of the conversation."

"Doesn't make it untrue."

"I know, Mia. I know. But you also know I can't. You're out here trying to have an orgasm because you want more sex, and the thought of having it at all freaks me out. Could you imagine James in that situation? Not only would I lose any chance I might ever have with him. I'd lose my job, and I can't do that."

"You're right. God, I hope one day you find the thing you need to help you."

"I hope you aren't pinning all of your hopes on a man, Mia. You know as well as I do how that works out."

"I know. And I promise you, I'm not. I want this. But I choose him to explore the option with."

"Then you have to talk to him."

"I have to talk to him."

"Yes. Now get off the phone with me and go tell that man you want him to help you find your orgasm. And Mia, I hope you're a multiple orgasm squirter."

"Oh, my God," I yelp, laughing "Gracie!"

"What?" She softly laughs with me. "I read about them."

"One day, we'll both be recipients of multiple orgasms."

"If only. Now stop stalling and go talk to the man."

"Yes, *Mom*."

I guess it's time to ask Demitri to help me find my missing orgasm.

CHAPTER TWENTY

DEMITRI

I'M PUTTING the finishing touches on lunch when Mia gets home. Grilled cheese and tomato soup with a side of pickles. It's feel-good food. Comfort. And sometimes she needs that when she gets home. These are the days I also try to stay out of her way. There are times she wants to talk about what was discussed, and other times she will disappear into her room for a few hours, resurfacing only after she's processed what she needed.

Today, she appears in the kitchen in her socked feet, and I know she's been crying, but that doesn't really tell me anything.

"Are you hungry?" I ask, offering her a plate with a sandwich on it.

"I am, actually." She gives me a small smile. "Thank you."

She takes her seat at the table while I prepare our soup. Carrying everything to the table, I sit and pass her a bowl. We've started eating the cheesy good stuff, but Mia seems off.

"Everything alright?" I finally ask.

She nods, not taking her eyes off her plate.

"Mia?"

"It's nothing," she says quickly. *Too* quickly.

"I'll be here when you're ready to tell me whatever it is you need to tell me."

"I know. I'm trying to figure out where to start."

"We've had this discussion, haven't we? You start at the beginning."

She rolls her eyes, sighing like I'm the bane of her existence. I grin at her.

"Fine. I have a band-aid, and I don't know how to peel it off."

"Huh? Where do you have a band-aid?"

"It's a figure of speech, Demitri. I have something hard to talk to you about, and I'm afraid. How about that?"

"Just say it?" I ask, taking a bite of my sandwich.

"I asked Dr. Malcome how to find my orgasm."

And now I'm choking. Chest pounding, gasping for air, there's a giant lump of bread and cheese in my throat, and I know my eyes are bugging out. Mia sits there, a smirk on her face as if to say 'you said just spit it out' and this is now all my fault. I might die by a grilled cheese and never find out what her doctor told her to do about the missing orgasm.

I finally get the food down my throat and take a drink of water, holding my finger up so she doesn't speak again while I'm drinking. After a few deep breaths and cracking my neck, I finally look at her.

"Now, what did you say?" I rasp.

Her smirk turns into an honest grin, and she waits a beat to make sure there's nothing to kill me.

"I asked her how to find my orgasm. Why can't I have one?"

"And she told you what?"

"She told me I needed to tell you. To explain why I can't."

"Okay. Why can't you, Mia?"

"Because I'm ashamed," she quietly replies.

I reach my hand across the table, lying it next to hers, letting her know I'm there. Not touching, but close enough that she can feel the warmth. She looks at our hands, mine scarred and still tinged with oil and engine grime, hers strong and callused from working at the bar. When she stretches her pinky out to rub mine, I feel like we might be making progress.

"What happened? Can you tell me?"

"It's about Brett. I know, shocking, right?" she tries to joke.

"Don't. Don't hide behind the humor, *Krasotka*. Be real with me, okay? Just me."

She looks at me, tears in her eyes, and nods.

"When he would...when I had to...when he would rape me, sometimes I would have an orgasm."

I don't react. Fuck, I don't even know what to say to that. The silence lingers, and I know she's waiting for me to make the next move. To either stay or run away. One day she'll figure it out, right? That I'm not going anywhere?

"Mia," I say quietly. "I don't understand why that's shameful. Can you explain it to me?"

She still won't look at me, but she nods. "If I had an orgasm, it means I enjoyed it, right? And that's wrong. I never enjoyed what he was doing to me. Not after he started hurting me."

"I don't think that. Not at all."

"You don't?"

"No. I know the theory is that it's different for men and women. That men are physical creatures while women are emotional. And that might be why you can't find your orgasm now, but Mia, at the end of the day, an orgasm is the effect of the cause. It's the physical. The cause in this case is friction. Rub anything enough in the right way, and it does what it does, you know?"

"But you rub me the right way, and I can't. Does that mean I'm just broken?"

"No!" I shake my head almost violently. "It means that you're so focused on the control aspect you can't release it. You pull back when the friction gets to be too much. Because you're scared."

"I do?"

"You do, *Krasotka*. You stop grinding as hard. You stop pulling me in as deep. You stop the friction before it can cause the effect."

"Fuck," she whispers. "I do. I do that, Demitri. Why didn't you ever say anything?"

I chuckle. "What was I supposed to say? Mia, the way you ride me is great, but it takes me five seconds longer to cum when you stop grinding that sweet pussy on me?"

She looks at me, her face completely slack, her eyes blank, blinking. And then she laughs. Not a small laugh, either. This is a full-bodied, feel-it-in-your soul kind of laugh. One that is a release of the demons.

"Dem," she wheezes.

"What?"

"That was funny."

"I wasn't trying to be funny, Mia. What is it you'd like me to say when you go inside your head instead of living in the moment?"

She sobers up, staring at our still touching pinkies. "I don't know. I don't know that there's anything you can say. But I'd like to try."

I take in her face, her body language. She's open, honest. Her eyes, still shiny from unshed tears, ask me to understand. To realize she's giving me all she can.

"*Krasotka*, can I touch you?"

"Yes," she whispers.

I stand up, lunch now a long-forgotten mess to deal with

later, and move around the table until I'm standing in front of her, our knees touching. I lean down, take her hands in mine, and help her stand until her body is angled into mine. I wrap her arms around my neck and mine around her waist, holding her as close as possible.

"I want to touch you, *Krasotka*. I want you to let me. Allow me to show you how to let go. Please."

"Yes."

"Right answer." I grin, waggling my brows. "Now let's have some fun."

Before she can react, I have her up in my arms, her legs unconsciously wrapping around my waist, her fingers weaving into my hair and gripping. The bite of pain isn't unpleasant. And the squeal she releases makes me laugh.

I don't waste any time walking through the house and up the stairs, only stopping when I've reached her bedroom and am standing at the bed.

"What now?" she asks, pulling her flushed face back enough to look me in the eyes.

"Now, I'm going to lay you down on this bed and show you how to let it all go."

"Demitri, what if I can't?" Her insecurities are coming through strong.

"Then you don't. Maybe we learn some things you like or don't like. Maybe we get you close, maybe not. If it doesn't happen, we try again later. And we'll keep trying until you see stars."

"Why are you so willing to do this?"

"Mia," I say her name before kissing the corner of her lips. "I'd give anything to see you fall apart and know it's because of something I did with you."

"You mean something you do to me."

I shake my head slowly, kissing her neck. "No. Because of something we do together, because you're going to help."

"What? How?"

"I'll show you," I murmur into her ear before sucking the lobe into my mouth, making her gasp.

Without another word, I lift Mia's shirt up and over her head, tossing it behind me. I then reach around her and remove her bra, dropping it as well. I lower myself to my knees, undoing the button of the jeans she's wearing and pulling down the zipper. I slowly draw the fabric over her hips and down her legs, helping her step out of them and leaving her standing in front of me with only her black panties and socks on.

"I'm going to take these off now, okay?" I look up at her while I finger the elastic band at her hip.

She nods, biting her lip. Before I pull them down, I lean forward and kiss one of her scars. It's faded over time, but I know it runs deep. When I lean back on my feet, I slide the material down her legs, revealing her sex to me. It's glistening, wet.

"Lie back on the bed for me, *Krasotka*."

She does as I ask, slowly sliding onto the mattress. Only when she's in position with her head on the pillows do I remove her socks, leaving her totally, gloriously naked.

"Now what?" she whispers, trepidation in her voice.

"Now, I'm going to kiss and lick and suck on every inch of your skin until you've melted into the mattress and don't have the energy to give the control any power."

"Good luck, I hope you're successful." She smiles.

"Have faith."

And then I get to work. Starting with her left foot, I lift it, kneading the arch, until she moans. I then kiss the top of her foot and make a trail of kisses up her left ankle, calf, and thigh. When I reach the apex, I inhale a deep breath, taking in her scent, spicy and musky and perfect, before I repeat the motions on her right leg. I then bypass her pussy and start at her hips, kissing from one side to the other, making sure any scars get special attention. I kiss and lick up her ribcage, only to pull my head back when I get to the underside of her tits, much to her obvious dismay.

"No fair!" she cries.

"Patience. Have patience."

I smile, already expecting her answer.

"I have none of that, Dem."

"I know." I smirk, kissing her palm and starting my way up her arm. "Tough."

After kissing both arms, I gently bite on that spot at her shoulder and neck, making her squirm under me. I kiss up her neck until I'm over her, holding my weight off her, knowing that might be a trigger.

"Now the fun begins." I grin before leaning in and touching my lips to hers. She opens immediately, our tongues dancing the dance of ages gone by.

I don't linger, knowing I have other places to put my mouth to work, and I kiss down the other side of her throat to her chest. Circling one nipple with my fingers, I trace the other with my tongue. When her breathing increases, I pull as much of her breast into my mouth as I can and suck. Her hips lift off the bed, her hands go to my head, trying to pull me close and push me away at the same time.

She cries out in pleasure, her body convulsing with each pull of my mouth. When she firmly pulls my hair, I release her tit with a pop and look up at her.

"What was that?" she pants.

I trail my eyes down her body to her pussy, seeing the evidence of her release.

"That, my dear, was an orgasm."

"But, how? How did you do that?"

I grin, feeling pretty proud of myself. "You did that. I just helped you get there."

"Think we can do it again?" She practically giggles.

"You're going to do it again, at least once. I'm not done feasting on you—as long as you can handle it."

"What are you going to do?"

"I'm going to lick your sweet pussy until you scream my name, *Krasotka*."

"What about you?"

"What about me?"

"Don't you want to...you know..."

"Later. This right here is all about you. I have four years of orgasms to repay you for."

I move until I'm between her legs, my hands running up and down her thighs. Being able to touch her is still blowing my mind, and I never want to take my hands off her. Mia's skin is so soft, like she bathes in silk.

"You don't have to," she says. "I know some guys don't like—"

"Enough," I stop her. "If you say some guys don't like the taste of pussy, those guys are nothing but idiots and lazy fuckers. And I can promise you I'm not that."

She nods, biting her bottom lip, and I go to work. Spreading her thighs apart, I settle my shoulders between them, opening her up to me. Her pussy is perfect. Trimmed hair, puffy lips, and wet. I inhale her scent again before licking a path up her slit. She breathes in sharply, but I'm going to feast as long as she'll let me.

Opening her with my thumbs, I circle her clit with my tongue, applying pressure before backing off, building her up but not letting her crest completely. She tries to grind against my face, but I pull back until she calms down, only for me to work her back up again.

"Demitri. Please," she begs.

It's the begging that gets me. The plea in her voice that she's *this* close to breaking.

Inserting one finger into her pussy, I feel her tense up but wait for her to relax into my touch before I rub against her inner wall while pulling her clit between my lips and sucking gently. And that's all it takes. She goes off like a firecracker, her hips bucking and her legs shaking.

"Demitri!" she yells while convulsing under my touch.

I slide my finger out while still lapping at her clit, making sure to extend her orgasm as long as possible.

"Demitri," she rasps. "Enough. Please. Stop. No more."

I immediately pull back, resting my head on her thigh, and look up at her face. Flushed, her eyes still unfocused, her hair spread out on the pillow beneath her, and her mouth slack. Her breathing labored, her hands still gripping my hair.

"Wow," she finally gasps. "That was new."

I chuckle against her, leaning in for one last kiss at the top of her slit before I pull myself away, moving up the bed until I'm beside her, both of us on our sides, staring at each other.

"You did it, *Krasotka*." I smile.

"You did it," she mumbles sleepily.

"Come here," I tell her, raising my arm.

Without hesitation, she moves over until she's in my arms, her head on my chest, her fingers playing with the hem of the shirt I'm still wearing. The dynamic of me being fully clothed and her being completely naked is not lost on me, but I reach over and pull the covers up over both of us

"Thank you," she quietly says, kissing my chest over my heart.

"Sleep."

And she does. I hold her as I drift off, knowing the break will come and that I'll be right next to her to help her through it.

CHAPTER TWENTY-ONE
MIA

I'm in bed with a man who gave me an orgasm. Two of them! They were honest to God, bone tingling, toe curling, hair-raising, rainbow colors exploding, breath stealing, fucking orgasms. And he didn't take anything for himself. I look over at his face, so peaceful in rest, and my only question is, when can we do it again?

I didn't freak out. I didn't pull away. Okay, I tried to pull away, but I didn't! Man, Dr. Malcome is going to be so proud of me. Because I just had an orgasm—two orgasms!—with the man I'm head over heels for. One who has been so patient and kind with me. I know he feels like he's intruding by being here all the time, but I love him being here. Something about his presence in my personal space makes me feel safe. Protected. Because I know he'd live up to the Pavlov name and kill anyone who tried to hurt me.

I want to tell my friends. Hell, I want to tell the world. Would it be too much to have a t-shirt made that says *This woman just had an orgasm?*

But more than that, he didn't want or demand anything in return. He didn't make me feel guilty, he didn't make it about him. And I didn't demand control. I willingly gave this man power over me, and I survived. I trust him. I want to be free with him, to stop hiding.

He stirs, opening his eyes and smiling when he finds me watching him.

"How long have you been awake?"

"Long enough to know if I'm going to freak out on you." I scrunch up my face but break into a smile.

"Well, what's the consensus?"

"Honestly? I feel pretty good. Fantastic, if I'm being honest."

"Really?" He sounds almost surprised, but then again, so am I.

"Yeah," I confirm. "Really."

"Do you want to talk about it?"

"I want to do something different."

"What's that?"

"I want to see you feel as good as you made me."

He stares at me, a thoughtful look on his face, before he breaks out in a giant grin and throws the covers off.

"Come with me. Also, you're going to *come* with me if we do this."

I don't think twice. I give him my hand so he can pull me up and right back into his arms.

"I never want to let you go," he confesses into my hair.

"I don't want you to let me go."

He doesn't let me get very far away from him, holding me while walking backwards into the bathroom and turning on the shower. Only then does he step back and start removing his clothes, his eyes never leaving mine. T-shirt off and thrown behind his head. Jeans undone and kicked to the side. Boxer briefs shucked off and added to the pile. I'll joke with him later over the color of those, but right now I'm too distracted by his dick to say anything. Standing hard and proud, hitting his lower stomach when he moves, my mouth has gone dry and started to water at the same time. Huh. I've only read about that happening, I didn't think it was real. Guess I was wrong.

I wonder what it would feel like in my hand. Would it be rough and veiny? Soft and velvety? What would he taste like?

"Don't go there," he interrupts my thoughts.

"Huh?" I startle. "Go where?"

"Wherever you were just going in your mind. It was either very good or very bad, and we don't have time for that right now."

I open my mouth to argue, but the look on his face stops me. He's right. I was not thinking good thoughts. I was thinking very bad thoughts. Maybe he should ask me what they are, but he won't. Not right now. Guess that discussion is going to have to wait. And I'm honestly not sure I'll ever be able to suck his dick and enjoy it.

"There," he points to my face. "Wherever that is, don't go there."

I nod, offering him a small smile. "Sorry."

"Nope, don't do that either. Guess I'm not doing a good enough job distracting you."

He crowds into my personal space. A space I would have protected with my everything a few short months ago, but here? Today? I don't mind it. Not with him.

"I'm going to touch you again," he warns me.

"Yes."

Demitri wraps his arms around me, pulling me into him, his cock between us straining for attention.

"Ignore him for now," he whispers into my neck. I think it's his new favorite place to touch.

"What if I don't want to?" I challenge.

"Patience. Did I not teach you anything earlier?"

"Nope. You did not."

He laughs, his body shaking against mine and doing weird things to me.

"Come on, *Krasotka*, let's take a shower."

He walks me into the walk-in shower, testing the water on himself before moving me under the spray. Seriously, did he read a book on how to be a gentleman?

"I thought we were going to do something different than shower," I muse just loud enough for him to hear.

"Tons of fun can be had in a shower, Mia. Soap makes a great lube." He smirks.

"Is that so?"

"Very much so. I have a question for you before I decide how this is going to go."

"What's that?"

"When was the last time you touched yourself?"

His blunt question throws me off. Not that I think anything is off limits between us anymore, but because I don't know how to answer and not sound pathetic.

"Has it been that long?"

I nod, avoiding his gaze.

"Hmm." He rubs his chin and assesses me, but not in a bad way. "That creates all kinds of opportunities."

I watch as he reaches around me to grab the body wash off the ledge, my knees going weak when he pauses to inhale the vanilla scent with a smile on his face. Pouring the soap into my upturned palm before returning it to its home, he then starts rubbing it all over my hand, coating my fingers. It's almost too intimate, but I want to see where this goes.

Demitri turns me around so my back is against his front, his cock seeming to throb against my ass.

"Touch yourself," he quietly commands.

"I don't know if I can," I admit.

"Let me help."

Placing his hand over mine, spreading the soap along his

fingers as well and intertwining our fingers, our hands move together up to my neck, caressing it, before sliding them to my breasts. He circles my palm over one nipple and then the other, making the little nubs harden like diamonds and giving me a zing right to my core. Back and forth he moves our joined hands, working me up just enough to frustrate me when he moves us away. Also, coming from nipple play shouldn't be the regular, right? But here I am, getting completely worked up and frustrated because he won't let me have what I want.

When he moves our hands down my stomach, my breath hitches. I haven't touched myself in years. My no-touching rule was for everyone, no exceptions. Our hands glide over my mound and finally between my legs. His free arm wraps around me, knowing if this keeps going, I'll need help standing.

"What are you doing?" I ask, my eyes locked on our joined hands.

"I'm going to show you how to make yourself feel good. How could you ever tell me what you like if you don't know?"

With pressure on my finger, he helps me circle my clit, adding pressure with each pass. I feel like I'm having an out-of-body experience, watching what's happening to me without understanding that I'm the one making the zings and shudders happen.

"That's it," he encourages. "Just like that."

We increase the speed of our fingers, and I understand what he means by friction now. This friction is fucking amazing. When my eyes close on their own, I know I'm almost there. My breathing increases, my mouth falls open, my chest tightens, and my legs shake almost violently. But it's the electricity that flows from my core, making my brain short-circuit, that feels completely new to me. This isn't the same as the orgasms I had earlier. This is not the explosions and toe curling, this is more like a wave. Cresting and washing away the negativity and shame I've felt for years.

"Demitri," I sigh. It's not the scream he keeps asking for, but something guttural, feral.

He holds me in his arms, the water washing the soap away, nuzzling my neck and whispering things in Russian I can't understand. His penis is still standing hard and proud between us, but he acts like it's not even there.

"I thought this was about you getting your release, not me." I grin over my shoulder.

"Eh, worth it." He smiles back.

I turn in his arms and rest my head on his chest, my legs still weak. His hold on me tightens, his heartbeat a steady rhythm against my ear. I love this man. No matter what's going on with his family, or the threats we're possibly up against, I know we'll be alright together.

"What's going through your beautiful head, *Krasotka*?" he asks.

"Just thinking how much I like this. You, here with me. I didn't know I would."

"I still hate the reasons I have to be here," he confesses, "but I don't want to be anywhere you aren't."

I don't say anything else, there really isn't anything to say. I rub my fingers through the light smattering of chest hair he has, his contented groan lighting me up in a way I didn't know was possible.

"Can I touch you?"

"Always. You always have my permission to touch me whenever you want, Mia. I trust you."

"I trust you, too."

I know he's grinning without having to look. I continue trailing my fingers over his chest and down his abs. His gloriously, wonderful abs, I might add. Until I reach the base of his cock. Encircling it in my hand, I gently squeeze and pump, going from root to tip. He sighs, and it emboldens me to be more aggressive. Jerking him off even faster, adding in a rotation that makes him shudder. I'm enjoying myself when the soap hits, and he's right—this is some good lube.

I increase my grip and slide along his shaft, working myself up again in the process. It's almost like we have the same brain, because as much as I'd love to jerk him off until he comes in my hand, I want more. His hold on me becomes tighter, his breathing increasing.

"Demitri, I want you. I want you inside me."

"Turn around."

It's a command and plea in one. It's something I have to obey. And I turn around.

"Put your hands on the wall and bend forward, *Krasotka*."

Following his directions, I do as he says.

"If this becomes too much, tell me. I'll stop. Understand?"

"I do."

He grips my hips and slides his cock up and down my ass before running it through my folds. His tip hits my clit a few times, making me jolt with pleasure.

"Ready for me?" he asks, lining himself up with my opening.

"Ready," I confirm.

With one hand on my hip holding me, he bends his knees and thrusts inside. Our earlier activities have left me wet and wanting, and he slides in to the hilt with no resistance on my part.

"God, you feel so good," he groans into my back, both hands gripping my hips.

I push back against him, lifting my ass up just enough that the angle changes and he rubs that spot he found earlier with his fingers. My eyes roll into the back of my head each time he hits it, and I know I'm going to have another orgasm.

"Demitri," I moan, my fingers trying to claw their way into the shower wall.

The water beats down on us as his motions become more erratic, and my pleasure builds.

"Going to come," he warns, speeding up his thrusts.

I feel my walls squeezing around him when he freezes behind me, shouting out his release before continuing to make shallow thrusts. His hand reaches around and grazes my clit, and that's all I need to throw me over the edge with him. I scream his name, and he wraps his arms around me as we both collapse to the shower floor. My legs have officially given out, and it seems so have his.

"You alright?" he asks, peppering my shoulder and neck in kisses.

I don't answer right away, feeling my emotions bubbling up.

"I think so," I tell him. "But I think I might also still cry."

"I've got you. Let it out."

And that's exactly what I do. Sitting on the shower floor, with Demitri's arms wrapped around me, I cry. I cry for the happiness he brings me and the relief I feel at being able to give him the gift of my orgasm. I cry for being able to orgasm. I cry for the young woman who had her innocence ripped away from her first by her father and then by Brett. Two men who were supposed to love and protect her. My father might not have ever physically touched me, but his mental and emotional manipulations opened me up to be taken advantage of, and Brett seized the opportunity.

I cry it all out, the water starting to run cold, when Demitri finally lifts my chin and looks at me.

"You're beautiful when you cry, *Krasotka*. But it's time to get out of the shower before we turn into prunes and freeze."

I smile, my tears drying up, and nod, not trusting my own voice right now.

Demitri helps me stand before pulling himself up to his full height and turning off the water. He grabs a towel and wraps it around me before he helps me step out of the shower and gets a towel for himself.

"It's time to return to the real world, isn't it?" I ask, grabbing another towel to wrap my hair up in.

"It is. You up for it?"

"If I must. Brodie's probably going to quit on me if I keep leaving him alone."

"Nah. The kid loves you. He's not going anywhere."

I laugh and we finish up in the bathroom. Demitri leaves me to get dressed and we meet up downstairs. It's time to get back to reality, but nothing seems the same. I'm not the same. And after a quick check in with my body, heart, and head, I realize I'm okay with that.

CHAPTER TWENTY-TWO
DEMITRI

LIFE HAS SETTLED into this weird little calm that I don't trust. I've returned to the garage for the most part, Mia drives herself to and from work, and I only come in a few nights for a bite to eat and to check in with whoever's on watch before I go back to Mia's and crash. We stopped at my place last weekend and it looks like it's abandoned. There was so much dust piled up that I had to wash clean clothes before I could wear them.

I held my tongue, but Mia told me to pack all my shit and make it real. As tempted as I am by the idea of fully moving in with her, I'm still not a hundred percent sure that she's not going to regret it all and demand I get out of her space. I told her that if we were moving in with each other, we needed to move to something 'ours' to keep the balance even. She didn't like my answer, but after thinking about it some, I think she understood where I was coming from.

I stick around after hours to work on this cherry fifty-seven Chevy Bel-Air. When we're done with her, she'll be the envy of everyone around. She's already a beauty, but we're going to make her purr like a kitten. My stomach growls and I realize it's time to go.

I'm closing down the back office when I hear noises and a hushed conversation outside the office window. I leave the lights as they are and slide up to the window as quietly as I can. The voices are Russian, and my skin crawls. I close my eyes to concentrate on what they are saying.

"I swear I saw him the other day. It's him, no doubt about it."

"We can't just go to her and say we found him. We need proof."

"How are we going to get that?"

"I don't know. Maybe something in the office will give us the guy's name."

"How are we going to get into the office?"

"Are you fucking stupid? We break in, idiot."

"I don't know about that, man."

"Look, Luka. You're in or you're out. You have to choose."

"What happens if I want out?"

"You run. You know she'll kill you if you don't."

"She'll kill me if I do."

"Then I guess you're in."

"The lights are still on. Let's come back when we know the place is empty. I don't want to have to hurt anyone just on a whim that this guy is Mr. Pavlov."

"Fuck you, I know who I saw, and it was him. Bet everything I have on it."

"Still think we should wait until we know the building's empty if you're so sure of everything."

"Fine. But I'm telling Ms. Pavlov if you pussy out. Let's get some food and come back, see if it's empty then."

Mr. Pavlov was my father. Not me. And there isn't anything here that would tie that name to the family. I rack my brain trying to remember a Luka. The only one I can think of was just a kid when I checked out. He wasn't too into anything back then, either. Where's he been the last few years since my father died? Why's he back?

I'm asking myself a million questions that I don't know the answers to as I listen to them scurry away like the rats they are. Think they can come into my place of business on a hunch and destroy what I've worked so hard to build? No, they didn't talk about doing that, but these are Pavlov men. They can't quietly go in, get the information they want, and get out. They have to create chaos and destruction on their way.

I pull out my phone.

> Demitri: Have eyes on the garage?

Joker: I can. What's up?

> Demitri: Two of the family. Want to break in and verify who I am. Need IDs on them if you can. One of them is Luka Novikov, I'm sure of it.

Joker: What do you want to do?

> Demitri: Stick around here until they come back and teach them a lesson?

Joker: What are you going to do?

> Demitri: Give you the information and let you handle it?

Joker: That's the right answer. We'll take care of it.

> Demitri: Going to the bar.

Joker: Grady's on duty.

Demitri: Why is it just Aiden and Grady pulling bar duty?

Joker: Have to ask them, man. They keep volunteering for it.

Demitri: They're insane. That's the only thing I can figure out.

Joker: No argument on that. I think we all have to be a little crazy to work here.

Demitri: I need to get to the bar. If they think they know who I really am, I need to stay close to Mia.

Joker: No worries. I got this.

Demitri: Let them in before you do anything. I want to talk to Luka.

Joker: You got it.

I put my phone in my pocket and grab the keys off my desk. I bypass the bay with my truck in it and go to the far wall. Pulling the cover off the car, I grin to myself, thinking about Mia's face when she sees it. My own 'Elenore', a completely restored and mint condition sixty-seven Ford Shelby GT. It's the first car I ever restored on my own. Found on my father's property, abandoned and forgotten after what I can only assume was a small fender bender. I had it transferred to John Smith's name as soon as I had the identification to do so, further removing it from the Pavlov family. Little known fact, my father loved cars. Loved them and left them as soon as he was tired of them. He also had a secret alias he used to procure the cars, and this one could never be traced to the Pavlov name.

I open up the bay door and slide behind the wheel, my hands gripping the steering wheel before sliding my fingers along the buttery soft leather encasing it. I look over to the passenger seat and briefly think I see Mika sitting here, smiling, the wind blowing her hair around her face through the open windows. I blink, and she's gone. This car is beautiful. But she's also haunted. Memories of days gone by, before my world crashed around me, assault me for a few more minutes. When I open my eyes, all the past thoughts disappear to be replaced with Mia's smiling face.

Sometimes you have to face the fact that it's time to move forward. To put the past where it belongs, to find your happiness in your future. I loved Mika. I'll never forget her. Or the pain her death caused me. But that love? It's not the same. It's not as big as the love I have for Mia. That might be because our opportunity for love was cut short, or it might be the realization that can only come with age. Regardless, I feel like I'm ready now. Ready to move on, to move forward. And in order to do that, I have to also be ready to move on from this car. I know of a buyer in Diamond Cove, some billionaire who runs a company with his brothers.

It's time to make the call. Time to move forward. Time to tell Mia what she means to me.

The bar is sleepy this Wednesday night. Grady is at his post in the far corner, a discarded basket and half empty pitcher of beer on the table. I slide in and look at him. He's obviously tired, like he should be sleeping instead of sitting here.

"Why are you doing this?" Skipping the greeting, I go right into the questions.

"Hello to you, too. Hope you had a great day. I see you survived. You're welcome for making sure your girlfriend is safe and no boogiemen are coming after her." He raises a brow at me.

"Yeah, yeah, I appreciate you, but you look like shit, friend. You need a real meal and sleep. So what's the deal?"

"You asking cause you care about me?" He smirks.

"Yeah, let's go with that. I care about you, Grady. Now spill the beans."

"The young people these days call it tea. You're showing your age with beans."

"Deflection. Stop with the bullshit."

"I'm here because I have to be." He sighs. "I'm here because I can't be anywhere else."

"Why? Why you and Aiden? Don't you fuckers have a whole staff under you that could do this?"

"Besides the point. We have to do this because we do."

I stare at him and replay what he said with what he didn't. There's more he isn't saying, but what is it? I follow his eyes to the bar and the empty corner where Mia's friends usually sit, and it hits me like a truck. Aiden's reluctance to talk about his secret obsession. Grady's insistence that he personally be here.

"I get it now."

He stares at me, trying to figure out if I'm the one bullshitting, but nods when he realizes I'm not.

"We all have our crosses to bear," he quietly states. "This is ours."

I don't ask him questions about which girl caught his eye. Not my business, and when or if he wants to talk about it, he will. We sit in silence, Grady's eyes constantly roaming the room, mine never straying far from watching Mia do what she does best.

Grady gets a text and reads it before looking up at me, a hardness to his features I've only seen a few times before.

"They have your guys. Caught them red-handed and inca-pacitated them."

"Where are they?"

"Place on the edge of town. Aiden's on his way here so we can go get answers."

"You're going, too?"

"I'm the one who gets the answers."

CHAPTER TWENTY-THREE
MIA

IT's dead in here tonight. Grady has been at his post all night looking both bored and on edge. He also looks like he needs a nap, if I'm being honest. I heard from Aiden that they had a call out this weekend to go help someone and it didn't go down as smoothly as they were hoping. I know what they do, and it's dangerous. Unstable people always are. I can only imagine how Brett would have reacted if a gang of bulked up guys had shown up to move me away from him. Someone would have ended up dead.

I'm counting inventory when Demitri comes in, looking a little stressed himself. He doesn't say anything to me, which is our normal. Hiding in plain sight, but not flaunting it. I pour him a coke and open a beer bottle for him before he even makes it to the bar.

"Thanks." No emotion, and he's not meeting my eyes.

"Long day?" Same question I'd ask any of my patrons.

"Yup."

He grabs the glass and bottle and nods before turning and going to the booth where Grady is. Something's wrong. I feel it in the pit of my stomach, but I can't get answers right now.

It's dead in here tonight, but not empty. There're a few couples out for an after-dinner drink and a group of friends playing pool.

I distract myself by going back to inventory and shooting the shit with Brodie through the window to the kitchen. I'm not sure how much time has passed, but when I see quick movement out of the corner of my eye, I turn around in time to watch Demitri and Grady rush across the bar and out the door, their faces set in stone. As soon as they exit, Aiden walks in, calm as a cucumber, like nothing odd is going on.

"What the hell?" I ask as he takes a seat at the bar.

"Don't know. But I'll take a beer."

"I'm not sure you deserve a beer with no answers." I grin at him.

"Story of my life, Mia."

"What is the story of your life, Aiden?" I grab a mug, moving to the taps and pulling a beer for him. "Actually, that can wait. Pull your phone out and figure out what the hell is going on first. Then story time."

He shakes his head but does just that, typing out a message and staring at the screen, waiting for the reply. Both of us are getting antsy when it finally comes through.

"Someone tried to break into the garage, and the guys want to talk to them."

"What? Where? Who?"

"If I knew that, I would have told you."

"We need to go to him."

"No, Mia, we don't. You don't need to be anywhere near what's going on. That's the whole point of us being here. To keep you out of whatever shit is happening. And you're going to stay out of it."

"I don't like you very much right now."

"That's fine. I'll take your anger and dislike over you being in danger any day of the week."

"Ugh." I toss my hands up. "Stop throwing logic in my face."

"Nope."

"Fine. Then tell me your story."

"The long, drawn-out version or the down and dirty?"

"Down and dirty, of course. I'll ask questions if I need more."

He takes a gulp of his beer. "Can I get cheese sticks with my story and maybe an Irish Old Fashioned?"

"I guess," I sigh. Turning, I shout through the window. "Order of mozz sticks!"

"You got it, Boss!" Brodie yells back, probably thankful to be doing something. Or pissed off that I'm interrupting his study time. I turn back to Aiden, grabbing a glass to make his drink. "Start talking."

"I'm from South Boston. Most of my family are either Southies or from Dorchester."

"That's where the accent comes from. I didn't think it was New York."

"Nah, never liked that city much. Boston all the way. My dad and mom are still together, married forty years. Ma had six kids."

"Six? She's a superhuman!"

"Eh, it's what she signed up for. Stay out of the way, stay out of business, and keep having babies to carry on the legacy."

"Legacy?"

He takes another swig of his beer and looks at me with a stoic face. "My family's Irish Mob. My daid runs the fucking thing with his brother."

I look at him, noticing his accent coming out even more than usual. It's a mix of Boston and Irish.

"How did you end up here if that's what you grew up in?"

"I got out. The old man wasn't happy, but he couldn't exactly fight the government, could he?"

"You joined the service."

"I did. Army. Went into basic with no clue what I was going to do. Figured I'd let them tell me when I got there."

"What happened with your family?"

"He cut me off. Stopped talking to me, stopped acknowledging that I was his son, removed me from everything in his life. Ma would call when she could get away with it, but my daid is a real fucking bastard, you know? She quit calling when he started hitting her for calling me."

"Why did he care if she gave him so many kids? Aren't there others who want to be there?"

"I have four sisters and one brother. Younger. He's a fucking twat. And you know girls aren't allowed to do anything but spread their legs for whoever their father determines is the right guy."

"So you miss the place, then?"

"Would it be bad to say that I do sometimes miss it? I haven't been back in twenty years. Went home at twenty on leave to tell them I'd been selected for Special Ops and couldn't even get in the front door. He refused to see me, said no son of his would have abandoned the family and he hoped I landed in some desert and didn't come back."

"Fuck. Aiden. He sounds like a monster."

"Sounds a lot like Dem's dad, honestly. They probably would have gotten along really great if they weren't mortal enemies. Irish, Russian, Italian—they all hate each other. It would really piss the fucker off if he knew Dem and I were friendly."

He says this with some self-satisfied smile, like he's getting away with something. Owning the man for being a decent human.

"If your sisters aren't allowed to have a say in their lives and your brother's incompetent, what's happening with your family?"

"My cousin Declan wasn't given the same chance to get out I was. He's the heir apparent, and he's also the one who keeps me informed when something might be happening around here."

"He doesn't hold it against you? That you left?"

"Yeah nah. He's wicked cool. He knows that life isn't for everyone, and that I had higher aspirations. He doesn't want to keep anyone in that doesn't want to be there. He's also secretly trying to go a little more legit than the old man. He's tired of burying cousins."

"He knows what you do with ANON?"

"He does. And he helps out sometimes. In his own way. He's not cool with the human shit that is the darker side of everything these families do."

"Are you afraid your dad is going to call you one day and demand you come home?"

"Every single day of my life."

I'm trying to think of what to say next when Brodie calls the sticks are done and Aiden's phone buzzes on the bar in front of him. I grab his food and slide it to him while he taps on his screen. He won't look at me, and he's practically gnawing on the inside of his mouth, a stress action I noticed the first time I met him.

"Demitri isn't going to make it home tonight, is he?" I ask, trying to stay calm.

"No. He's alright, though."

"Oh. Okay."

I turn away from him and busy myself rearranging the bottles I was trying to count earlier. I don't want him to see my face and worry about me. I'll be fine. I've had many nights alone. What's one more?

"You aren't going to be alone," Aiden says. "You won't be left unprotected."

I nod but don't say anything, biting my lip to hold back the sob I want to let loose. I look up and meet Brodie's eyes in the window, and he turns to leave the kitchen. When he gets behind the bar, I walk away, feeling Aiden's eyes bore into my back. I stop in the bathroom, splashing cold water on my face and taking deep breaths.

I pull my phone out of my pocket and look at the time. It's still earlyish.

Mia: Could use some friends if you're still up.

Grace: Be there in ten.

Nola: On my way

Sofie: Walking out the door.

I put my phone in my back pocket and sigh in relief. There are friends and then there's my girls. All of us would drop whatever we're doing for each other. I wash my hands and walk out from the bathroom, not looking at Aiden as I take my spot behind the bar again, thanking Brodie.

I stare at the door, willing my girls to come in, but when it opens, it's not them. Aunt Linda walks through, finding me immediately and giving me a reassuring smile.

"How about something fun to drink tonight?" she asks, hoisting herself up onto a stool.

"I think we can probably do that. What brings you in?"

"I can't just stop in for a drink?"

"Barlowe's is closer."

"Ahh, Pat's great and all, but his ass doesn't look as good as yours."

I laugh, shaking my head while pulling a glass out and placing it on the bar. I grab the bottles of gin and vermouth from the display and a bottle of bitters. I fill the mixing cup with ice, add the liquid, and shake it up, pouring it into the glass and grabbing an orange twist for the garnish. I slide it across the bar to Aunt Linda with a dare in my eyes.

She narrows her eyes at me before lifting the glass and taking a sip. Her eyes widen and she licks her lips. "What the hell is that?" she asks.

"It's called a Hanky-Panky."

She laughs, slapping her hand on the bar. "I love it. I'll have to remember this. I bet old Pat couldn't make this one."

"Who do you think told me about it?" I challenge.

"Touché, girl."

She continues to sip her drink, and I check on the few other people in the place. On my way back to the bar, the door opens and Sofie and Nola walk through, grins on their faces.

"We're here. The fun can begin now." Nola smiles at me.

I roll my eyes and keep walking until I'm back behind the bar. I pull out two glasses, filling both with ice. I grab the coconut rum and a bottle of pineapple juice, mixing both and sliding them to their usual spots. Aiden stiffens at the sight of the women, and Nola almost trips before she sits down hard, holding onto the bar. Sofie looks around the room, and if I'm not mistaken, she sits down with a look of disappointment on her face.

I open my mouth to ask what's wrong with them when the door opens, and Grace comes in with two bags in her hands. I recognize the logo immediately and can't help my smile.

"Chips and salsa make everything better." She grins at me.

I grab a wine glass and fill it with Moscato, placing it in front of her. "Agreed. Thanks."

"Oh, good, all of you are here. We can get this all done in

one conversation," Aunt Linda says before taking another sip of her drink.

"What do you mean?"

"I'm here to make sure you know your boy is okay, and he's helping an old friend. You have nothing to worry about."

"If I have nothing to worry about, you could have just texted me."

She smiles behind the rim of her glass. "Could have but didn't."

"There's something you aren't telling us," Grace observes.

"Possible. But we can get into that later. Tonight, all of us are having a sleepover at my place."

"Where do you live?" Nola asks.

"Over behind the community center in Briar Mountain."

Sofie starts shaking her head while Grace goes pale. Nola freezes.

"I don't think that's a good idea," I tell her.

"Bullshit. It's a fantastic idea."

"I can't do that." Grace, quiet and calm, but with an edge of panic in her voice, looks at Aunt Linda.

"You can. You will," she assures her.

"We don't..." Sofie fades, not even finishing her thought.

I turn to Aunt Linda. "None of us are particularly comfortable in Briar Mountain, Aunt Linda. I'm the only one who regularly goes over there, and I only stay as long as I have to."

"I understand that, dear, I really do. But it's been a long time since that man was allowed to hurt you, and he's dead now. He can't ever do it again."

"His father—" Grace starts.

"Is also dead and gone. His mother is in therapy in a different state, living with her sister, and his cousin is never going to be a problem for anyone ever again. The whole fucking clan was removed from the face of our town."

"What about the other cops? The ones who helped them?" Nola asks.

"Cleaned out, kicked out, and not given glowing recommendations. None of them will ever be in a position to aid a monster again."

"Nate will also be close to you all night. I'll be with him," Aiden speaks up.

"Both of you need to be there? You can't go home and get some sleep?" I ask, looking at him for the first time since he told me Demitri wasn't coming home for the night.

"I'll be there." There's no room for argument in his tone or words. Just the calm assurance that he'll be watching over us, no matter where we are.

"Seems like a done deal." Aunt Linda pats the bar. "Let Brodie close up tonight, Mia. I think he can handle it."

"You seem to know a lot about Brodie."

"I'll fill you in later. At my place."

Oh, that woman knows exactly what she's doing. Dangling information like that over our heads, knowing we can't resist.

"I have to be back for work in the morning," Grace tries one more time.

"James is going to be late tomorrow, Grace, dear. He's helping out tonight."

That causes all of us to pause and stare at the older lady. She really does know everything, doesn't she?

"We don't have any clothes with us," Sofie tries.

"Bullshit. I happen to know that each of you carries an emergency bag in the trunks of your vehicles. Inside that bag are enough clothes for a week and all of your toiletries. Next excuse?"

"I have to feed my neighbor's dog?" Nola doesn't even look like she believes her own lie.

"Nope. Neighbor doesn't have any pets other than a goldfish. She also isn't out of town this week, she just got back from a business trip three days ago, and her company won't send her out for another three weeks."

All of them are looking defeated, when Aunt Linda adds in the pièce de résistance. "Waffles are on me at Sandy's in the morning."

The collective gasp from my friends makes her smile. She knows she's got us.

"I don't think I like you very much," Grace calmly tells her. "You don't play fair."

"Never have, never will. And I can teach you my ways. At my place. Go tell Brodie you're leaving. Bring the chips and salsa."

I hang my head and turn to the window. How does she do this? How does she always get her way? And, really, how the fuck does she know so much? I hear Demitri's voice in my head saying, *'Aunt Linda knows all'*.

Guess we're having a sleepover. In Briar Mountain.

CHAPTER TWENTY-FOUR
DEMITRI

"Sorry we didn't get a formal greeting before all that, but I'm James Covey." The tall man sticks out his hand, and I shake it.

"John Smith."

"Or Demitri Pavlov." He grins. "I'm the lawyer who processed your name change for Aunt Linda."

"Oh. Well, nice to meet you. Did you say Covey?"

"Yes."

"You know Grace?"

"My paralegal."

The possessiveness in his voice with those two words catches me off guard.

"She's nice."

"Yes, she is. And she's off limits."

"Let you in on a little secret," I tell him, leaning in. "All my limits start and end with Mia. Your Grace is just a friend."

He straightens up, and I swear if he were wearing a tie, he'd adjust it. "She's not 'my' Grace."

"Oh, my bad. Anyway, thanks for your help with Luka tonight."

"It's what I do."

Without another word, he turns away from me and speaks in hushed tones to Grady before leaving.

"What did you say to him?" Grady asks after we watch the other man leave.

"I just asked if he's who Grace works for. Man straight up looked like he wanted to kill me for even knowing she exists."

Grady laughs. "He's, umm, protective of his paralegal."

"You could say that again. Thanks for your help with Luka. Glad you didn't have to kill him."

"I don't kill them." He gives me a scary as fuck grin. Seriously, I think he's been taking notes from Joker. That guy's terrifying. "Just maim them every once in a while."

"What's going to happen to the other guy?"

"He was dropped off at the police department. His full confession taped and delivered."

"Guess we know I'm definitely made now, huh?"

"Probably. But isn't that what you wanted?"

"It is, but not this way. I'm afraid all of you are in danger now. Two of their *kryshas* have been removed from the ranks. You know he's not going to stay silent, and as soon as he gets a phone call, he'll call Sasha."

"You let us worry about us. You worry about yourself and staying safe."

"Part of me wants to talk to her. Find out what she really wants. If it's the money, fuck, she can have it."

"I think we both know it's not just the money. She needs you."

"Why?"

"Because you have what she doesn't. It resides between your legs. You were born with it, and therefore, are always a threat to her. If she can't get you to join her, then she has to eliminate you to demonstrate her power over the 'rightful heir'."

"You sure know a lot about crime families and how they work."

"Had to. Special Ops. We did all kinds of interesting things. I spent a lot of time in areas where the mafia ran everything."

"Were all of you in the super-secret military society?"

"Not all of us. Some of us were just Rangers."

"Fuck off," Daniel calls from the other side of the room where he's working on a computer with Joker.

"Yeah, fuck off." Joker grins and I shiver.

See, that grin is terrifying. Grady has some practice to do.

I shake my head, chuckling at the group. What they all have is something I've never experienced. Being in the military has made them all family, even if they didn't serve together or at the same time. I never wanted to be a part of my family, and I knew from an early age I didn't want to be like my father.

I pull out my phone. Four-thirty in the morning. Mia's going to kill me.

"I need to get home. Mia's either worried or pissed, and I'd prefer to grovel as soon as possible."

"No need to rush, she's not there." Grady smirks.

"What do you mean, she's not there? Is she alright?"

"I don't know if she's alright, but she's safe. Aunt Linda called for a sleepover. All the girls are there."

"I'm not sure how I feel about Aunt Linda getting so close to Mia," I confess. "She knows too much, and that could be dangerous."

Daniel walks over to us, a knowing look on his face. "I can promise she's alright."

"What do you know?"

"Not allowed to talk about it, but it's not bad."

"I'll believe it when I know what you do. Until then, I'm going to remain skeptical. I don't like not knowing the secrets."

"I know you don't, but all I know is that there's an idea being floated. No more, I swear."

"I need to get to Aunt Linda's."

"Nope. We just did a damn fine job not breaking the guy's legs and turning him over to the cops. We're going to celebrate with breakfast."

"Nothing's open," I point out.

"Sandy's is." I want to punch the grin off the guy's face, but fuck. Sandy's breakfast is the best food in the world. Her waffles can make a grown man cry.

"Fine, fuckers. Sandy's."

Grady, Daniel, and even Joker laugh at that, knowing they'd all say the same thing. I once told Sandy I loved her after eating those waffles. And shakes. Woman knows her shit when it comes to perfect diner food.

"George, look who it is!" Sandy yells over her shoulder as soon as I walk through the door. "Our lost boy is back!"

"Mama Sandy." I smile at her, letting her pull me into a hug.

When I first met Aunt Linda, she brought me here for breakfast in the pre-dawn hour. I'd just unloaded twenty-plus years of pain and rejection and heartache on the woman, and I thought she was ridiculous for suggesting waffles at four in the morning. She neglected to tell me the fucking things are magical. Sandy took one look at me and pulled me in for a hug. It was one that only a mother can give, and it had been so long since I'd felt any kind of affection that wasn't attached to strings that I broke. Right there in the middle of the diner. I was a snotty, blubbering mess. That woman held me for what felt like hours, shooing away anyone who came near. Including Aunt Linda.

When I pulled myself together enough that I could let go of her, her husband, George, took me into the kitchen and taught me how to make an old-fashioned milkshake. For a few months, I practically lived in this place. They fed me, and Sandy brought me clothes that her son had left when he moved out.

George isn't behind the stove anymore, mainly sitting at the counter bullshitting with the other customers because of a back injury. Hasn't stopped him from being everyone's favorite with his big, sparkling white teeth etched in his dark skin with laugh lines showing how well he's lived.

"How's my boy this morning?" Sandy asks, gripping my chin and turning my face left and right, like she's checking for damage. Did she call me her boy? Yes. Am I almost a foot taller than her and probably seventy pounds heavier? Also, yes. Will I ever stop her? Hell no.

"I'm alright, Mama S. Just had a long night."

She turns to Grady, Daniel, Joker, and Aiden and narrows her eyes at them. "You better not be upsetting my boy here. Or getting him into trouble."

"Sandy, you wound me." Daniel grins, giving her a side hug. "You know I'd never."

"Bullshit, Danny. I know too well you would."

He laughs, moving past us and grabbing the corner booth. Each man, in turn, stops to give Sandy a hug. She's the town mom if there ever was one. I look out the windows and see James on the sidewalk, making a call. That man is so strange.

Sandy takes my arm and pulls me over to George, who gives me his own once over.

"I'm alright, you two, promise," I tell them.

"You do look better than the last time we saw you. You got a girl or something?" George asks, his smile firmly in place.

"Ahh, well..." I rub the back of my neck, my face getting hot.

"Tell us all about her," Sandy demands.

"She's perfect." I smile. "She's a smartass who puts me in my place, but she loves her people hard."

"Sounds like a winner. And when are you bringing her in for some good cooking?"

I laugh, shaking my head. "I don't know. She doesn't come over the mountain very often."

As I'm speaking, the door opens, and it takes me a minute to realize what I'm seeing. Mia, Grace, Nola, and Sofie all flank Aunt Linda.

"Unless she does," I say more to myself, watching the group. Grace looks more pale than normal, her eyes darting from one side of the diner to the other. Nola and Sofie look like they might have been on a bender all night, and Mia is swaying a little bit, too. But she's got this goofy grin on her face as she meets my eyes, and I can't look away.

"Ladies," Sandy greets before freezing in her tracks. "My girls."

The way she says it, like she's feeling everything they've ever been through. Like it's a relief to see them alive, and like it's been a lifetime since she's laid her own two eyes on them. She lets go of my arm, almost like she's lost the ability to hold on, and her feet carry her to the women.

They all stare at each other, not sure what to do, when Sandy decides for them. She pushes Aunt Linda out of the way and grabs all four women at once. It's almost comical, but this isn't a funny moment. This is a healing moment.

"My girls," Sandy repeats, tears in her eyes.

All five women are crying now, Sandy pulling each one in for the same hug she gave me. Each with the same heart-healing arms. No words are spoken, but you can almost see the love they all have for each other.

"George, your wife is an amazing woman." I lean into his shoulder.

"You're damn right she is," he quietly replies. "Which one is yours?"

"Mia. Mia is mine."

"That's a fine choice, son." He nods. "She needs someone like you to help her through it. You won't leave when it isn't easy, and she needs that."

"I know."

"So," Sandy says, wiping her eyes. "Who's ready for waffles?"

The girls all blink away their own tears and raise their hands. The guys in the corner, who have been watching all of this, also yell their answers, and James opens the door, eyeballing us until he notices Grace in the group. Without a word, he walks to her, takes her arm, and guides her to one of the tables by the guys. The other girls follow her, with Mia squeezing my hand as she walks by.

"Your girl is Mia?" Sandy asks, stopping to stand by me.

"For as long as she'll have me," I confirm.

"Treat her well. I'd hate to have to cut off your supply."

"If that's not a horrible idea, I don't know what is."

We laugh, and Sandy takes my arm again, guiding me to the group where we'll all pretend that last night didn't happen.

CHAPTER TWENTY-FIVE
MIA

"I'm stuffed," I whine, pushing my plate away and rubbing my now hurting stomach. "Who let me eat so much?"

A napkin comes flying at my face, Nola grinning. "We don't let you do anything. You did that all on your own."

Both of us turn to look at Sofie, who is still stuffing her face. "I think Sofie's hollow leg has been activated. It's the only place for the food to go."

"Shut up," she mumbles around a mouthful of food. "It's too good. I can't stop."

"Well, if you'd come see me more often, you wouldn't be needing your fix so bad," Sandy playfully snips as she refills coffee cups.

Grace, Nola, and Sofie all tense at the words, casting their eyes downward.

"Oh, girls, I'm sorry. I know this place has bad memories for you. I've just missed you all so much. I understand why you don't stop in, but know when you do, I'll take care of you."

"Thanks, Sandy. We miss you, too." I smile at her.

"Ha! You just miss my waffles."

We share a laugh, and I look around at this motley crew that have somehow become like family to me in the last few months. It's like Demitri and I did some weird meshing of people who happen to all get along. As we finish up, I excuse myself to go to the bathroom.

When I step out of the bathroom, Grace's boss, James, stops me before I can exit the hallway.

"Hey, James. What's going on?"

"How well do you know, uh, John?"

The look I give him must make him realize how idiotic he sounds, and he sighs, restating his question.

"You know who Demitri is?"

"I do."

"Do you trust him?"

"With my life. I'd trust him to stand in front of a moving train for not only me, but every person sitting out there. Well, maybe not Daniel, but that's a different story."

He huffs out a laugh. "I just worry about you."

"I appreciate your worry but know that I am well aware of where he comes from, and it doesn't matter to me."

"You'll call me if you need help?"

"No offense or anything, but if I'm in the way of bodily harm, I'm probably going to call one of those guys out there with the military background and training who know how to kill a man with their pinkies."

"Alright." he holds his hands up in defeat. "I earned that. But don't forget that if you need me, I'm here."

"Thanks, James. I appreciate it. We should get back before someone misses us," I tell him.

"Too late for that," Demitri says, coming up and pulling me to him then wrapping his arms around me. A clear, possessive move. Can't say I'm mad about it. "Mr. Covey."

James sighs and pinches the bridge of his nose like an old

man who's tired of dealing with everyone's shit. "It's James. And if I was an ass earlier, I apologize."

I feel Demitri's grin on the side of my head, and I wait for his response.

"No worries, friend. But next time you want to grill my girl about me, you should go ahead and include me in the conversation."

"You heard that?" I tilt my face to see him.

"We all heard it. Lesson one: Never have a 'private' conversation in Sandy's in the hallway to the bathrooms because it's nothing but an amplifier to the dining room."

James has the good sense to look at least a little ashamed.

"Good. Then everyone out there will know that I take care of my family, and those women are my family."

"Then we agree. We protect our family. But what we aren't going to do? Judge anyone based on their past, their families, or what they've done to survive. Understand?" Demitri asks him, the pain in his voice at being judged evident.

James regards him for a minute before rewarding us with a small hitch of his lips. That's about the only smile you get from the guy, ever, so it's big. "Understood."

"Good. So, how about we start over and realize we both want the same things?"

Demitri sticks out his hand and waits. James rolls his eyes before shaking hands.

"I'm John, but my friends call me Demitri." It's a challenge. We all know it.

"James. Nice to meet you, Demitri."

"Kiss and make up so we can get out of here. I have a hot wife to go home to!" Joker gives us shit from the table, making everyone laugh—the girls—or groan—the guys.

"You heard the man. If we don't get out there, he's going to start talking about what he wants to do to his wife," Grady hollers.

"Let's go, boys." I grin at them. "No need to make everyone else miserable while you're deciding if your pissing match is over."

Demitri chuckles, and James shakes his head. We all exit the hallway to cheers. Crisis averted, I guess.

We take care of the bill and bid a somewhat teary farewell to Sandy and George, who, in a rare occurrence, stands up from his perch at the bar to hug a number of us. When we walk outside, I'm stopped in my tracks by the most beautiful car I've ever seen.

"Is that a sixty-seven Shelby?" I ask, turning to Demitri.

"Yeah." He almost looks embarrassed.

"You've had that beautiful girl and never told me?"

"I didn't think about it?"

"Demitri! You don't hide a car like that. You show her off, you show her love, you treat her right!"

"Oh, shit," Nola says from behind us. "Here we go."

Demitri turns to look at her, but I'm on a roll now.

"This is a nineteen-sixty-seven Ford Shelby GT500. Carroll Shelby designed it, and it's still thought of as a superior racing machine today. She's sleek. She's fast. She's got a big-block V8 engine. She's got not one, but two 600-CFM Holley carburetors. She's sexy. Fuck, Demitri, can I touch her?" I ask, practically jumping out of my skin.

He stares at me, slack jawed, and I swear I see love in his eyes. He cracks a grin, and with a husky voice, replies, "Yeah, *Krasotka*, you can touch her."

I think I hear the other guys laughing, but I pay them no mind. I slowly walk to the car, sticking my hand out, and finally run my fingers along her body.

"We should just go," Grace says quietly. "We've lost her. She's not leaving that car."

"I didn't know she had such a big thing for cars," Demitri whispers loudly behind me.

"Not cars. *One* car."

"Why?"

"You'll have to ask her."

I know the others are leaving. I hear car doors and engines start, but I'll worry about them later. I can't take my fingers off the beautiful front quarter panel.

"Wanna go for a ride?" Demitri breathes into my ear, making me shiver.

"Can I drive her?"

"One day."

I turn to him with a pout and sad eyes, and that bastard just laughs.

"It was really windy on the pass coming over. And other people are stupid when it's windy on the mountain. I don't want you or her to get hurt, okay? I promise I'll take you out and let you drive her all fucking day, okay?"

"That makes me feel marginally better."

"How about I let you squeeze the stick the entire ride back?"

"I feel like there's an inappropriate joke there somewhere."

"Probably." He grins, shrugging one shoulder. "Your chariot awaits, milady." He holds his arm out for me and walks me to the passenger door, opening it and helping me sit down.

I'm pretty sure I moan when my ass hits the buttery leather seats. And there's no way in hell I can keep my hands to myself. I touch everything. The door handle, the gear stick, the dash.

Demitri gets behind the wheel and turns to grin at me. "Care to tell me why you love this car so much?"

"My uncle had one. We'd spend entire weekends tuning it up and cleaning her."

"That's nice. But why do I feel like there's something not so nice coming?"

"He was killed in a car accident. Some kid high on meth

ran him off the road and into a tree. He was killed instantly, and the car was totaled."

"I'm sorry."

"Me too. More than the car, he was the only relative I had that tried to protect me."

"How old were you when he died?"

"Fifteen. The summer I grew boobs. Bad timing on the tweaker's part, that's for sure." I turn my head against the seat and look at Demitri. "This car reminds me of him and the good memories. Thank you."

"I haven't done anything yet." He smirks. And then he starts the engine. I think I might orgasm right here. Maybe the trick was a Shelby all along. Hell, the rumble coming from under the hood vibrating the seat is doing a damn fine job of getting me close.

"Demitri, take me home."

"Yes, ma'am."

CHAPTER TWENTY-SIX
DEMITRI

So, a muscle car turns Mia on. Of course, it's the one I'm going to sell. Fuck, I need to find another one of these babies and get her to help me restore it. The thing is, I do love the car, but the memories attached to it have become too much. I can't look at this car and not think about my father, something I actively try to avoid.

"Tell me about the car," Mia demands once we're on the road. "Why do you hate her?"

"What makes you think I hate it?" I hedge, really wishing we could avoid this conversation completely.

"Really? The way you look at her, firstly. Oh, and the way you barely touch her, and show her no love. There's no caressing going on over on that steering wheel. Also, the way you call her an it. This is a Shelby."

"Fuck, you really do see everything, don't you?"

"Pretty much. So, spill it."

"It belonged to my father."

"That would explain it. Why do you have her?"

"He left it alone in a garage on the back of the property for years. It fell into trash, basically, and I brought her back to life.

The cars were a secret of his, bought with an alias only a few of us knew. And none of those are still alive to track it down."

"What are you going to do with her?"

"I have a buyer. In Diamond Cove. Some billionaire guy."

"If you must sell it to someone, he's probably a good choice. Richie Rich's tend to take care of their toys or at least pay someone to do it for them."

"You aren't upset that I'm selling it—her?"

"No. I'm upset that you feel like you have to because of the memories tied to her. And while she is my favorite car ever in existence of, well, ever, she's not mine. She's yours to do with what you need to."

"You are extremely understanding and all together confusing."

She laughs, shrugging. "What can I say? I have multiple ideas and feelings all at the same time. I'm complex, Demitri."

Now I laugh, looking in the mirror to change lanes. Mia goes quiet, her fingers never breaking contact with the interior of the car. We sit in comfortable silence for a while, then Mia stiffens in the seat beside us.

"Dem." Her voice is quiet and calm. Too calm. "Look in the rear-view mirror and tell me what you see."

I do as she requests, and at first I don't see anything, just the normal flow of traffic. And then I do. Two big, black SUVs speeding through traffic. Normally it wouldn't be something I cared about, but these SUVs aren't your normal oversized cars. They scream 'special'. They're Russian-made. If I had to guess, I'd say they are UAZ Patriots. They go by a different name here, but that doesn't matter. What does is that there are two Russian SUVs going high speed on a mountain road.

"You think they could just be assholes speeding on a high accident-pass?" Mia asks.

"Sure. They could."

"But?"

"But it's too much of a coincidence that I pull out this car and they follow it."

"I thought everyone was dead that might know your connection to the car?"

"Maybe I was wrong. But I'm going to need you to activate that watch and let Joker know what's going on and then hold on, baby, we're going to see what this ol' gal can do."

Mia fumbles with the watch Joker gave her, sending him whatever information she can. She then sits up straight, checking her seatbelt, and grabs the door handle. She was concentrating so much she didn't realize I'd already increased our speed by fifteen MPH.

"What's your speed?" she asks. Okay, maybe she did realize.

"Fifty-eight and climbing."

"Can you keep that up on the mountain, Demitri?"

"If anything can, it's a Shelby."

I hit the gas and feel the vibrations of the engine in my seat. The sound loud and powerful. The way she handles the curves is like nothing else I've ever driven. Foreign sports cars are one of the specialties of the garage, but this baby? She's a dream to drive. The purr from under the hood is almost erotic.

"Demitri, they sped up," Mia tells me, watching through the mirrors.

"I'll keep you safe."

We finally make it through the curves of the mountain to the straight pass that will take us to Rock Hill. I continue to increase my speed, hoping we can continue to avoid any cops that might be out, and weave my way through traffic.

I downshift the gear and hit the brakes so I can make a turn, and immediately shift and hit the gas again once we've made it. I do this a few more times until I'm sure we've lost them. I can hear Mia breathing hard in the passenger seat, turning her body to look out the small window in the back.

She finally sighs. "I think we've lost them. Time to hide this badass car."

I make a few more turns, hitting a button on my phone as we slide into the lot of the garage, the door already opening.

"You don't think they'll come straight here?" she asks, an edge of panic in her voice.

"They'll never see us," I assure her, pulling into the bay and hitting the button on my phone to lower the bay door again. "Can't see in from the windows."

"Oh, that's nifty to have."

"Plan for everything. Hope it never comes in handy."

I put the car in park and turn off the engine. The vibrations still rattle through my body even in the silence.

"Wow. That was something."

We sit there in the quiet, both of us jumping when my phone rings.

"Joker," I answer and put it on speaker. "I'm with Mia. She can hear you, too."

"Good. It was both of them, Andrey and Sasha. Grabbed the plates off a camera on the mountain."

"Of course it was. That was quick."

"Our friend went right to them."

"How did they know where we were? To follow us?" Mia asks.

"I don't know," he admits. "But we need to do some more digging. Where are you now?"

"At the garage," I answer.

"Does it have what you need for a little while?"

"Yeah. We'll be fine."

"What about work? I have a business to run." Mia's stubborn streak is showing.

"Brodie's going to have to cover things, Mia," Joker breaks the news to her.

"It's Thursday. College night. He can't do it alone. I need to be there."

"I hear you. And just this once, I'm going to have to tell you no," Joker replies, his voice brokering no argument. "I'll call around. We'll get you some help for the night. Stay safe and I'll talk to you later."

When she lowers the phone, I turn to Mia. "I'm sorry. This is why I should have walked away. I put you in danger today. Because of me, because of who I am."

"Fuck you, Demitri."

Before I can respond, she flings open the door and exits, slamming it closed behind her. I jump out as quickly as I can and round the hood to get to her.

"I'm sorry."

"Damnit, I don't want your apologies!"

She turns away from me but doesn't really have anywhere to go. I reach out and take her hand, pulling her into my arms.

"I'm sorry, *Krasotka*. I'm so sorry your life is crazy because of me. I never wanted this to happen."

She buries her face in my chest. "Is this why you left me before? Why you disappeared?"

"Yes."

"I swear, if you do that again, I'll hunt you down and kill you myself, Demitri. Do you understand me?"

I don't answer, but I lift her chin up and capture her lips in mine. The kiss starts soft and gentle, but quickly turns almost feral. Both of us waging war with our control. Our tongues battle, doing the dance of lovers everywhere. I turn her, pressing her back against the car. My hands grasp the sides of her face, my thumbs tracing her cheeks, my cock growing hard and demanding.

She's unbuttoning my flannel and running her hands up

under my shirt, first on my chest, then around my waist, pulling me closer to her.

"Are you sure you want this?" I ask, kissing down her neck, gently biting the tender skin at her shoulder.

"You are not going to fuck me against a Shelby," she moans out as I suck at her skin.

"Fine," I agree, picking her up and wrapping her legs around my waist. I turn, finding a work bench that's blessedly free of clutter, and sit her on top of it. "How about here?"

"Yeah, works." She pulls at my clothes. "Less clothing."

I help her by removing my flannel and pulling the undershirt over my head and tossing it on the table beside her. She starts to fumble with my belt, her eager fingers threatening to unman me before we get started. I step back, much to her ire, and smirk.

"*Krasotka*, you have too many clothes on. I can't devour you when you're dressed."

She looks down at herself and huffs out a laugh, like she forgot she was wearing anything.

"Keep going, Mister," she demands as she pulls her shirt over her head, dropping it at her side.

She kicks off her shoes and shimmies out of her jeans, sitting on the table in only a white lace bra and mismatched blue panties with an obvious wet spot on them.

"Are you turned on?" I ask as I pull off my work boots and shuck my jeans.

"Yes. Get over here." I raise my brow and she grins. "Please?"

"I can't resist you when you're polite," I groan, moving between her legs.

"I don't want you to resist me," she says, pulling me in for another kiss. Just as heated as the last, but less violent.

She runs her hands over my body, like she's memorizing all the details.

"I want you," she whispers, kissing up my neck, her hands sliding inside my boxer briefs, gripping my dick.

"Mia," I grunt at her touch. "I want you, too."

"Now."

"So demanding." I shake my head, removing her hand and kissing her palm before sitting it down on her thigh.

I kiss down her chest, pulling her tits out of the cups of her bra, sucking first one nipple into my mouth and then the other, working her up. She's squirming on the hard surface, but I'm giving her what she wants. What she needs.

My hand skims down her stomach and I tease the band of her panties, but don't go under. Instead, I use the fabric. Feeling the wet spot, and adding pressure on the area, Mia gasps. It only lasts for a few seconds, my need for her too much. I can't tease her. Kneeling between her legs, I'm at the perfect height for what I want to do. Helping her remove the now offensive fabric and put them on the table next to her, her scent invades my senses, heady and intoxicating.

Kissing up her thighs, her hands automatically go to my hair, gripping it like she's trying to find gravity. Her legs spread for me, and I'm looking at the promised land. Her pussy is glistening with her arousal, and my mouth waters at what I know awaits me.

I flick out my tongue, getting my first taste. Mia moans softly, wanting this as much as I do. I circle her clit, pulling the nub into my mouth, and her grip on my hair tightens. Taking a finger, I run it through her wetness, enjoying her shivers of pleasure then slowly insert it into her pussy. Her walls are already clamping down, looking for relief, and I am here to deliver. I get to work, sliding my finger in and out, my tongue striking her clit with a mission. Make her come on my face.

Thrust. Flick. Rub. Suck.

"Demitri!" she screams, and I swear she's pulling my hair out.

Her orgasm rocks her body, her cry silent. My cock begs for attention. This woman always turns me the fuck on, but when she allows herself to fall apart in my arms? It's an aphrodisiac that's incomparable to anything else in the world. I continue to lick her pussy until she pulls me away from her.

"I can't," she pants. "I can't take any more."

I slowly stand, stopping to give her tits some more love.

"Demitri. I want you inside of me."

"Of course." I grin at her.

She reaches forward, lowering my boxer briefs until my dick springs free. And then, like the temptress she is, she leans back on her hands and spreads her thighs. A challenge. A need.

I step between her legs and pull her ass to the edge of the table. I line my cock with her pussy and feed myself into her opening. Slowly. She might be the demanding one, but I have some control. Because I know what she likes and what she needs. I've learned to read her body and face.

Once I'm connected to her in the most intimate way, I look her in the eyes, checking in to see how she's doing. She's breathing hard, her face flushed, eyelids hooded.

"You still with me, *Krasotka*?"

"Yes."

I pull out, almost to the tip, and thrust back in, slow and steady. Mia pushes against me, creating a new friction that hits us both.

"How do you do this?" she keens. "How do you keep doing this?"

"I've learned your body. What you like." Thrust. "What you need." Thrust and swivel.

Her eyes roll to the back of her head and pussy grips me. I adjust with small, quick thrusts, my body hitting her clit with every drive. The ripples of her walls telling me more than any words could.

"You're close," I growl. "Get there. Come for me."

Her arms start to shake from holding up her body and she drops to her elbows, creating a whole new sensation and angle and that's all it takes. I feel her orgasm in every cell of my body and hold off on my own to ensure she gets the maximum pleasure.

When she starts to whimper from being too sensitive, I let my release go. Aiming right at her g-spot, sending her into a mini-orgasm. She drops to her back, her fingers curled around the edge of the table with white knuckles.

I collapse on top of her, my head on her chest, and once she's regained function, I feel her hands in my hair again, almost massaging my scalp.

"So that was a first," she finally says when her breathing has calmed some.

"What was?" I lift my head to look at her, and she grins.

"I've heard about adrenaline sex, but never knew I would be able to have it."

"What you're telling me is that a car chase turned you on?"

"Maybe?" She laughs. "Still need to figure out how we get the hell out of here, though."

"I have an apartment upstairs. Don't even have to go outside. No one will ever know we're there."

"You're telling me you had access to a bed this whole time?"

"You telling me that this wasn't hot as fuck, and you want to do it again sometime?"

"Touché."

I pull her up into my arms, bridal style, and walk to the stairs at the back of the garage.

"What about our clothes?"

"I'll grab them later. I have something you can wear for now." I don't stop walking until we're in the apartment and I flip on a light switch. "Living and kitchen, bedroom behind that door, and bathroom."

I step into the small room and sit her on the sink. I turn on the shower and grab two towels out of the closet.

"This is nice for an over a garage apartment."

"It's not big, and probably needs to be updated, but it suits my needs when I forget to stop working or one of the guys doesn't feel good or needs a place to crash."

"Never thought we'd be the ones who needed a place to crash."

"Yeah, not like this anyway. Let's get in the shower and check in with Joker and see what's going on."

"We're showering together?" Mia raises her brow at me, a knowing glint in her eye.

"Yup. We are."

"How's the water heater in this place? Because you know damn good and well that we can't just shower."

"It's a big one. Now get in there so I can dirty you up a little bit more before I clean you off."

She giggles and hops down from her perch, sashaying that perfect ass by me on her way into the shower. Fuck, she's perfect. And she's mine.

CHAPTER TWENTY-SEVEN
TEXT MESSAGES FROM EVERYONE

THE GIRLS

Grace: Well, this is interesting.

Mia: What?

Grace: Your replacement bartender is here.

Mia: Who is it?

Sofie: It's Grady.

Mia: WHAT?!?!?

Nola: Oh, yeah. He's slinging drinks like it's
his day job.

Sofie: Yeah, he is.

Mia: No man-handling the bartender!

Grace: He's doing a really good job.
Wanted you to know someone is here and
everything's fine.

Nola: Are you okay?

Mia: Fine.

Grace: But?

Mia: I hate hiding.

Sofie: It's to keep you safe. Alive is always
better.

Nola: And you get to hide with that fine-
ass-man who's in love with you.

Mia: He is pretty fine.

Grace: He gave you another orgasm,
didn't he?

Mia: …

Nola: Don't hold out on us! We're all living
vicariously through you!

Sofie: Teach us your ways.

Mia: You'll have to ask him! Seriously, I
don't know how. I only know when he
touches me, I don't panic. He's taught me
how to let go and, well, find my fucking
orgasm.

Grace: I'm really happy for you.

Mia: You know…

Grace: Nope. Not going there.

Mia: Fine. I'm going to go have another orgasm. Just for you all.

Sofie: Get it, girl!

Nola: I love you. And hate you.

Grace: Bitch.

Mia: Love you, too!

THE GUYS

Demitri: What do we know?

Joker: They found your house. Been camped out for a couple of hours.

Demitri: Joke's on them. I haven't been home more than a few minutes in over a month.

Aiden: It also gives us the chance to track them.

Nate: I'm almost in their system now. They have to be working with someone who knows their shit. The firewall is decent.

Demitri: Don't put anything past them. Anything on the 'sister'?

Aiden: Nothing. She's gone under.

Joker: She'll resurface soon.

Demitri: I wish she would so we could get this over with.

Daniel: She's not completely quiet. Batch of designer drugs found on campus. Same ones that went around the high schools.

Joker: Fuck! Those aren't anything to fuck with. They can kill.

Daniel: Sammy's working with PD to find how they got there.

Demitri: She's starting. First the drugs. Then the violence.

Daniel: Hopefully she works slow.

Demitri: Grady's quiet. What's up with him?

Aiden: *Picture of Grady behind the bar at City Brews* He's your very popular bartender tonight.

Demitri: Oh, shit!

Aiden: All these college girls with a daddy kink. They're all drooling and trying to slide numbers his way. Keep calling him their very own Bryant.

Aiden: Now they're talking about Stella Moore and her Daddy romances?

Demitri: Guess we need to go book
shopping?

Aiden: One of them just gave me the name
of one, said it was their favorite. I'll send it
to you later.

Demitri: Brodie must be jealous.

Aiden: Not sure it's Brodie you should be
asking about. The girls are here and are
being very…protective of our boy.

Demitri: Is that so?

Aiden: Grace is glaring, Nola is talking shit
about every one of them, and Sofie might
be growling?

Demitri: I'm sure he's eating up every bit of
it. How long do we need to stay here?

Daniel: To be determined. We'll arrange a
food drop off tomorrow. You good for
tonight?

Demitri: Stale soda and canned ravioli for
the win, I guess. We'll survive.

Daniel: Talk to you in the morning. Also,
need to come up with a plan for next
weekend. We've got an out-of-town job.
This one might require everyone.

Demitri: We'll figure it out. Can't put your
lives on hold for me. I appreciate what
you've done already.

Daniel: You are our job, too.

Demitri: Thanks. See you in the morning.

MIA AND AUNT LINDA

Aunt Linda: How you holding up?

Mia: Could be worse, I guess?

Aunt Linda: Make sure he's taking care of you.

Mia: He is.

Aunt Linda: Good. Don't forget what we talked about.

Mia: I haven't.

Aunt Linda: I think you're a good choice.

Mia: We'll see. Only time will tell, right?

Aunt Linda: Try to get some rest. Have a feeling shit's going to hit the fan sooner rather than later.

Mia: It is what it is.

Aunt Linda: Atta girl.

CHAPTER TWENTY-EIGHT
MIA

"We've been here for a week, Demitri. I can't stay here any longer," I tell the man who has done everything in his power to keep me sane this week.

"It's one more night."

"Promise?"

"Yes," he chuckles. "Promise."

"I'm sorry. I know I'm being bitchy."

"No, you're not. You don't owe me an apology, either. This is not normal. None of it is."

"Are they still watching your house?"

"They are."

"What are we going to do?"

"I don't know. I know I haven't been home, but at some point, they are going to track me down."

"And if you're at my house, it puts me in danger," I finish his unspoken words.

"I can't do that, *Krasotka*."

"You're going to leave me again, aren't you?"

"Only as the very last resort."

He pulls me into his arms, planting a kiss on my lips that

leaves me breathless and momentarily stunned. Long enough that he can escape to the garage below.

I watch him retreat and know I'm being irrational. Am I being overly whiny today? Yes. Am I losing my mind from not being able to leave this apartment for a week? Also, yes. Am I due for a breakdown? Fuck yes. I had a phone call with Dr. Malcome because everyone agreed it would be bad for me not to stay in the apartment. It wasn't enough. It didn't feel private enough to really talk. She did put me in touch with Dr. Thorpe in Briar Mountain. She's a busy lady, but she was finally able to get her to nail down some availability for me. She thought I should still go see her, even though I've found my missing orgasm.

Oh, and orgasms? Let's just say that Demitri is very, very sorry I'm cooped up in this place and has decided naked games are a wonderful distraction. I'm not going to disagree with him on that one. It is, in fact, a very nice way to pass the time. Unfortunately, there's only so many surfaces one can get freaky on in this place, and we obviously need more space.

I never thought I'd be adventurous when it came to sex, but here we are.

Demitri has been going down into the office for a little while every day because even he realizes that we can't both stay naked twenty-four hours a day and might need some separation from each other. I've been able to pull up the bar information on his laptop and get some work done, but it's not the same. I need the wood grain of the bar under my fingertips. I need the interaction with the people who come to my place to get away from the real world for a little while. To play pool with their friends, to find someone to keep them company for the night. To talk to the bartender about what troubles their souls. I need Brodie complaining about the fryer going on the fritz again. My girls sitting in their corner talking about their wants and needs and how their day was.

After Brett took so much from me, I tried to be alone. I thought it would be better for everyone if I stayed away, kept to myself, stayed silent. I learned quickly that I am not that person. I feed off other people's energy.

Which is why I'm sitting in the dark at the top of the stairs, listening to the guys in the garage below talking shit to each other. Demitri included. It's still so odd to me that they know him as John. I will always struggle to reconcile that man with my Demitri.

"So you gonna tell us about the girl you got hidden upstairs?" one of the guys asks.

I've learned their names are David, Cameron, and Seth. All Rock Hill natives.

"Nope. You don't need to know."

"Aww, come on, John. You're obviously getting laid. You're too fucking happy."

"Not your business, Cam."

"Must be some magical pussy he doesn't want to share."

"Fuck you, David."

"Oh, look at him, getting all hot and bothered. She must be something special."

"She is special. And she's mine. You don't need to know about her pussy because if you ever even think about getting close to it, I'll fucking kill you with my bare hands. The subject is closed. Understand?"

"Touchy, touchy. Sorry, man. Just giving you shit."

"Look, guys. That woman is special to me. She's not a barfly. She's not a groupie girl. She's not a one-night stand that's extended for the week. She's here because she's with me and I need her by my side. One day, if you all can get your minds off of your dicks, I might even introduce you to her."

"Wow. Boss is in love, boys!"

Whoops and laughter follow that statement, but I'm not smiling. I'm too stunned that he's admitting his feelings for me to other people. What he says to me is one thing. I have the magic pussy, after all. And all men say those things when they want that, right? But to hear him say it to the guys that work with him? They don't know who the real man behind the John name is, but they know he's serious about me? That tells me more than any of his sweet words ever could.

"If I am, I won't be telling you assholes first. But when you do finally meet her? Ask her about the Shelby. I think she could probably school you sorry sons of bitches some."

"Wait. She's a car girl?"

"She's a Shelby girl."

"A woman with standards. Good for you, boss. She still let you drive her around in that old truck?"

"Don't knock Betty, asshole. She's my first lady."

I continue to listen, laughing at their antics. Am I offended he referred to his truck as his first lady? Nope, not at all. He's a car guy in his soul. I'd be more upset if he didn't. I look at the time on my phone and know I need to get ready. I finally get to return to the real world tonight, and the energy running through my veins at the thought has me hopping up and practically skipping to the shower.

"I'll be in the office watching all the cameras. With the volume up." Demitri winks, his arms wrapped around me in the office.

"I know. I'll behave."

"You be you. Just try not to be too flirty with the cute guys?"

I laugh, kissing his cheek. He frowns and pulls me closer for a proper kiss before smacking my ass and laughing when I squeak.

"Asshole. I'll get you back for that one."

"I'd be disappointed if you didn't."

I wave to Brodie as I pass the kitchen.

"Yo, Boss. Good to have you back. Maybe all the hotties will pay attention to me now!"

"Jealous much? Green's not your color."

"I don't like competition."

I walk behind the bar, sighing at the feeling of coming home. I run my fingers over the grain, the familiar grooves bringing me a peace I haven't felt in days. My anxiety calms, my stress seems to dissipate. This is where I belong. I look at the room in front of me, breathing in the air before the crush of bodies that usually come with the weekend make their way in. The guys who flirt because they want a heavy pour, the women who get the heavy pour because they are polite. The shit talking at the pool table. The couples canoodling in the booths. The groups who take up the big tables in the middle and yell insults good naturedly at their friends.

Yeah, this is where I'm meant to be.

"Ten minutes to open!" I yell through the window to Brodie, who grunts his response. Typical.

I walk through the room, wiping off the tables one more time before going to the door and flipping on the open sign and unlocking the door. Not surprisingly, it's my girls who walk through right away, like they were on the other side waiting.

"It's about time," Nola pouts. "It's getting chilly out there!"

"Why didn't you knock?"

"We were letting you tell the bar how much you loved it since you've been gone for a while." Grace smiles, moving past me.

"Bitches," I laugh.

"Your bitches." Sofie grins, hugging me as she comes in.

I don't wait for them to order, walking behind the bar and making their drinks. There's something calming for me in pouring wine or mixing a Sex on the Beach. It's precise in its chaos. You can do anything with a drink, the control is all yours. Want to double pour the alcohol? Sure. Asshole ordering? Short him the normal pour. Then charge him double. And tell him it's an asshole tax. It's good to be in charge.

"What have I missed?" I ask as I pass out their drinks.

"A bunch of girls hitting on Grady," Sofie and Nola say at the same time, both of their faces pinched in jealousy. Hmm.

"Is that right?"

"I got new reading material out of it." Grace blushes.

"What?"

"Someone recommended Stella Moore. She writes Daddy/littles romances."

"And you've been reading?"

"Umm-hmm," Grace confirms.

"I've heard about her, too!" Demitri yells from my office. "Aiden told me all about it."

"Go back to hiding and forget you heard anything!" Grace yells back before covering her face in embarrassment. "I didn't know he was back there."

"Sorry." I grimace. "He'll be listening all night."

"Terrific. At least now I know."

My phone buzzes from its place under the bar.

> Demitri: Tell her I'm sorry, and that I'd love to talk books with her if it won't embarrass her more.

I turn the screen around and show Grace, much to Nola and Sofie's amusement. She flips off the camera, and I hear Demitri's laughter from the office.

"I don't think I like him anymore," she grouses.

"Yes, you do. And he's serious about the books. The man

has read every book I own and packages keep showing up with more."

"Serious?"

"Very. Seriously, he's got thoughts."

She narrows her eyes at the camera but doesn't say anything. The door opens and the first customers of the night walk in, a big group of men in suits, pulling at their ties. Businessmen. Cheap whiskey and fancy mixed drinks. The next group is my frat bros that come almost every weekend to play pool. Pitchers of beer on repeat all night. Next up are the younger women, probably from the University. They all look disappointed that it's me behind the bar and not Grady. Mixed drinks and shots for them with names like Sex on the Beach and Flaming Orgasm. Blowjob and Buttery Nipple.

The room starts to fill up, and the night is going great. Brodie's bringing food from the back and I'm busy. Wonder if Grady would be up to a part time gig on the weekends when we're slammed?

I'm making another round of tonight's sex drink, a Wet Pussy, when the door opens, and our mystery woman walks in. I make brief eye contact with her before I go back to making the drinks. I side eye the girls, all of whom are trying not to look directly at her, but they've obviously seen her. I finish my drink order and slide them across the bar to the girls.

I hit the button under the bar that notifies Brodie I need assistance. Usually, I'd just yell through the window I had to pee, but this will let him know something's going on out of the normal.

"What's up, Boss?" He rounds the corner, looking at me worriedly.

"I need to grab some change from the office."

"Sure thing. I'll keep an eye out. Nothing's cooking at the moment."

I don't turn around and look at the girls. I scoot around

Brodie and out from the back of the bar, making a beeline to my office, not stopping to talk to anyone.

"What do we do?" I ask as soon as I make it through my office door and close it behind me.

"Nothing," Demitri replies.

"What the fuck do you mean, nothing?"

"Mia, do we want her here? No. But has she done anything? Technically, no. Tonight, we watch. We wait."

"What if she says something to me?"

"Like what?"

"Like 'I know you're fucking my brother, and I want his money!'"

"Oh, *Krasotka*. What we do is not fucking. Earth shattering, orgasm inducing, dehydration causing, but not fucking."

"Enough. Stop distracting me with your sexy words and broody eyes. What am I going to do?"

"You're going to go back out there and do your job. Run the bar that you built and make your customers proud."

"And?"

"And deal with what comes your way when it happens. Wait for her to come to you. She isn't stupid enough to make a scene in front of everyone out there. Too many witnesses. Maybe she just likes your bar."

"Yeah, and maybe she has another listening device she wants to drop off."

"Go. I've got you. I won't let her hurt you, okay?"

"Okay."

Demitri stands and does my favorite thing. He holds his hand out to me. I know it's because he doesn't want to move away from the cameras, but that gesture, asking me to put my faith in him. It melts my heart every time. I give him my hand and he tugs me to him, kissing me gently.

"I'm here. We do this together," he tells me when he pulls back.

I nod, letting him hold me for one more minute before letting go and stepping away. I trudge back behind the bar and laugh at Brodie, who's hitting on the college girls. I make a sweep of the room and see the woman sitting in the same booth as last time, drink already in her hand. Well, at least I don't have to talk to her yet.

All of a sudden, my safe place doesn't feel very safe with her here. It's going to be a long night, isn't it?

CHAPTER TWENTY-NINE
DEMITRI

"COME ON, ANSWER THE DAMN PHONE," I say to myself, calling Aiden.

No answer.

Grady.

No answer.

Daniel.

No answer.

Joker.

No answer.

Nate.

No answer.

"Fuck!" I growl, tossing the phone on the desk. "Who's a guy supposed to call when his maybe half-sister who probably wants him dead is in his girlfriend's bar unannounced?"

I take a breath and pick the phone back up. I text them all.

Demitri: Lady is in the bar. Who can I call?

Joker: We need five. Keep calm.

Keep calm. Keep calm? Fucker really told me to keep calm? Fuck him. I zoom the camera in to get a better look at her. She's dressed like she just left a business meeting. Black slacks, white blouse, black jacket. Minimal makeup. Her hair is straight and hanging down her back. She keeps looking at the dainty watch on her wrist, and then checking her phone. We need cameras from the other side so I can see what's on the screen. I make a mental note to install those tomorrow.

I nervously tap the desk, staring at the screen, flinching every fucking time the lady moves. When my phone rings, I practically jump out of my skin.

"Talk to me. Tell me something good."

"We are in the middle of fucking nowhere, but I have help on the way," Joker replies.

"Who?"

"Couple of friends."

"Mia wants to know what she's supposed to be doing."

"What did you tell her?"

"To do her job."

"Good answer." His dry reply almost makes me laugh, but I'm too keyed up to find it amusing.

"It's like she knew you all were gone."

"Maybe she did."

"How?"

"Don't know yet."

"You really aren't much help, you know that?"

"Look, I'm doing what I can, alright? We've got a woman with multiple broken bones and five kids under the age of eight. All in various states of abuse. Right now, they are my priority. I'm worried about you guys, too, but I have to deal with the people whose lives are actually at stake right this minute."

I lean back in the chair, rubbing my face, trying to release some of the tension. It doesn't help.

"Fuck, I'm sorry. You need to help those people."

"I am. All of us are. But I've got help coming your way, too."

"Thanks."

"Take a breath, keep your eyes on the cameras, and you won't be alone for long. Oh, and text Aunt Linda. Let her know what's going on."

"What can she do?"

"That woman is a better shot than all of us put together. Just do it."

I hang up and text Aunt Linda.

> Demitri: The woman is here. ANON is out of commission this weekend.

I don't expect a reply, and one doesn't come. I continue to watch the camera feeds. And wait.

And wait.

And wait some more.

After what feels like hours, but has been under one, the door opens and three men walk in. Big, burly dudes that look like they're right out of an MC romance. I recognize one of them as Davis. His long hair is down, something I've never seen. A few seconds later, two other men come in, and these, I recognize immediately as Sarge from Boulder Canyon and Sammy, the cop from Briar Mountain. The first two, though? Never seen them in my life.

One of the guys that I don't know avoids facing where the woman is sitting, but the others scan the room like it's their business. They pause briefly when they land on the woman, but that's it. They go to the bar and lean in, speaking to Mia.

"Our friend said you have some funny drinks on the menu." This guy is huge. Like size of a barn huge.

"Your friend, huh? He have a name?" Mia quirks an eyebrow at him. Thatta girl.

"Let's say his name is ANON for now, shall we?"

Mia grins, nods her head, and pulls out a glass. "All of you want something funny to drink?"

"Beer," the other guys answer in unison.

I smile as I watch Mia pull the Midori and peach schnapps off the wall and grab a shot glass, mixing the shot and sliding it across the bar.

"What's it called?" He eyes the glass skeptically before downing it without waiting for Mia's reply. "Huh. You guys should have one of those." He grins at the men behind him.

Davis grins and winks. I swear, he's too good looking, and he knows it. If it weren't for the band on his finger, I'd be planning his murder. "I don't need any Kermit the Frog Piss tonight, bud. But that was the perfect drink for you."

The big guy turns to Mia and his smile gets even bigger. "You just gave me Kermit piss?"

"Yup. Want a beer now?"

He laughs, loud and free, drawing the attention of other patrons in the bar, including the woman. "That'd be great. Tap all around."

"And seriously, can I get names?"

"Later." Sarge smiles at her. "We're here all night."

She winks at him, turning to eyeball the camera. Yeah, she's met the old guy a few times and knows I called in the help. "Bathrooms are down that hall across from my office," she quietly tells them.

They don't reply, just grab their beers and move to an empty table in eyesight of the woman.

Mia looks at the girls, all with varying faces of awe.

"How come everyone who comes in here that might be a helper looks like a Greek God with tattoos?" Nola blows out a breath, fanning her face. "Even the old one looks like a hot Santa with his graying beard! How does that happen?"

"You've got Christmas on the brain, huh?" Mia laughs. Smart girl, ignoring the hot Santa part of her declaration.

"Who wouldn't want to sit on that lap?"

Mia flings her towel. "I want you to go over there and try it."

"What?" She sits back, and the look on her face is hilariously terrified. "No way! I could never!"

"But you'll sit here like a thirsty ho and comment all night?"

"Exactly. It's what I do!"

"Wouldn't it be so much easier if we could get laid?" Sofie bemoans beside her. "All look, but don't touch. That's our life. You're the lucky one."

"Just have to find you a guy with the patience of a saint. It's what I did."

Does Mia's statement make me smile? Yes. Punch the air with how wonderful she thinks I am? Of course. More than that, it was the way she could objectively see a group of decent looking men and not have to fan her face. Does she really think I have the patience of a saint? Well, maybe when it comes to her, I do.

I go back to watching the camera and the woman they keep trying to tell me is my sister. In my experiences, that doesn't mean much. Blood has never done anything but cause me pain. Nothing from this situation makes me think anything is different. I'm on edge, wanting to be out there, a barrier between that woman and my girl, but I know the safest place for me to be is here. Doesn't mean I like it.

"You look like you're constipated."

I look up at the man standing at the door smirking at me.

"Sarge." I stand up and reach out to shake his hand.

"John." The way he looks at me, like he knows that name is a lie, almost makes me feel like a little boy with his hand in the cookie jar.

"Should I even bother asking how much you know?"

"Probably not. But I'm asking, what do you need?"

"I need you to protect Mia. Please."

"You love her?"

"Yes."

"You told her that?"

"Not yet. We've been a little busy lately."

"No time like the present, son. You don't tell her now, who can guarantee you have the opportunity to tell her later?"

I nod, knowing he's right.

"So that woman out there, that's who we need to protect your girl from?"

"That's the plan."

"Who is she?"

"They tell me she's my sister."

"Fuck, son."

"Welcome to the shit show that is my life."

"We'll be here all night. You know we'll keep her safe."

"Who is we?"

"Those are my boys. Two of them served with me, one of them was also with Daniel. And you know Davis and Sammy."

"Does he have to wear his hair down and flowy like that? I didn't recognize him at first."

"You two can catch up later. He's the one who filled us in on the way down who you were. And don't worry, I'm not mad. You do what you have to in this life to survive."

"Thanks. I think I needed to hear that."

"Anytime. You know I'm good for motivational speaking."

We both laugh, knowing he's full of shit but also telling the truth.

"She's on the move." Sarge points to the screen beside me. "I'll go back out."

"Yeah," I answer without looking away from the screen.

He doesn't say another word. He closes the door, and I see him enter the frame a few seconds later. I turn up the volume and zoom the camera in.

"What can I get you?" Mia asks. Only someone who knows her as well as I do could tell she's nervous right now.

"I'd love another glass of wine, please."

"Red, right?"

"Yes, please. You remember?"

"I tend to remember people who aren't beer."

She laughs, and I want to puke. It sounds so forced, so fake.

"Are you going to visit the campus again?"

"Huh?" she starts, momentarily caught off guard. Ha! She's not perfect. "Oh, uh, no. Not this time."

"Did Brodie start a tab for you?"

"No. He offered, but I wasn't sure how long I'd be here tonight." She looks distracted, like Mia is throwing her off with her questions. Or not asking the questions she thinks Mia should ask. "I'm sorry, it's just really loud in here. Do you have somewhere we can talk? I have a question for you, and I'm sorry it's during a busy Saturday, but it's business related."

"Oh, well, sure. Let me get Brodie back out here. We can go to my office."

Mia turns to the window into the kitchen, her eyes wide and wild, looking up at the camera like she hopes I'm listening. Like there was any doubt about that. I look around her office. It's a plain room without much in it, but she does have a small half bath. I immediately turn off the monitors, knowing everything will still be recorded, and head into the bathroom. Closing the door most of the way, I perch on the toilet seat and hold my breath. I pull out my phone, opening the voice memo app, and get ready. I don't know what this woman wants, but whatever it is, I'm pretty sure I'm not going to like it.

CHAPTER THIRTY

MIA

I HATE THIS. With every fiber of my being, I do not want to be in a room alone with this woman. But I lead her down the hallway into the office, trusting that Demitri heard everything and is hiding.

I slowly open the door and glance inside, internally breathing a sigh of relief. I step in and allow the woman to enter before softly pushing the door mostly closed.

She looks at the crack like it's offending her, but this is how it is.

"Brodie is out there alone on a Saturday night. If shit goes sideways, I need to hear it," I offer by way of explanation.

She seems to accept it and sits on the couch across from my desk, crossing her legs.

"My name is Katya Sokolova-Pavlov."

She says it slowly, watching my reaction. I keep my face a mask of indifference. She can't hurt me. She can't touch me. Nothing she can say will surprise me.

"Nice to meet you. I'm Mia Alexander."

"And you own this bar?"

"I do."

"Are you the only owner?"

"If you're here to conduct business, are you telling me you didn't do your homework before stepping foot in here the first time?" I challenge, raising my brow.

Her lips quirk and she tips her chin in acknowledgement that I'm right. And that she did do her homework.

"Just because your name is the only one on the paperwork doesn't mean you did it alone, you know."

"I'm aware. How can I help you, Ms. Sokolova-Pavlov?"

"I have a rather delicate proposition for you. One that you would greatly benefit from."

"I'm listening."

Fuck, I hope I'm not the only one.

"I have a few...associates who want to get into the bar business, but they don't know how to run a bar. I was wondering if we could work out a trade? They would work here, under your mentorship and knowledge."

"Like an internship?"

"Exactly like an internship."

"And what do you get?"

"I get knowledgeable bartenders and business owners that can then come work a new opportunity for me."

"Bullshit. What do you really get? No one works for free anymore. Hell, most internships are paid positions these days. Also, you want me to train someone to be a bartender and business owner? They have schools for both of those. And books for the lazy ones who can't get out of bed in time for class."

"I don't need to explain the whys, just the money."

"I'm waiting."

The look on her face tells me I need to back up a little, to not be such a hard-ass, but she sounds like a fucking moron. Seriously, she thinks anyone with any business sense would fall for this?

"I would pay you ten thousand a week."

I stare at her, my face devoid of emotion.

"You want to pay me half a million dollars a year to let people come in here and work for free. What's the catch?"

"You might need to turn your head from time to time."

"Why?"

She blinks a few times, like me asking that question is unheard of.

"Did you hear my last name?"

"Yes."

"And do you know what that last name means?"

"Should I?"

She rolls her eyes at me, like she's dealing with a child.

"My father is the head of the Russian Bratva. He's a very powerful man."

"If he's so powerful, why isn't he here asking me this himself?"

"You think he'd lower himself to do the actual work? He's got other, bigger things to worry about."

"Is that so?"

Yes, I can play the stupid and innocent game.

"It is. So he sent me. This is at his request. And you don't fuck with a man at his level."

"What is it exactly you want my bar for, Katya?"

I'm internally smiling at the look of incredulity on her face that I would have the audacity to use her first name.

"We need your *bar*," she spits the word like it's dirty, "to move some things."

"Drugs?"

"Among others."

"What others?"

"I wouldn't worry about it."

"The answer is no."

"What do you mean, no?"

"I mean, if you can't be upfront and totally honest with me, I don't want to do business with you."

"I'm trying to give you plausible deniability."

"Big words, little meaning. You think I believe for one minute that you wouldn't throw me under the bus at the first sign of trouble?"

"You would just have to trust me."

"Except I don't trust you. The answer is no."

"This isn't over."

"Of course not. How about you send your dead father in here to ask me next time?"

Her head snaps up, her eyes narrowing.

"You think just because I own a little bar in a small town that I don't know anything? I watch the news. Your first mistake was lying to me about him. Your next was trying to manipulate me with money to do your illegal shit. I would appreciate it if you got the hell out of my bar and never come back."

"You'll regret this."

"I'm sure you'll try to make me, but you aren't close to the worst person I've ever had the displeasure of dealing with."

She looks like she's ready to throw a tantrum. I don't need this. I need her gone so I can have a proper meltdown.

I stand, putting us on an even level, and I look her in the eyes. "You should leave this place, this town, and the people that live here alone. We don't want your drugs, we don't want your family, and we don't want you. Get. Out."

The woman actually stomps her foot before turning on her red bottomed heels and storming out of the office, flinging the door open for added dramatics.

I'm frozen in the middle of my office. Unable to move, or breathe, or call for help. I feel my legs trying to give out, the desk feeling too far away to hold on to for support. I start to go down, but before I hit the ground, two strong arms are around me, pulling me up and against a chest I now know intimately.

"Shhh, *Krasotka*. She's gone. I have you. Everything's okay now."

"She, she didn't want you. She wasn't here for you. She wanted me to..."

"I know, baby. I know. But she's gone now. And you were such a fucking boss lady. I'm so proud of you."

I hear the edge of panic in his voice, the same panic I feel.

"I'm going to lose the bar, aren't I? She's going to do something to it. Set it on fire, break in and trash the place. We already know they can get in. I fucked up, didn't I?"

"No. You didn't fuck up. You responded to her ridiculous request exactly how you should have."

He sits down on the couch, pulling me down next to him, holding me to him. The older man, the one the girls referred to as Hot Santa, is the first to the door.

"Everything okay?"

"It will be. She gone?" Demitri asks her.

"Stormed out of here like a madwoman."

"At least she's gone."

"Your girl alright?"

"My girl is fucking epic. She burned the shit out of that woman without even raising her voice. Fucking rockstar."

"You don't fuck with my bar," I finally lift my head enough to say. "Or my family."

Her declaration hits me like a gut punch.

"Family protects you," Sarge replies. "No matter what that family looks like to you. Blood ain't shit if they stink."

Mia smiles a little. "I'm Mia." She gives a little wave.

"I remember. I'm Sarge. The idiots out there are Davis, Tiny, and Ranger."

"I've also had the pleasure of meeting Davis. And, let me guess, the oversized giant of a man is Tiny, right?"

He laughs, nodding. "You got it. I'd say blame the Army for bad nicknames, but he came with that one already in place."

"Thank you for coming tonight. I'm so sorry you had to give up a night for me."

"Nonsense. Family, remember? My family called me and I'm here for you."

"Who did you call?" I ask Demitri.

"Joker."

"Hmm. That tracks. Only he would know people crazy enough to come out in the middle of the night to watch a person they didn't know."

Sarge laughs again, making Mia smile.

"I like this one. She's feisty. Reminds me of my Rosie."

"Is she okay?" Grace asks, rushing through the door, stopping short when she sees me. She lets out a sigh of relief. "Thank God. I thought she might have killed you back here. What did she want?"

"She wanted to plant her men and run business out of here," I tell her.

"Fuck that."

"That's pretty much what I told her."

"Of course you did." She grins at me.

"Is Brodie good out there?" I ask.

"He's giving body shots off the bar." She shrugs.

"I don't know if you're fucking with me or not, Gracie. And right now, my brain can't decide if it cares."

"Davis is helping behind the bar," Sarge offers. "He's got experience. Owns his own up in Boulder Canyon."

"That's right. He owns Zach's."

"He's like a local legend up there. Former FBI guy turned bar owner."

"Of course he is. And I bet all the single ladies in town come in to see the man with the luscious locks."

"Co-Owner. His wife would be really upset if you left her out of it. And don't let his momma hear you compliment the hair. She's been trying to get him to cut it for years."

"Of course." I grin at him.

"What's the plan?" Grace asks. "Want me to start kicking everyone out?"

"No," I laugh. "No point in it. Nothing's going to get solved tonight. Tell Brodie I need ten more minutes and he better have his shirt on when I get out there or he's fired."

I grin at her, both of us knowing I'd never fire that man.

"You sure you don't want to close for the night?" Demitri quietly asks.

"I'm sure. I just pissed off the unofficial, self-proclaimed, wannabe head of the Bratva. We're staying open to celebrate."

"Okay then. You heard the lady."

"We'll see you out there." Sarge tips his chin before leaving us alone in the office.

When we're alone, I turn to Demitri. "What do we do now?"

"I don't know. Right this minute, I guess you go out there and run your bar. I'll touch base with Joker, and when you close, we'll debrief before we go home. How's that sound?"

"*Home*-home or the apartment?"

"Home. I think if I take you back to the apartment, you'll lose your mind." He smirks at me.

"You're probably right," I return his grin, "but I think I'll sit here in your arms for a few more minutes before I go back out there into the real world."

"This is real, too, *Krasotka*. Don't doubt that."

He tips my chin up, kissing me softly, his lips pressing against mine in a promise.

If only I could stay here for the rest of the night, but he's right. Reality is all around us and it's time I deal with it.

CHAPTER THIRTY-ONE
TEXT MESSAGES FROM THE GUYS

SATURDAY NIGHT

Joker: How's it going?

Demitri: Fine. Mia took the bitch down like the bad-ass boss lady she is.

Joker: Of course she did. Was there any doubt?

Aiden: That's our girl.

Demitri: Excuse me?

Aiden: Sorry, that's your girl!

Demitri: That's what I thought, asshole.

Grady: How are the other girls? Are they okay?

Demitri: Fine. Staying to hang out with the new friends. Thanks for sending them, by the way.

Aiden: What new friends?

Joker: The Boulder Canyon gang. Davis and friends.

Grady: Why'd you send them?

Joker: Because they could help?

Aiden: Who was with Davis?

Joker: Sarge, Tiny, Ranger.

Aiden: Seriously, fucker? You sent in the hot guy brigade?

Joker: You worried?

Grady: Fuck you.

Joker: Touchy, touchy.

Daniel: Demitri, I'm glad everything's okay. We'll be back Monday. Check in then?

Demitri: You're playing dad and having to separate the boys, aren't you?

Daniel: Yes. It's like they forgot these guys were there for us, too, and that they are all very happily married.

Demitri: Jealousy is not logical.

Daniel: Now if only they could decide who they are jealous over.

Grady: Fuck you.

Aiden: Fuck off.

Demitri: At least they are in agreement there.

SUNDAY NIGHT

Demitri: All's quiet on the western front.

Nate: Wasn't that a book about World War 1?

Demitri: Yes.

Nate: Germans?

Demitri: Yes. It was pretty anti-war.

Nate: Is this where I make an inappropriate joke about you being Russian?

Demitri: You can try but doesn't change that it was a good book.

Nate: You take all the fun out of things.

Demitri: I try.

MONDAY MORNING

Demitri: When will you all be back?

Joker: What's wrong?

Demitri: She didn't wait too long to retaliate. The bar's been vandalized.

Daniel: How bad?

Demitri: Not sure yet. We haven't gone inside. Window's broken out though, and we can see damage on the inside.

Aiden: ETA is about an hour.

Joker: I called Sammy. He's calling some of the guys he knows on Rock Hill PD.

Demitri: Do we have to involve the cops?

Joker: Yes. You need a report to file a claim on your insurance. At a minimum.

Demitri: She's going to hate that.

Daniel: I know she's not a fan of them with her history, but we're calling in the good guys.

Demitri: I know. Thanks. I'll try to keep her out until you get here.

Joker: Don't touch anything.

Demitri: You got it.

"At least she didn't burn it down, right?" Mia says, trying to justify what's happened.

"Nobody got hurt, Mia. This could have been so much worse."

I pull her into my arms, knowing my words are really helping right now, but also remembering all the times I was forced to join the crew as they did to others what has just happened to her. And I've seen so much worse. Someone let her off easy, and I don't know why.

"Do you think the alarm scared them away before they could really do some damage? That they'll come back to finish the job?"

"They did what they wanted to do. No alarm was going to scare them, *Krasotka*. They wanted to send a message, and they still need this place for whatever they have working, so they aren't going to completely destroy it. Just make your life hell for a while."

"Until I give in."

"Or they run you off completely and they can step in and take over."

"They want my place as a front to launder money, don't they?"

"And drugs, women, goods."

"Fuck."

She leans back, looking around me, trying to see how bad the inside is. I don't want her to go in. Even if the damage is minimal, I want to protect her from all of it.

"Mia," I whisper. "I'm so fucking sorry this happened. Everything bad keeps happening, and it's all my fault."

"How can you say that? None of this is your fault, Demitri!"

"But it is. If I weren't here—"

"Your father would have still slept with the maids and had children you didn't know about. He would have still been an evil man, running an empire of illegal operations. I would have still been a target for that woman because she wants something from me. She would have done this even if you weren't here. But you are here. I have you to lean on. You to love me."

"I do, you know." I shrug. "I love you. Every part."

"I love you, too. Now, suck it up and realize this isn't all on you, not even a little bit."

"Yes, ma'am." I nod.

"Good. See how easy things are when you listen to me?"

I shake my head and kiss her in a very not safe for outside in public way, but she comes willingly. No more running from me, no more avoiding my touch. No more. And this is just us. A declaration of love in its simplicity. No over-the-top antics to go with it, just us, standing in the middle of a parking lot. And her giving me shit immediately after. I love this woman.

"The guys will be here in an hour, and Sammy is sending some of his cop friends. They said to tell you they are 'good ones' to ease your mind."

She laughs, shaking her head. "Just because Brett was an asshole cop and his dad ran a corrupted department doesn't mean I think all cops are bad, Demitri. I rely on them all the time with the bar, and they keep me safe. I know all the guys and gals on Rock Hill's PD. I'd trust all of them to do me right."

"That's good to know for the future, I guess."

Still smiling, she reaches into my pocket and pulls out my phone. "Go ahead and text the guys that I'm alright with cops coming. They need to anyway. Insurance."

"Damnit, that's what Daniel said." I take the phone from her and text the guys that cops are alright. I hate being wrong, especially to him, but I suck it up and do it for her.

The gang pulls into the lot less than an hour later. The cops are here, talking with Mia. We're still standing outside. None of us have gone in yet, almost as if the cops were waiting for them to get here.

"Have you gone in yet?" Daniel asks, joining our little circle.

"No, sir," one of the officers answers. "We were getting some basic information from Ms. Alexander."

"Good. It alright if I send a man in with you when do you finally go?"

"If Ms. Alexander is alright with it, I don't see a problem."

"Thanks." Daniel nods our way and goes to talk to Joker about whatever he's got up his sleeve.

We're answering the last few questions when the girls show up.

"Oh, my God, Mia." Grace walks up to us, tears in her eyes, looking at the building. "Are you alright?"

"I'm fine. I wasn't here when it happened."

"Thank goodness," Sofie adds.

"What can we do to help?" Nola asks.

"Nothing right now. We're getting ready to go see how bad it is."

"Let us know what you need. We're here for you."

The girls all hug, and I take Mia's hand. She's not going in without me either. One of the officers meets us at the door, and we all step inside. I know what I'm looking for. The real damage beyond the flipped tables and chairs. Because my family doesn't do things half-assed. But I don't see it. I don't see burn marks on the floors or cracks in the walls. Some of the liquor bottles are missing, but none have been broken to leave glass on the floor.

"We'll need an inventory of what's missing from behind the bar. And a list of any damages," the officer tells Mia.

But she's seeing the same thing I am. A few overturned tables and chairs, some missing booze, and not much else.

"Window guy will be here in thirty to replace this one," Daniel says through the broken window.

"Thanks," Mia graciously tells him. "What else do you need?" She turns to the cop.

"I think we're good. You'll get us a list to add to the report?"

"Sure thing. When can we open?"

"As soon as you want, I guess. I figure some kids got a little too enthusiastic."

"Could be," Mia replies absentmindedly.

The cop leaves, and Joker shakes his head.

"I swear. They didn't even take prints, so convinced it's 'just kids'," he says, using finger quotes. "Fuckers. Nate and Aiden are coming in to check for prints."

"We already know who it was," Mia replies. "Are prints really going to change our minds on that?"

I look around the room again. "Mia, I'm not sure it was them. This is too...clean."

"What do you mean?" Daniel asks, coming in through the back with some equipment.

"I mean, Russians aren't known for their polite destruction. They aren't known for leaving messages without damage. I don't see a ton of true damage."

"He's right," Mia says from behind the bar. "I've seen bars that were broken into and busted up. Biker bars, trying to run someone out of town for competition back home. The first thing they would do is damage the actual bar." She runs her hands over the still smooth wood. "There's no harm to mine."

"No bottles busted up," Joker adds, taking a closer look. It seems all of them are noticing what I already did. "No pool cues broken. Tables and chairs just tipped on their sides."

"Demitri," Mia quietly calls my name, looking at something behind the bar.

I quickly go to her side, where she points to where my bottle of vodka has been for four years. It's missing. In its place is a different bottle, one that's dark instead of clear, and there's no liquid in it. I lift it up and Mia gasps.

"There's something in it."

Mia reaches in with a pair of skinny tongs and pulls out a piece of folded paper. Joker comes over with gloves on and opens the note so we don't touch it. All of us crowd around, all of us looking at it. Then they all look at me.

"What's it say? Can you read it?" Mia asks.

Ты не один. Я здесь, чтобы помочь.

"You are not alone. I am here to help." I look up at everyone, adding, "And the initials SP."

"Your uncle?" She looks at me, and I know the hope and fear in her eyes reflect my own.

"I don't know. I don't know who else it would be."

Daniel's face hardens as he pulls out his phone. "I need to make a call."

He walks to the far corner, bitching someone out in low tones, but we can't make out any of the words.

"Fuck. He's going to be in a mood all day." Joker frowns.

"What else are you all doing before we can start straightening up in here?" Mia asks, distracting us from Daniel.

"Let me just scan the room, and then we're good to go."

Joker picks up the piece of equipment Daniel brought in and starts walking around the room. I don't know what it is, but these guys have some fun tech toys.

"Let's start making a list of the booze that's missing?" I ask Mia.

"Grr. More inventory. I hate inventory."

I chuckle as she walks to the back office to print out a list. Looks like we're doing a full inventory before we can open back up. I watch her walk away, unable to help myself for admiring her ass.

"We've got an issue," Daniel quietly says when he returns to the bar.

"What's that?"

"Aunt Linda knows shit she's been keeping from us. Big stuff, man."

"What do you mean?" I ask, looking from him to the hallway.

"She's on her way to explain it all. It's time she comes clean with all of us."

Mia returns and we get to work updating her inventory list. All the vodka is missing. Of course it is. But the gin, rum, and bourbon are also coming up in much shorter supply than there should be.

"At least they didn't touch the kegs. Those are a pain in the ass to replace." Mia sighs when we finally finish.

The other guys have flipped all the tables right side up, and the girls have reappeared with food for everyone from the Mexican place down the street. We've finished wiping everything down when the door busts open and Aunt Linda walks in.

"Welp, guess it's time to fess up, huh?" she announces, pulling out a chair and sitting down, immediately reaching for a chip. "Can I get a drink? Got any rum left?"

Mia stares at her, frozen for a second, before standing and going behind the bar.

I stare at the older woman, seeing her in a new light. She's not just 'everyone's aunt who keeps their secrets,' but she's an actual secret keeper. And that makes her even more dangerous. The problem is, I don't know where the danger will land, with us or with the other side.

CHAPTER THIRTY-THREE
MIA

I stare at Aunt Linda, my face slack. Hell, my mouth might even be hanging open. What she just told us has all of us in some form of frozen shock. I break away from her face to look at Demitri, who is barely holding his shit together. I know when a person is close to breaking, and he's at his limit.

I don't say anything, but they all turn to me when I stand and move to Demitri's side, taking his hand and pulling him up. I make eye contact with each person at the table, silently telling them to leave us alone. The girls get it. Hell, they can probably read my mind at this point. Daniel spares me a small glance before continuing to glare at Aunt Linda. Grady and Aiden both nod their heads in understanding and Joker and Nate tip their chins before going back to their laptops.

Brodie is also here now, having come to see what he could do and sticking around for story time. He looks lost.

I pull Demitri into the office and close the door. I don't let his hand go until we're sitting side by side on the couch. I gently tug on his arm, and he puts his head in my lap, holding my thighs. He squeezes his eyes shut, but I know he's reliving memories I can't see behind the lids.

"Wanna talk about it?" I gently ask, running my fingers through his hair.

"I don't know what to say," he replies, sounding so lost. "I feel like I've just had my entire world flipped on edge."

Aunt Linda told us she's been keeping secrets. Lots of secrets. About Demitri, his family, and who the bad guys are.

"Sasha was never a good guy, Mia. He's done unfathomable things in his life that he will never be able to atone for. Violence was always a part of him. I don't understand."

"Do you believe what she said?"

"That he's tired of the blood and hate and doesn't want the family to continue? I have no idea what to believe."

"Are you going to talk to him? I'll go with you."

"No. I don't want you anywhere near that monster."

"How will you ever get answers if you don't talk to him, Demitri?"

"I don't know that I want the answers. Does that make me a bad person?"

"No, Dem, it doesn't. It makes you human."

"I don't think I want to be human right now."

I lean over and kiss his forehead. He pulls me back, kissing my lips with a sad desperation I've never felt from him before.

"*Krasotka*, I need you," he whispers. "Please."

"Yes," I whisper my reply.

He sits up and helps me stand. This isn't going to be sweet or seductive. It's going to be a release of emotions he's not ready to face. It's going to be quick and naughty. I check in on my mind and body, and they both understand that this is what the man I love needs, and we can provide it. He's not using us or wanting to hurt us. He's leaning on us. Me. He needs *me*.

His eyes remain locked with mine as he tugs the drawstring on the sweats I stole from him a few weeks ago. They were also the first thing I found to throw on when the alarm went off this morning. I kick off my tennis shoes while he slides the fabric down my legs, helping me out of them. He then pulls down my panties, leaving me bare under an over-sized t-shirt—also stolen from him.

"You're hot as fuck in my clothes, Mia. But even hotter out of them."

He lifts up from the couch, yanking his own pants down far enough for his cock to spring free. I straddle his thighs, his hands running up mine and lifting the fabric of my shirt to cup my ass. He holds me to him, crushing our lips, his tongue darting out to lick the seam of my mouth. I open, letting him in, and he groans. Without ending the kiss, he lifts my body while I adjust his cock under me and slide onto his shaft.

I place my hands on his shoulders and use his body as leverage to rise and fall, lifting until just the tip remains and sliding back down again. My pussy grips him, pulling him in more with each downward motion.

"I want you to come too, Mia. I need you to."

"I'll try," I promise.

"I'll help you get there."

He removes one of his hands from my backside and brings it around to my front, flattening his palm on my lower belly and pressing his thumb against my clit. He's circling it, dragging his thumb lower with each circle, gathering the wetness that's growing from where he's entering my body. The dual sensations of his cock and finger builds me up.

I'm almost there when he throws me over the edge with his words.

"You're the most beautiful woman I've ever met in my life. The way you care for me, love me, want me. You are the best part of my existence."

My body pulses around him, pulling him in even deeper. He growls my name as he climaxes, his face buried in the crook of my neck.

"I guess we've mastered the quiet quickie." I giggle into his hair.

I feel him laughing under me, his body creating extended waves of pleasure to course through me.

"You know they're going to worry if I killed you."

"Or if I killed you," I agree.

"You know they call orgasms 'mini deaths'. Does that mean we killed each other?"

"The fact I want to laugh at that just proves how fucked up we are, right?"

"Fucked up together, baby." He smirks, patting my ass before helping me stand.

He follows and leads me into the bathroom, where he helps me clean up.

"You ready to face those people again?" I ask, looking at the door.

"I guess. If I have to."

"We've had a long, already shitty day, Dem. We can do whatever the fuck we want."

"After you order a new bottle of Beluga Gold."

"You'll have to settle for a different kind of shot today."

"Fine. Let's do this."

Two hours is how long it takes for Aunt Linda to get everything set up. Enough time for me to worry a tread into the floor of the bar worrying about Demitri. He's quiet. Too quiet. He's separated himself from the rest of the people here, sitting in a corner booth on his own. The don't-fuck-with-me vibe he's putting off keeps everyone away. I don't blame him.

He's about to meet his uncle for the first time in years, and he's afraid.

He's upset that I won't leave. That I won't leave him alone to meet the monster. I understand he doesn't want me involved, but what he doesn't get is that I already am. I became involved the first time I went home with him. And when that bitch walked into *MY* bar offering me money to look the other way? Well, it became personal.

"He's going to chew his lip off before this begins." Grace frowns, standing beside me.

"It's his tell. Next, he'll start running his hand through his hair and gripping the back of his neck. And then he'll start tapping on the table with his thumb."

Grace side-eyes me. "This thing between you is real, isn't it? It's not just fun or sex or forced proximity?"

"It's always been real, Gracie. I only had to quit fighting it to let it happen."

"I'm happy for you."

"And sad for you," I reply, tugging on her arm and pulling her into a hug. "It'll happen for you one day, too. You'll open your eyes and your heart and realize your perfect match is standing in front of you, begging you to let them love you."

"I hope you're right, but let's not hold our breaths, okay?"

I snort, holding in a laugh. When is this woman going to realize that she's an amazing human? That Brett could steal so much from us, but he could never take our will to survive. To fight the demons he left with us. I know each of us still has some of those to slay, but we do it little by little each day. And one day, we will all be able to look back on that time in our lives and realize the scars might still be there, but the pain that went with them has faded and we are stronger now.

I'm not totally prepared when the door opens and the brute that broke into my bar comes through the back door with Aunt Linda at his side. He looks older than his years. I guess that's what being a monster will do to you. Or I'm just a bad judge of age after they reach twenty-one.

Demitri looks up, determination and a bit of fear in his eyes. I feel so bad for him. I want to take that fear away, but I don't know how.

"You broke into my bar," I say, standing.

"I did," he replies, his Russian accent still thick. "I did what I had to do."

I scoff, rolling my eyes. "Why are you here?"

"For my *plemiannik*. My nephew."

"What do you want with me, *Dyadya*? You spent years hurting people. Hurting me. Are you back to finish the job?"

"Demitri. Please. Can we sit and talk?"

I look between the men and can see the resemblance. While Sasha looks like he's lived a hard life, he shares the same eyes, the same jawline. Where Demitri is tall and lean with muscles, Sasha is shorter, stooped from the years of living.

Demitri looks at me, an unspoken need radiating from his entire being. I immediately move closer and take his hand. Sasha doesn't miss the action, a sad smile on his face.

"I need you to know the truth. About me. About our life."

"Start talking."

Demitri sits back down in the booth and I join him, our hands still clasped under the table, resting on his thigh. Sasha joins us, and I notice everyone else in the bar moving closer, sitting at the closest tables. I don't blame them. I'd want to hear all of this, too. The only person who remains standing is Aunt Linda, and for the first time, she looks like she doesn't have the answers.

We all watch as she goes behind the bar and grabs four shot glasses before returning to the booth and sliding in next to Sasha. There is no fear in her as she sits so close to this monster, this killer and trafficker. She places the shot glasses on the table and pulls a bottle of clear liquor out of her bag. A bottle of Beluga Gold. Without saying a word, she opens the bottle and pours the liquid into the glasses before passing them around to us.

"*Za tvoyo zdorovye*," she announces, picking up her glass.

"To your health," Demitri translates as he also picks up his shot.

I follow, and we all down the drink.

"You stole my bottle of vodka," I say to Sasha.

"I haven't had a drop out of it and will make sure it finds its way safely back to you."

Demitri squeezes my hand and looks at his uncle. "Why are you here? Why did you come back? What do you want? Is it about the money?"

The older man laughs, ending in a cough. Aunt Linda hurries to get out of the booth and runs over behind the bar, pouring the man a glass of water. She returns and sets it in front of the older man before taking her seat next to him. It's like she's taking care of him. Like she cares for him.

"Demitri, I don't need your money, nor do I want it. I have my own, dear boy."

"Then why?"

"To protect you. And your *ledi*." He gestures to me. "I couldn't let anything happen to you."

"To protect us?"

"Yes."

"Why should I believe that? *Dyadya*, I watched you. For years, I saw what you did. The women you hurt."

"You saw what I wanted you to see, Demi."

Demitri flinches at the nickname. One he doesn't use. Dem? Yes. Demi? No.

"What does that even mean?"

"You saw me remove women. You saw me hand them over to other men. Men you assumed were just as evil as your *otetz*."

"Exactly! You sold those women to other men without any remorse or resistance!"

"Demitri, those men? They were government agents. I was helping those girls get out. To safety."

Demitri's head flings back like he's been punched. I feel the blow, too.

"You killed Mika!"

"No, I didn't. That wasn't me. That was your father and Andrey."

"What do you mean?"

He sighs, like the weight of the world has been on his shoulders for way too long. He gives me a look asking for forgiveness as he reaches for the bottle Aunt Linda left on the table and pours another shot. After downing it, he turns to Aunt Linda, who nods her head with a gentle smile on her face.

"I guess I should start at the beginning."

CHAPTER THIRTY-FOUR
DEMITRI

I LOOK AT MIA, who raises a brow at me. Challenging me to say something to him about his comment. Guess it runs in the family.

"That is usually the best place to start," I tell him.

"You know some of the family history. You know that our great-great-great something-or-other worked for that man's great-great-great whatever." He nods his head to Daniel, who sits up straight, listening hard. "You know the families broke ties when one of ours and one of theirs ran away together in the name of love."

I nod. I'd heard the family history my whole life.

"Our father was sent back home. He was told to raise the good Russian sons and not come back until we were powerful enough to take over from them." He looks at Daniel again. "My father was a cruel man. Hard. Taught us in fists and blood, power and money. He did not love us, only loved what we would be able to do for him when we were big and strong."

I know very little about my grandfather other than the old stories. I nod at Sasha to continue.

"We did what our *dedushka* wanted. We became big and

strong and mean. We came back and Ivan took care of business. He wanted it more. Not only had he been beaten by our *otetz*, but by us. He was the baby. We made him what he was, Demi. It was all our fault."

"Hush," Aunt Linda admonishes. "Not your fault." She turns to us, rolling her eyes. "I've been telling him for years this wasn't his fault. He wouldn't believe me."

"And we'll be coming back around to that statement." I glare at Aunt Linda, who has the good graces to look a little ashamed. "Go on."

"I knew if we were going to succeed here, we had to get smart. Not just strong. We all went to school for things that would help the family. Stanislav went into finance. Ivan got his MBA. Misha and Sergi went into IT. I went into criminal justice and eventually earned my Juris Doctorate—my law degree."

I raise my brows in surprise at that. "Law?"

"How can you break the rules if you don't know them?" He shrugs. "It was during that time I met someone. Someone I knew would make the family very unhappy."

He stares at Aunt Linda and my stomach drops. "You... and...Aunt Linda?"

He nods. "*Da*. For over forty years. She's been my confidant, my partner, my keeper, and my wife."

The room is eerily quiet. It's like everyone has quit breathing.

"Demitri, I've been a government asset for decades. I was the mole. I was the one who connected you to Linda. Gently pushing you all those years to be better than we all were. To not become what Ivan did. Or your sister."

I flinch at the mention of my sister, but she's not the one we should be talking about now. At least I know she's not out here wreaking havoc. She's behind bars, where she'll stay for the rest of her life.

"I thought Davis pushed me in that direction?"

Sasha stares at me, not saying a word, waiting for me to connect the dots.

"But he broke his cover for me."

"At my request, Demi. Even he knew you weren't going to listen to me, and he wanted to help."

"What is your deal with this other woman who says she's my sister?"

"I'm a Pavlov. I've been in hiding since the heat began, that's all they needed to know. Someone wants to grow their power in the Pavlov family? They need a Pavlov behind them. They asked no questions."

"So you're here to what? Get information and turn it over to the feds?"

"I'm here to make sure she doesn't hurt you. First and foremost, I protect you. Then I share what I know with the people I work for."

"I don't know how to respond to this. I can't believe it." I look at Linda. "And you. You made me trust you. Lean on you. You were like family when I thought all of my family had turned on me. You kept this secret from me. Why? Was it like a sick fucking game? Did you get off on it?"

Do I notice the hurt in Linda's eyes? Yes. Am I going to take back what I said? Abso-fucking-lutley not.

Mia stops me by putting her palm against my cheek and turning my face to her. "Demitri, baby, take a breath." I do as she says. "Good. Now take another. Do you need a break?"

I stare at her, the love on her face making me weak. "Maybe."

"Good enough. We need a break." She turns to the group, who have all been very vested in what Sasha has been saying. "You can grill them while we're gone and fill us in when we get back. Gracie, you're on."

Mia stands and pulls me up by our still connected hands,

walking us past everyone and into the hallway. Before we make it to her office, she pulls me into her body, wrapping my arms around her shoulders and hers around my waist.

We stand there for what could be seconds or hours. I don't know, but I need this. I need her to keep me calm. Her presence quiets the demons that have haunted me for years.

"I'm so sorry, Demitri," she soothes, rubbing my back.

"I don't know what to think, *Krasotka*. Or what to do."

"What's upsetting you the most?"

"Would it be completely wrong to say it's that Aunt Linda is my actual fucking aunt?"

She chuckles, and I can't help but join her.

"No. I don't think that's wrong."

"I feel betrayed. I feel like they used me like a fucking puppet. Pulled my strings and made me do things I might not have done otherwise."

"Do you really feel that? Or are you upset that they omitted the entire truth to you?"

"I don't know."

"It's okay that you don't know. Makes you human, Dem. I think you need time to process everything. You wanted to hear him out, so do that. Then get away from them for a little while. Sort through your feelings and figure out what you need to know more than the rest. Start there."

"Thank you."

I pull her in tighter and close my eyes, taking a deep breath.

When I wake up, I'm in a room I don't recognize. Alone. I'm in a chair, with my arms bound behind me and my legs tied.

There's a desk, one of those old things that looks like it's about to rust through. No lights are on, but there's a window letting in the fading light of day. Or it's so covered it looks later than it is, I can't tell. Two doors, one leading to what has to be the exit and one that I'm guessing is either a bathroom or a closet. I check in on my body, and nothing seems to be broken. I feel a bit sluggish, but not too bad.

I practice the breathing exercises Mia showed me that help her through a panic attack. I'm sure my family has something to do with this, and the last thing I can afford to do now is panic. I test the bonds on my hands and arms. Tied with precision, of course. I'm not getting out of them. My legs are bound as well, but looser. I know this tactic, of course. They can't play someone who watched the game for as long as me. I know the loose ties are to make me think I can escape. But, really, it just means someone is planning pain.

I try to feel my back pocket for my phone, but it's gone. Not a surprise. It's a shame I don't have one of those watches Joker gave Mia. That would come in handy right about now. I'm being a sarcastic ass to myself to pass the time when the door finally opens.

"Look, the *printz* is awake. It's my lucky day."

"Andrey. I'm so surprised to see you."

"*Poshyol te nakhuy.*"

"No thanks." I smirk, antagonizing him.

"I promised you I'd make you pay for turning on the family." He grins at me. It's evil and makes my skin crawl. "And now I can."

"You know, if you kill me, you'll never see the money."

"Who said I was going to kill you? Today anyway."

He moves close, so close I can smell the alcohol oozing from his pours, the sweat stench in his clothes. He looks like he's aged twenty years in the last five. Time has not been kind to him.

"Aren't you supposed to let my dear sister talk to me and tell me what she wants before you start hurting me?"

That gives him pause. But not for nearly enough time. "I'll make sure you still have your tongue when she gets here."

Well, fuck.

He grabs my left hand, and I'm not sure what's worse. Not being able to see what he's doing and knowing it's going to hurt, or if I could see.

When he twists my pinky and I feel the pop of it breaking, the pain momentarily takes my breath away. Yeah, not knowing and being able to prepare is way worse. But I don't give him the satisfaction of hearing me cry out in pain. He's forgotten who raised me.

"One down. Nine more to go." He chuckles behind me, grabbing the second finger and bending it until it also breaks.

Pain shoots up my hand into my arm, and I flinch, but don't give him any more than that. I refuse to let him see that he's got any control over me, even if we both know he has all of it.

"Oh, you already started." Katya tsks as she comes into the room. "What a shame."

"Hello, dear *sestra*," I say through gritted teeth.

"*Bratt*," she replies. "We haven't been formally introduced yet, have we?"

"Is that necessary? I figure why waste the time when you're just going to let Andrey here kill me when you get what you want."

"You might be right. And do you know what I want?"

"The money."

"Of course I want the money. I had to pay for being the bastard daughter of Ivan Pavlov my entire life. I'm due. You got to grow up in the life of luxury with our father. Now, it's my turn to live the good life."

I laugh. My entire hand is swelling and going numb. My

fingers throb through it. I laugh because this isn't the first time they've been broken.

"What's so funny?" Katya asks.

"You think I had a good life because our father accepted me as his son?"

"Of course. You were the son. The chosen one. The one allowed to stay because your mother was the lucky one who spread her legs first and got a ring."

"Oh, lady." I shake my head, still chuckling. "You were the lucky one. See this bastard right here?" I tilt my chin to Andrey. "Want to know what he got to do on random Tuesdays when my father was in a bad mood? He got to take me out to the barn and beat me. For shits and giggles. While our *otetz* beat my mother. His job was to make me tough. My mother's job was to turn a blind eye to all the whores my father slept with. Employed. Like yours."

She comes up and slaps me. "You will not talk about my mother!"

"Did you even know her? Did you know anything about her?" I spit back.

"I know enough to know she protected me!"

"You're right. Because if Ivan and Andrey here had found you when he was alive, they would have killed you."

She takes a step back, staring at Andrey like she's seeing him for the first time.

"You're lying."

"Am I? You sure about that?"

Andrey doesn't say anything. He's not going to tell the woman signing his current paycheck that I'm right. He's a brute. He's a horrible human being. But he's not stupid.

"Hurt him," she commands.

"With pleasure." Andrey dips his chin.

He walks over to the desk and pulls out a crowbar. I try to control my breathing. The last thing I need is to pass out from pain. And I know whatever he's got in mind is going to fucking hurt.

Andrey raises the iron rod over his head and swings with precision right at my elbow. I grit my teeth together to keep from making a sound and I absorb the blow. FUCK! That hurts like a motherfucker!

"More?" he leans in close to ask me. "Or are you ready to shut up and do what we want you to do?"

"Fuck you!" I spit at him. Then I laugh. "You aren't going to get shit. Do you really think I'm stupid? If something happens to me, the money is gone, asshole."

Punch.

Fuck! Right in the nose.

I feel the blood run down my face, can taste it in my throat. Not the first broken nose I've ever had. Probably won't be the last.

"Do you ever shut up?" Katya asks, grimacing at my newly rearranged face.

"Nah. What's the fun in that?"

"How about self-preservation?"

"You'll never survive this life if you're afraid of getting hurt, *malenkaya sestrichka.*"

"What does that even mean?" she asks, completely clueless.

I see Andrey roll his eyes at how fucking stupid the woman is.

"You want to take over as head of a Bratva that's already died out once and you don't know any fucking Russian, *little sister*?"

"I don't need to know the language to run the family."

"You probably also don't think you need a dick. You'd be wrong there, too."

"Not true. The family has progressed since our father's death."

I look at Andrey as best I can with my eyes swelling shut. "You haven't told her?"

He snarls at me and shakes his head. "No point. *Tupaya suka* wouldn't listen to me, anyway."

"You know, it could be the pain I'm in, but this is pretty funny shit."

"I'm done listening. You're going to sign our father's money over to me so I can do what he would have wanted and make this family strong and powerful again. Do what he couldn't with the goods I have access to."

"Gonna be hard to do with the feds breathing down your throat, won't it?"

"What feds? You're the only snitch left. Your uncles have been disposed of. They thought they got away, could lie low and come back, but we took care of that. And Uncle Sasha loves me like his own princess."

I might not ever shut up when I'm under stress like this, but I know when to keep my mouth shut. If she doesn't know Sasha *is* the mole, I'm not going to be the one to tell her. I don't see her being alive much longer, anyway. If she succeeds in getting the money from me, she's useless.

"Let me give you a little tip. The longer I'm alive and have the money, the longer you stay alive."

"Hurt him," she commands Andrey.

Fuck. Me. Try to help your sister out and this is how she repays you?

I brace for impact, knowing it's going to hurt. Will it be a kidney shot? Jaw breaker? Another finger?

Oh, my ankle. The iron hits and I think I might throw up from the pain. He's having way too much fun with this.

"Fuck, Andrey!" I finally yell, giving him what he wants. "Fucker!"

Punch.

And there it is, my jaw. Maybe a couple of teeth. Asshole can throw a fucking punch, that's for sure.

"Shut up."

"Fug vu fashol." There. I told him. I'm sure he understood. He's been breaking jaws for decades.

"Get his fingerprints," Katya says, moving to the door. "Let's see what we can do. Leave him in here when you're finished, in case we need something else."

Once she's out, Andrey looks at me, shaking his head. "You never learn, do you? I didn't want to do this, asshole."

I roll my eyes at him, my head lulling to one side.

"Not this way. I wanted to pick the time and place. My rules."

I blink my swollen eyes at him. "Ver wules," I mock.

"*Poshyol te nakhuy*. I survive by my rules. Beating you when you were a kid? So I didn't get beat. Taking out the trash in the family? Well, he never took me out, did he? I fucking survived. That *suka* doesn't have the authority. She doesn't know the rules or care to find out. We only let her think she's in charge. You, however, walked away. You told our secrets. This is what you deserve."

I know if I keep staring at him, he'll spill his life story, but I don't care. My hand is numb, my arm is throbbing, my ankle is screaming for help, and my face? Fuck, Mia's going to think I'm ugly now, isn't she?

Mia. I'll survive this for her. Fuck all of them if they think I'll give up and leave her alone. Mia. I swear I hear her voice. If I close my eyes, I swear I hear her calling my name.

"DEMITRI!"

CHAPTER THIRTY-FIVE

MIA

"DEMITRI!" I scream his name. I know he's here. He has to hear me.

"Mia!" Aunt Linda grabs my shoulders, and I swear it looks like she might slap me. "Honey, pull yourself together. They are going to get him out."

"He has to be okay," I whisper, my eyes tearing up.

"You did your part. You thought ahead. You found a way for him to carry something that could track him and no one would think twice about it."

"I just wanted to keep him safe. And I couldn't."

"This isn't on you. None of this is on you. Oh, my sweet, darling girl."

She pulls me into a hug, holding me like a mother holds a child, and I melt into her arms. I haven't had a mother's hug or love in so many years.

"Tell me he's going to be okay," I beg her. "Lie to me if you have to. Please."

"He's strong. Been through more shit than both of us can imagine. If anyone can survive, it's him."

"I said lie to me, Linda."

She chuckles. "That's Aunt Linda to you, young lady. And he's going to be fine."

Neither of us truly believe it, but the alternative? A world without Demitri? Unthinkable.

"I'm sorry, *malenkyi*. I didn't know this was the plan," Sasha quietly tells me, staring at the building we've all gathered in front of.

Aiden found me at the bar, passed out against the wall outside my office. The back door was standing wide open. I was groggy but not hurt.

"I really want to trust you, Sasha. I do. But you were the last one that came in that door, and then this happened?"

"Mia," Aunt Linda admonishes me.

"No, *moya lyubov*, I deserve her judgement. She's right. I was the last one in, and I'm the least trustworthy here. All I can do is hope she believes me when I tell her I didn't do this."

"Then save him," I tell him. "Go in there and get him for me."

"Not a chance in hell." Mary, the DEA agent, appears at my side. "It's time to let us do our jobs. Never thought in a million years this is what we'd finally get Andrey Novikov on."

"Kill him if you have to. I'd be alright with that," I tell her.

She grins but shakes her head. "Sorry. No can do. We follow the book on this one. We will only shoot to kill if necessary."

"Can you shoot him in the shin at least? I mean, that would hurt really bad, right?"

"As someone who's been shot, I don't know that I'd even want that for my worst enemy." Grady purses his lips. "Yeah, okay, maybe one in the shin would be alright."

I know what they're doing. Distracting me with their morbidly dark humor. Which I am trying to appreciate. But it's too hard knowing that they have Demitri.

I watch the agents Mary brought with her surround the

building, an old two-story building on the outskirts of town. I think it used to be some kind of factory but couldn't honestly tell you. It's been empty and falling down since I've been here.

Mary has kept our crowd far enough away so we can't impede with her people doing their job. The Rock Hill and Briar Mountain police departments are both here, and there are a couple of ambulances, just in case. They tried to put me in one, but I refused. Everyone threw a fit until I promised to get checked out as soon as we have Demitri.

Aiden made the girls stay at the bar, which didn't really go over well until James showed up and told them they were staying where they were. Daniel, Joker, Nate, and Grady are here. Aiden offered to stay back with my girls.

"Okay, people, we're going in." Mary's quiet announcement is like a blanket over my world. Everything goes silent. My vision narrows to the entry door on the front of the building. I watch as they silently go in, one by one, throwing up hand signals I don't understand.

Mary comes to my side with a tablet and shows it to me. It's a live feed of what's going on split into four sectors.

"These are the four leads. We have angles from everyone who just went into that building so we can switch if we need to."

"Am I supposed to be watching this?"

"No. So, don't look. I'm going to stand right here and do my job."

"I don't know if you're a really good agent or not."

"I'm an agent who doesn't give a fuck anymore. I do what I want within the limits of the law, and fuck everything else."

"Fuck, yeah." Joker fist bumps her. "You are my favorite DEA agent."

"Only because Davis wasn't DEA," she deadpans.

Joker grins. "You're still salty he got your score, aren't you?"

"I had to work in an office and deal with hormonal newly freed college kids, Joker. Davis got to be the cool bartender. You tell me."

Mary flips him off and then touches her ear. "I hear you. Subjects located on second floor. Notify when places set."

I look at the second-floor windows, saying prayers to any God that will listen to me. *Please let him be okay.* The windows are cracked. Some boarded up, like they gave up long ago. And still others so covered I'd be surprised if light filters through.

"On my mark. Go. Go. Go." Mary starts tapping on the tablet, and I stare at it, holding my breath. With the press of a button, she makes the voices of those inside the building audible.

"Unit one, go. Unit two, follow."

"I've found them. Unit one, upper quadrant."

"DEA! Arms up!"

"Put the weapon down!"

"On the ground. Get on the ground!"

And then I see him. Demitri. His head is hanging to one side, and he looks like someone hit him with a two by four. His eyes are swollen, blood coming out of his nose, his jaw is at an odd angle. His arms are tied behind his back and his legs have been restrained, too. The pain etched on his face is evident. In his whole body. His shoulder is sticking at an odd angle, his foot looks wrong. He's not well, that's for fucking sure.

"Oh, God. Is he breathing?" I ask.

"Verify life," Mary calls into her earpiece thing.

"Verified. Vic is breathing on his own. Some damage, but I'm pretty sure he'll live."

The voice coming through the tablet is my lifeline. Demitri's breathing.

"Let's take care of business so we can get him the help he needs. Wrap it up quick."

Mary taps the screen, probably turning off the volume, and smiles at me. "We'll get him out as soon as we can."

"Thank you," I mouth, unable to talk. My eyes overflow with the tears I've barely kept at bay so I could watch the screen.

I pull out my phone, and through blurry eyes I text Grace to let everyone know we found him and he is going to be okay.

Aunt Linda pulls me in for another hug, and I completely break down. She doesn't stop me, which I'm surprised by since this woman isn't usually one to let us get away with things like having breakdowns.

And it only lasts a couple of minutes.

"Time to buck up, girl. Those assholes are being led out."

Well, I guess if there's ever a time to stop crying, it's watching the people who kidnapped the love of your life get dragged away, right?

I turn and watch as four large men in black tactical gear lead Katya and Andrey out, their arms held behind their backs by the much larger men. I know I'm too far away for her to make out anyone clearly, but I swear, she's staring at me—*into* me. It makes a shiver go down my spine. Andrey looks nothing like what I imagined. He's short, balding, with a very well-fed midsection. But he's a barrel. His arms are huge, he has no neck, and his chest almost matches his gut. I wish I could see his face up close, but I can't. And maybe that's a good thing.

As they get to the SUVs waiting to take them away, Andrey turns and, in a move straight from a horror movie, kicks the man holding him and charges toward us. Everyone freezes, not knowing what to do, until he's about fifty yards away. Sasha steps forward, calmly and a little scarily, raises his arm and shoots. The men holding Andrey let him go as he goes down, immediately holding his leg, screaming what can only be obscenities in Russian.

Sasha, still cool as a cucumber, turns to me, handing his firearm to Mary, and smiles. "You asked for him to be shot in the shin, *da, malenkyi?*"

"You're doing the paperwork for this," Mary deadpans while I nod and smile at him. She puts the earpiece back in. "We're going to need that backup bus."

"Thank you," I mouth to Sasha, who bows his head.

Two EMTs, paying the man writhing on the ground no attention, run into the building with a stretcher. I look at Mary, who nods her head.

"Second floor. To the back."

She really doesn't give a shit, does she?

I take off running, not giving anyone the chance to hold me back or stop me.

"Demitri!" I yell, running up the stairs. "Dem!"

I find them in the back room, two of Mary's guys still with him, his arms now unbound from the chair and the rope that had been around his legs gone. They're moving him onto the stretcher, and I freeze. He looks like everything hurts. He's holding his body wrong, and his face. Well, his face has seen better days.

As soon as they have him on the stretcher, I find my feet again and rush to his side. His arm is sticking out weirdly, and the EMT stops me before I can get too close.

"Ma'am, might want to go to the other side."

They don't even question if I should be there, and it's a good thing. They don't deserve all these big emotions I have coursing through my body. I quickly move to his other side and take his hand.

"I'm here, Dem. I'm here."

His eyes try to open, but they are so swollen he can't. Instead, he squeezes my hand, pulling me closer. I lean over him, and he mumbles something, but I can't understand what it is. He tries again, his face contorting in pain.

"Wuv vu."

"Oh, you idiot." I cry-laugh. "Don't talk. I love you, too."

He nods, and it's almost as if he needed to hear that before he could pass out for a little while. I worriedly look at the EMT, who smiles.

"He'll be fine. Just needs a nap, and that shot of good stuff we gave him knocked his ass out."

I nod and walk with them out of the room, following them down the stairs and to the back of the ambulance.

"We'll follow you," Daniel tells me before they close the back doors. "And you're getting checked out as soon as we get there."

I roll my eyes. "I'm fine."

"Don't care."

"Okay, Dad."

He shakes his head and chuckles. I watch him join the others and start to load up as they close the doors after doing some checks. I don't let go of Demitri's hand until I'm forced to when we arrive at the hospital.

"Hey, honey. Gotta let me check you out," the nurse tells me, and it takes me a minute to realize I know her.

"Lizzy?"

"Yeah, babe. I'm in disguise as the mean ER nurse tonight. Let's go get you looked over."

I watch them wheel Demitri through the doors and away from me.

"He'll be okay," she tells me. "They wouldn't let you in that far, anyway."

I nod and let her lead me to a bed in the ER where they take my blood and give me a once over. Joker comes to tell me the news as the doctor is writing up my clearance papers.

"He's in surgery. It's gonna to be awhile."

"What's wrong with him?"

"Broken ankle, shattered elbow, a couple broken fingers, and nose and jaw."

"Five minutes. I want five minutes with that cunt. Can you arrange that?" I look at him, meaning every word I just said.

Lizzy laughs, shaking her head. "I think we've all been there, haven't we?"

"Yeah, I guess we have."

"Well, come on. I'll walk up with you to see my brother-in-law and the gang."

"Does Daniel ever drive you crazy with his 'I'm in charge and you will do what I say' attitude?" I ask her as we get in the elevator, Joker snorting behind us.

"All the time. That man is crazy protective of Vic, and by extension all of us. He's a pretty good brother to have on your side, though."

She leaves me with a hug in the waiting room. Everyone is there with us. Daniel and his entire crew, the girls, James, Aunt Linda and Sasha, Mary. We all settle in for the wait. Knowing they're all here for Demitri warms my heart. Now, we just need him to wake up and recover.

CHAPTER THIRTY-SIX
DEMITRI

THE ROOM IS quiet except for the beeping. I've always wondered why they don't turn the volume on those things down when the first thing they tell you is 'get some rest'? My body feels like it weighs a thousand pounds, and everything hurts. I try to open my eyes, and pain shoots through my face, making me moan.

"Demitri?" It's a whisper, but I know it's Mia. She takes my hand, and I squeeze it. "Are you in pain? Squeeze once for yes and twice for no?" I hear the humor in her voice at the question, and I wish I could laugh, but I'm afraid that might actually kill me.

I squeeze her hand once, and I feel her reaching over my body to hopefully hit the button. The door opens almost immediately, and a nurse comes in.

"Ahh, Mr. Smith. It's good to see you kind of awake. Let me look at a few things and I'll get something for that pain. You've been through it."

She fiddles with a few things. I feel the blood pressure cuff tighten on my arm and the thermometer drag across my forehead.

"Okay, be right back with something for you. Try to get some rest, okay?"

See. What the fuck did I say? I hmm at her, because I can't open my mouth.

"They wired your jaw, Dem. No talking or solid food."

Well, fuck. I can't talk, can't see, can't move. Think Mia would put on a naughty nurse outfit and give me a sponge bath? Fuck, I wouldn't be able to see it if she did.

"Not sure what you're thinking about there, Romeo, but that nurse is going to come back in to see little Demitri waving hello." She laughs.

"Nngty nnse," I manage to push out through my teeth.

"No clue what you're trying to say, but I'm going to imagine it's about me naked or something cause if Nurse Hilda turned you on, we have some issues other than your broken bones."

I shake with laughter. Making everything hurt, but I don't care. I'm alive. Mia's fine. I'll feel the pain.

"Oh, look. I guess you aren't a masochist. Little Dem is gone."

I try to shake my head and stop that right quick when everything spins from the pain.

"Stop, please. I'll behave. Let's just go back to hand holding, okay?" she begs, a desperate tone in her voice. "I can't stand to see you in pain."

I squeeze her hand, rubbing my thumb on her skin. It's nice to know I can still feel her.

"Alrighty, Mr. Smith. Let's see if this helps with that pain. Once you're out, I've got an icepack for your face. It'll help with the swelling, so hopefully you can open your eyes soon."

Two days. That's how long it takes for my eyes to open. I've been in and out of consciousness, mostly from the really good shit they keep shooting into my veins. Mia has been here every time I've regained my senses, only for them to fade away again when she calls the nurse.

But this morning? This morning, my right eye opens. Sort of. Enough that I can see things close up. Everything beyond about three feet is blurry, but it's a start. Fucker really went hard on my face.

I fell asleep after looking at Mia for a few minutes, rubbing her palm with my hand. Her eyes full of tears and her face in a big, wobbly smile. Waking up this time, I immediately know something is different. Mia's not here. I can feel her absence. I tap my hand on the mattress. Pretty much the only form of communication I have right now.

"Hey, there. Look who's awake," Joker's voice fills the room. "Don't flip out, she just went to get something to eat. Okay, she didn't go, she was forced. That nurse, Lizzy? She barged in here and told her if she didn't get off her ass and get some food, she was going to get security to kick her out. She's a badass. Also, Grace was behind her. Did you know they look just alike? It was kinda freaky, man. Anyway, I'm on Demitri duty until she gets back, so I thought I'd fill you in on all the shit you've missed."

I give him a thumbs up, letting him know I heard him. Then I roll my hand. The universal 'get the fuck on with it' symbol.

"You're seriously in a hurry? Got a hot date or something?" he jokes. I flip him off. "Fine. Okay, here's what's happened. Your Uncle Sasha is officially retired. From both federal whatever the fuck he was and playing Russian bad guy. He said all his brothers were dead that weren't locked up. You are his only family, and he's going to take a break. Try to get to know you if you let him, but I think that was his story to tell you, so when you talk to him, don't tell him you know all this."

My chest shakes with my laughter, and it doesn't hurt as bad as it did. Either we've managed to keep up with the pain or maybe there's hope I'm getting better.

"Your bitchy sister is crying her eyes out, talking about it not being fair, that you don't deserve anything, blah blah blah. Anyway. She's not getting out. Judge refused to set bail. She's a flight risk."

The way he says this with so much joy makes me smile. Except that's still a no go. Hurts like a bitch.

"Andrey is saying it was all her, that he was just a witness. Of course, no one believes that. No way could that woman do to you what was done to you. He's behind bars, too. Kidnapping, multiple counts of assault, possession. Man had enough powder in his pocket to get the entire county high."

I nod. Coke was always his favorite.

"That about catches you up, right? You're broken in a few places, but they'll mend. Have some new screws in your ankle and your arm. But I'm sure you already knew what he broke. Also, your fingers are fucking gnarly, man. They had to operate on them to get the bones back into place. At one point, there was a question on if you were even going to be able to keep them. Your girl went nuts and said she needed you returned with every part of you intact."

I love when that woman gets mean. As long as it's directed at someone else, that is.

"Anyway, Grady's been working with Brodie at the bar to keep it open. Everyone's been coming in asking what happened, and if Mia's alright. The town really loves her, you know? I know not as much as you do, but, hey, gotta share the girl when she's Mia."

I growl, and he laughs.

"I know. I feel that way about my wife."

"I don't think I've ever heard you say so many words in a row, Joker. Is this a new skill or one you save for super-secret conversations with your buddies?" Mia asks, coming into the room. I immediately feel better having her close.

There's a pause, and Mia laughs. I can almost see her shaking her head.

"You think that look works on me? Hate to burst your bubble, funny man, but it doesn't."

"Damn," he mutters, turning to me. "You sure *this* is the woman of your dreams? That look can scare the pee out of some people."

I slowly nod, trying to make eye contact with Mia. She pushes Joker out of the way and grabs my hand. Of course, we all know the only reason he moved is because he was okay with moving. He's a scary fucker when you get down to it, and I'm glad he's on my side.

He says his goodbyes and leaves the room. With him gone, and Mia here, I give in to the need to rest some more. How can I sleep so much? I mean, after so long, isn't it just enough and you need to stay awake for a while?

"It's okay, Dem. Sleep. Heal." Mia kisses my forehead, letting her lips linger. I feel her fingers feather down my face, and everywhere they touch, the pain magically goes away. It's the last thing I remember before sleep overtakes me again and I dream about Mia.

I've now been in the hospital a solid week. Seven. Fucking. Days. Between the post-surgery infection worries, the government trying to be extra special with me, and the jaw that's wired shut, I'm tired, cranky, hungry, and feel like my insides are pure liquid.

They've gotten me up a couple of times, but it's fucking impossible to use crutches when you have an elbow that's completely useless. They brought in one of those things on wheels that you steer and prop your leg on, and again—fucking impossible. Can't drive with your right hand when it's your left side that's fucked and you can only use one hand.

So, they stand me up long enough to change the bed and I show how good my balance is on one leg before I collapse back into bed and pass out because just that little bit of energy zaps me. Because I can't fucking eat and this food substitution they have running through my veins is fucking stupid. I did mention I'm cranky, right?

My only bright spot is Mia. And, oddly, the girls and nurse Lizzy. They have been on rotation, making Mia take breaks to see something other than my ugly mug and the walls of my room. Lizzy showed her where the nurse's room is so she can get some sleep, and Grace, Nola, or Sofie take over, making sure I survive the couple of hours when Mia leaves me.

Today, Aiden and Joker are keeping an eye on me. Staring at me, waiting for something to happen.

I flip them off.

It makes them laugh.

"I come with gifts." Joker grins that grin that would terrify small children while lifting a bag. "You're too quiet, I need some words."

I stare at him. "Fug vu."

"That's my boy. Way to go. That fug was really close to a fuck!"

Aiden smirks at the exchange, but he seems distracted. I give him the manly chin tilt, and he returns it, but I see it. He's worried about something. I raise my brow, asking without words, and he shakes his head, waving me off.

I turn back to Joker, who pulls out some tech gadget and waves it in front of my face to get it to unlock. It's a giant keyboard.

"The only AI I trust. Because I built it myself."

I give him a thumbs up.

"Asshole. You don't even know what it is."

I circle my hand. It's the 'show me' motion. Maybe the 'get on with it' motion.

"You type. It talks for you. It's not perfect, and it's not going to sound like you, but it's something, right? Better than thumbs and middle fingers?"

I flip him the bird. Because I can.

"Here, try that again."

He hands me the tablet, and I type.

"*Fuck you, asshole.*" The mechanical voice sounds Australian.

Joker and Aiden both grin. "Sorry, no Russian voice available."

I flip him off. Mainly because it's fun.

"*What do we know?*" I type, trying not to cringe at the voice.

"Your buddy, Andrey, is singing like a canary. He's flipped on everyone he's ever met."

"*Doesn't surprise me. Andrey takes care of Andrey first.*" I type.

"Well, he tried to turn on Sasha. That didn't go over too well. I think Sasha threatened to shoot his other shin."

I quirk my lips. That's as much of a smile as I can do right now, but it's enough.

"*I have to talk to him, don't I?*"

"You do," Aiden tells me. "There are things he knows that you need to know, too."

"I know it's hard," Joker adds. "Family sucks, and yours

has some real issues, but I think you owe it to yourself to hear him out."

"*I don't like when you make sense.*"

"Don't worry, I'll be back to my regular smartassery in no time."

Mia enters the room, wearing a new pair of my sweats, her clothing of choice this week, and smiles at the guys. They say their goodbyes and Mia takes her position in the chair next to the bed, immediately taking my hand.

I rub her thumb with mine before pulling it out and using the new toy Joker left for me.

"*I love you. Thank you for being here.*"

She blinks at the Australian guy speaking for me and laughs. "Joker?" I nod. "Figures. And I love you, too. But I miss your voice."

I shrug, the pain of moving getting less each day. I look at the woman I'm going to spend the rest of my life with, even if she doesn't know it yet, and type the words I know I need to, but hate all the same. "*Can you call Sasha and Linda? I think we need to talk.*"

She nods. "I'll set it up."

Guess I need to get all my emotions in check and my questions figured out.

CHAPTER THIRTY-SEVEN
MIA

THE DAY AFTER HE ASKED, Sasha and Aunt Linda come to see Demitri and me. Daniel trails in behind them, a silent observer. And probably a peacekeeper, if we need one.

"Demi." Sasha nods. "You look much better."

Using his fancy new talking toy, Demitri types. *"Can't talk, don't say anything about the voice."*

Sasha laughs, shaking his head. "Good thing that boy went army. He'd have driven us all crazy in the agency."

"What agency exactly?"

"That's hard to explain. Linda?"

Aunt Linda steps up to the bed, rubbing Demitri's good foot. "We work for an unknown. We don't have letters, and we answer to two people."

"Who?"

"The President. And the Chairman of the Joint Chiefs of Staff."

Demitri blinks at them. I blink at them. Daniel says nothing.

"Surprise?" Aunt Linda uses jazz hands and an awkward grin. Demitri closes his eyes and shakes his head.

"*You did this my whole life?*"

"Yes. I was recruited while in college. Imagine if that news had gotten out."

"*You'd be dead. Why?*"

"I didn't want that life. I fell in love." Sasha looks at Linda. "I didn't want her life to be in danger every day. Nor do I think she would have stayed with me if I didn't find a way. So I found a way."

"I was recruited at the same time. Aunt Marley recruited me, Uncle Frank, Sasha. They were professors in the ethics class we took together in undergrad. They were looking at retirement and wanted us to take over."

"How many of you are there?" I ask.

"Not many."

"*Why didn't you ever try to help me?*"

I look at Demitri's face, and it's full of a lifetime of hurt. Pain. Fear. This isn't adult Demitri asking. It's a scared little boy who grew up in a life he never should have had.

"I tried, Demi. I pushed for boarding school. Military school. Hell, I tried to get your *otetz* to send you to your *babushka* back home. He wouldn't let you go."

"*Who killed the others? The siblings?*"

"It might have been Andrey. But he wasn't much of a kid killer. Couldn't torture them like he likes." Sasha pauses to look at Demitri's hand, silently proving his point. "He might have beat you when you were younger, but I know for a fact he went easy on you. Never broke a bone then. We have a different theory."

"Daniel and his team have been helping us with that," Aunt Linda says, looking back at the man himself. "We don't know for sure, and the records and people have been lost to time in some cases."

"When the family was brought down the first time, it was by Davis Mills, who you know. His keeper, Marks, with the

FBI, is currently serving jail time for assisting the enemy. When we started looking into her, there was a direct line between her and Katya, who we knew as Karina."

"What do you mean?" I ask again, hoping these are the things Demitri wants to know.

"Karina had no past. No family, no record, nothing. She was too clean, which raised flags for us. No one is that squeaky. Joker couldn't break her file. She had help. After we learned her real name, we were able to start piecing things together. Marks grew up in the same foster home as Katya. They became close, and from what we can tell, Marks helped Katya hide. She turned a blind eye to her when drug investigations were going down. She provided her with the information on the inheritance Ivan had, and what part of it was legal."

"*She betrayed her office.*"

"And put a lot of people in danger. Life-threatening danger."

"Why would she help Ivan get away with everything if she was Katya's friend?" I ask.

"Money. Plain and simple. The woman was greedy and at the end of the day only out to take care of herself. Sure, she'd help her friend get a new identity, find others who would help her, stuff like that. But Ivan was the money and Marks was making money."

"*What happened to the other uncles? Katya said they were disposed of.*"

Sasha clears his throat, looking away from both of us. "Andrey. Katya found them and asked for their help before I made myself findable. They didn't want to help."

"Where does Demitri come into all of this?" I ask, needing to know.

"I needed to keep him protected. Linda has been the watcher of the family since I joined. She was my handler, for lack of a better term. But she watched the family for me. She kept tabs on everyone coming and going through the house and the family. The women Ivan had, what happened to them, where they ended up. The lower levels that disappeared. She helped me keep my cover by remembering the details I couldn't think about."

"*My siblings?*"

"Yes," Aunt Linda replies. "I know all of their names and where they are. I know what's happened to all of them."

"*Mika? What really happened?*"

Sasha bows his head, doing the cross over himself. "I couldn't save her, Demi. I didn't get there in time."

Demitri folds in on himself. He still feels the pain in his heart that will never heal. I don't blame him. There's a part of me that will always be jagged with scars. He reaches for my hand, pulling it to his lips and pressing my palm against them.

Sasha stands, coming to our sides, putting his hands on both of us. "I'm done. I'm an old man, *plemiannik*. I want to enjoy what time I have left. I want to spend it with my real family. With my wife, with you, if you'll have me. It's time."

"What about you?" I ask Aunt Linda, already knowing what her plans are, but asking for Demitri's sake. "What are your plans?"

Without hesitation, she pulls out a box and hands it to me. "This is for you. When you're ready. We hope that you and Demitri will think long and hard and come to the same decision Sasha and I did."

The couple stands and says their goodbyes, leaving us to stare after them.

"*You know?*"

Daniel looks at Demitri and nods his head. "I guess in some ways, no matter how removed we are from 'the family', we're never really too far away, are we?"

"*Are you embracing your Italian roots?*"

"Hanging out with you and the Irish man too much." Daniel grins back.

When Daniel leaves I hold up the box between us, not sure if it's a gift or a time-bomb.

"Open it."

I do as he asks, and on top is a letter. Opening it, I scan it quickly before quietly reading out loud to Demitri:

'My dear Mia, I know all of this is shocking and a little terrifying, but you, my dear girl, can handle it. Inside this box is everything you need to get started. The key to the apartment I've used for years to meet with those who had secrets to tell. I've moved anything personal out, and it's yours now. Use it, or return the key to Daniel, and he will know what to do.

You and Demitri are the ones we've been searching for, waiting for. The first time I saw you, I knew you were the one. That you fell into our Demitri's arms and he couldn't find it in himself to leave you, we knew you would be the next generation to take over. To watch, to learn, and to listen. To hear the secrets others were afraid of.

Both of you are uniquely qualified because of your individual pasts. The resilience both of you have shown to survive and flip off those assholes of yesteryear shows your strength, both mentally and physically.

Please do not go into this thinking there is no risk. You will face them. And you will overcome them. We will train you on how to handle them. We'd never leave you out there completely on your own. If you decide to do this, we are here for you. Both of you. Together, you are unstoppable. All our love, Aunt Linda and Sasha.'

The letter goes on to list all the names and locations of Demitri's half-siblings and the locations of both the office we are to contact if we choose to do this and the house that Aunt Linda and Sasha have owned for the entirety of their lives together.

We stare at each other, not sure what to say. I look back into the box and find a keyring with six keys on it, all the same cut. Perplexed, I look back to Demitri, who shrugs.

"Something we find out when the time is right, maybe?" I quietly ask.

He nods, not releasing my hand to type.

Guess we have some thinking to do.

SIX MONTHS LATER

"Brodie, need an order of mozz!" I call through the window.

"On it, Boss."

Thursday nights are still rocking with the college kids, and they do love their alcohol and fried foods. We've made it through the semester break and the holidays. I look at the ring Demitri gave me on New Year's Eve when he asked me to marry him. We were on the beach in Diamond Cove visiting Aunt Linda and Sasha. And yes, she's still Aunt Linda to us. Guess she always will be.

I look at the corner of the bar, full of my family. The one I made. The girls are all here, as well as some of the guys. Aiden sits with them next to Demitri. Grady is behind the bar with me, now a regular part-time bartender when he isn't out rescuing people or guarding their bodies with his life. Demitri smiles when I look at him. His face is still a bit crooked, but I don't mind. His injuries have mostly healed, but the scars will last forever. He's not as adept in the garage as he was because of his fingers. His elbow causes him so much pain when the weather changes, and he's got a slight limp from the broken ankle, but that hasn't stopped him.

He goes out running every morning. Mostly to prove to himself he can. Then he comes home, drags me to the shower, and greets me with a good morning orgasm before we start our day. I'm not mad about it.

Both of us are in touch with the therapist on ANON's staff, Claire. Demitri has been able to talk out so many of his demons from the past, and he's lighter somehow. He doesn't carry the weight of guilt anymore. Claire introduced us to her friend—and Daniel's mother-in-law—Gloria, who it turns out was the therapist I was being recommended to. Small world, right? We all laughed about the coincidence, and she praised my man for his patience and gentleness with me. We met her a few times, and I still speak with her on occasion when I'm in Briar Mountain, but my own mental health is much better as well.

"Um, hi," a small voice interrupts my daydreaming. "I'm sorry to bother you, but, um, I have a question?"

I stare at the girl, who doesn't even look old enough to be in the bar, taking note of her appearance. Her clothes seem faded and too big, like she's lost weight. Her face is pale, gaunt. She needs a good meal, that's for sure. Her hair looks dull, clean, but a few days past a fresh wash. However, it's her eyes that have my attention. The haunted look. It takes me a few minutes, but I recognize the girl.

"Lacy?"

She nods, and I look over at Demitri, who immediately stands and slowly moves to us.

"What do you need, sweet girl?" I ask.

"I need to know where I can find Aunt Mia? I was told she would be here."

I nod, having already guessed. I smile at her and she relaxes. "I'm Aunt Mia," I confide. "And that man walking toward us? That's Uncle John. How would you feel about Brodie making you something to eat and we can go talk in the office?"

She smiles, and a little of the Lacy I remember is there. "I'd like that, but I'm not sure what I can eat."

"I've got just the thing."

I point to the office and speak quietly to Grady. Demitri has already moved to the kitchen to talk to Brodie, and I make eye contact with the girls before removing myself from behind the bar. All of them blow me a kiss, knowing I might not be back out tonight, and I meet Demitri at the kitchen doors. I pull out my phone and show him the screen.

Source: It's time to give Brodie the key and make it official. He's now family.

"Will we ever figure out who that is?" Demitri asks.

"Don't know, but we can worry about it later."

"Just one thing before we do this." He smirks, pulling me in for what would normally be a panty-melting kiss, our tongues dancing with each other before he pulls back. "It's been too long since I've done that, needed to fix it."

"I love you."

"I love you, too, *Krasotka*. Let's go help our new *plemiannica*."

"Together."

"Forever."

EPILOGUE
DEMITRI

SIX MONTHS LATER

"Are we all set up?" I speak into the phone.

"Sure are," the voice replies.

I hang up, stuffing the phone in my pocket, staring out the window in the kitchen, and wait for Mia to show herself.

"I'm ready," she mumbles as she tumbles into the kitchen trying to get her shoes on.

"It's too early for you, isn't it?" I ask, trying to hide my grin. I hand her the cup of coffee I made, and she gulps it like her life depends on it.

"Wouldn't have been if the hot man in my bed last night hadn't demanded multiple rounds."

"He'd apologize, but he's really not that sorry." When she's close enough, I pull her into my arms. "How's life treating you, Aunt Mia?"

She snorts into her cup. "This is fucked up, isn't it? All of this?"

"I never saw it coming, that's for sure."

She looks at the clock on the microwave and grimaces. "Thought we were on a timetable today?"

"Yeah, we need to go."

"Are you telling me where we're going?"

"Nope, but you're driving."

We walk outside and, as expected, Mia turns to her car, but I move to the garage.

"Where are you going?" she asks, confusion covering her face.

"We're taking the Shelby."

"And I'm driving?" She raises her brow. It's a fair question. I've been telling her for a year I had to work on it and she couldn't drive it.

"You are."

"But I don't know where we're going."

"Diamond Cove."

She stares at me, the wheels in her brain turning. "You're doing it, aren't you? You're selling the Shelby?"

I nod, knowing this part of the day will upset her. "Sarge is going to meet us over there and bring us home."

"Isn't it out of his way?"

"Nah. He doesn't mind."

I toss her the keys and she looks like she still doesn't believe she gets to drive her. But that only lasts a few seconds, and she's sliding behind the wheel and making her adjustments.

"Who are you selling her to?"

"Some rich guy. Sebastian Workman?"

"From the Workman Group?" She looks at me, her eyes widening.

"Yeah, you heard of them?"

"Sure. They are like PR on speed. Corporate fixing, celebrity PR. They are magicians at making bad shit disappear, but it's like they have ethics, too," Mia replies, a hint of awe in her voice.

"Huh. PR people with ethics?"

"I know, right? But I hear they are good guys. And they have enough money to drop on a Shelby."

"In this instance, that's all that matters, right?"

"Let's drive." Mia bounces in her seat, the smile on her face making all the planning and plotting and secrecy of the day totally worth it.

I watch my girl ease into the engine of the Shelby, shifting gears like it's nothing, giving her gas when we have a stretch, and I can't help but think how far we've both come in the last year. I know some people thought I was a fool for taking her drips and scraps for four years, but if I hadn't been me, and she wasn't who she was at the time, we wouldn't be here. Blissfully happy. Together.

The last year has changed everything. I have a relationship with a man I swore I would never willingly be in the same room with. He's told me old family secrets and histories that would have been lost. He's guided me on helping others in need. He's helped me come to terms with the extended family members I have out there who may or may not know about me and their origins.

But most of all, Sasha and Linda—she dropped the aunt bullshit once semi-retirement hit her—have guided both Mia and myself on this new journey of helping people in a way that's both meaningful and just. I don't know how word gets out about us. I feel like the ANON guys have a hand in some of it, but the number of people who have come to the bar asking for help has been astounding. While Linda focused on the dealings with the Pavlov family and their criminal organization, we've branched into helping women who've been hurt, men who have seen things they absolutely shouldn't have, and others who need someone to keep their secrets.

We've met some interesting people. Some have families doing bad things, like I did. We take their confessions and get the information to those who can do the most to help. Because of the relationship we have with Mary and the DEA, we loop her in on as much as possible. For the ones who need help to get out of their current situations, we connect them with ANON. Grady working part-time at the bar is part of that. And the guy just enjoys it.

Aiden and I have become even closer. His understanding of my life and the family demands makes him an invaluable friend to lean on. I happily return the favor when he hears news from Boston and doesn't know how to process it. He's become a fixture at the bar as well.

Nurse Lizzy? She's started to join the other girls to talk about life and moving on from her past with bad men. It's good to see that it's not just Mia who has been able to live a happy and open life. It gives me hope that I can watch Grace, Nola, and Sofie do the same when they're ready. I hope I can be a shoulder for them when the time comes as well.

"We're here," Mia interrupts my thoughts.

She's driven to the offices of the Workman Group, and I can already see Sebastian standing at the door, his brothers behind him. They are giants. Reminds me of Tiny, Sarge's friend.

"I'll leave you two alone for a minute so you can say your goodbyes." I grin at Mia. She leans over the clutch and pulls me in for a quick kiss.

"Thanks. Take your time."

I shake my head as I get out of the car and walk to the doors. The men all come outside to greet me.

"You didn't drive her?" Sebastian asks after introducing me to his brothers.

"Not today. Had to let my girl get a drive in before you got the keys."

"She's into cars?"

"Just one," I laugh. "I'm breaking her heart a little, but I'm going to make it up to her."

Mia gets out of the car, tossing her hair behind her back while she lovingly caresses the hood.

"If I had that, and she loved that, I wouldn't get rid of it for anything, man."

I smirk at him. "I do have that, and you have no fucking shot, car or not."

He laughs, one of his brothers smacking him on the head. "You wanted the car. Don't make him regret it by being an ass about his woman."

The brothers argue until Mia joins us, the keys looped around her finger, her eyes a little glassy from saying her farewells to the Shelby.

"Which of you overgrown apes gets the Shelby?"

Sebastian steps forward, smacking his hands back at his brothers. "That would be me, ma'am."

"Before you get these keys, you need to know a few things."

"Yes, ma'am."

"One, it's Mia, not ma'am. Two, you will treat her with the respect you would give your mother. Take her out and treat her well. Spend some money on her. Make her feel loved and she'll love you in return. And no matter what, you do not drive her drunk or on drugs. Ever. Understand? Because I will know. And I'll kick your ass. I will be your worst fucking nightmare if you hurt that Shelby."

My shoulders are shaking, and I have to bite my lips to not laugh. I'm pretty sure the stare-down she's giving the man could put Joker's glare to shame. The brothers are all trying to hold in their laugher, as well, and Sebastian looks properly chastised.

"I understand, Mia. I'll make sure no harm comes to her."

"And if you need someone to work on her, you will call no one else but John. When and if the time comes, and he's no longer working on cars, he will decide who you go to next. And I don't care that we're over an hour away. You're rich. Find a way."

"I will."

Mia hands him the keys, narrowing her eyes at him one more time, and I swear he visibly shrinks under her stare.

"Come on, hard ass. Let the guy play with his new car. Sarge is here."

"Nice to meet you all." Mia smiles and waves at the Workman brothers and turns to skip to Sarge's truck.

"Fuck me. Does she have a sister?" I hear behind me.

Without looking back, I answer. "Nope. She's one of a kind. And all mine. Enjoy the Shelby. I'm going to enjoy my life with my girl."

I join Sarge and Mia in his truck, pulling her to my side as I wrap my arm around her, Sarge already laughing.

"This isn't the way home. Where are we going?" Mia asks when we've been on the road about forty-five minutes.

"Need to make a pit stop if that's alright with you?" Sarge asks from behind the wheel.

"Sure. Any good food places?"

"Boulder Canyon has a diner. Ms. Mable will take good care of you, but Rockton has the best pizza around."

Sarge pulls up to the garage, and I already see her. She's covered, on the back of a truck, ready for transport.

I get out of the truck and help Mia down. Sarge hands me the keys with a smile on his face.

"What's going on?" Mia asks.

"I have a surprise for you, *Krasotka.*"

"What is it?"

"Yo, Tiny!" Sarge yells. "Pull the cover!"

The man in question steps from around the truck and pulls the cloth from the car on the back. A nineteen-sixty-seven Shelby. One in much worse shape than the mint baby we just delivered.

"Dem," Mia whispers so only I can here. "What's going on?"

"I got you something."

"But you, but, what?"

"The Shelby you worked on with your uncle is gone, baby. The Shelby we just sold has memories I'd rather forget. I thought we could work on one together and make her ours."

The tears are fast. Spilling from her eyes without thought. She looks at me, the love shining through her eyes warming me from the inside out. She tugs on my shirt and kisses me. It quickly turns feral. A kiss others should not be watching, but I don't care. Anytime this woman wants to kiss me, I'm all in.

"Let's get married," she says, grinning.

I laugh. "I already asked you to do that. Remember?"

"Yeah, but let's do it now. We can go to your uncle's on the beach."

"Right now? Just us?"

"Just us. We'll let Sasha and Linda watch."

"I'm registered to marry people in the state." Sarge grins at us.

"How do you feel about driving back to Diamond Cove, friend?"

"Terrific. But we need a license."

I stare at Mia, knowing she needs this. "Marry us today. Just us and my aunt and uncle. We'll plan a bigger thing later and have the formal license. That work for you?"

"Works for me. Tiny, want to come with us?"

"Sure. Let me call my wife and let her know I'll be late. We can swing by and see my brothers."

"Ask your brother if you can drive his new car." Mia grins at him. Now I can see the similarities are too much to be a coincidence. Tall, big, cocky.

"Want to ride the bike back?" Sarge asks. "Have a spare you can use. Pick up this gal later?"

"Perfect. Shall we?" I ask Mia.

"Let's do this."

On the way back to Diamond Cove, I feel my phone vibrate with a new message. At a stop, I pull out the phone and my stomach drops.

"What's wrong?" Mia asks.

"Trouble's coming. Might be small, but it's still trouble."

"Do we need to turn back?"

"Fuck no. I'm marrying you today, *Krasotka*. Nothing we can do about it until tomorrow, anyway."

"I love you, Demitri."

"I love you, too."

Before we take off, I show her the message on the phone.

Aiden: I think we have a problem. My uncle and cousin are both coming to town. Prepare yourself.

BONUS EPILOGUE

MIA

"Why do I have to take this class again?" I ask.

"Because you're weak. We need to know if something happens, and you get pulled into some shit, you can take care of yourself," Aunt Linda replies.

"What about me? Why am I here?" Demitri asks, narrowing his eyes at the woman.

"Because you're supporting your woman, and I said so."

He grins at her, shaking his head before looking at me and blowing a kiss.

"Don't worry, you'll get to blow up shit next."

"Oh, now that I agree to do," he enthusiastically tells her.

"Care to make a wager on the better shot?" I challenge.

"Nope. I know who the better shot is," he replies. "It's Aunt Linda."

I stare at the woman, who bats her eyes and smiles innocently. Hmm. Has he forgotten where I grew up?

"I'll take that challenge." I smile back at the two of them.

"Not until you prove you can take Demitri down," Sasha chuckles.

"Have you thought about getting in touch with your siblings yet?" I ask Demitri, circling him, looking for his weak spot.

"No. I'm not sure what I want to do yet."

"You should think about it."

"You ever going to tell me about all those secret meetings and phone calls you had with Aunt Linda?"

"She better not!" Aunt Linda yells from across the gym she commandeered at the community center in Briar Mountain.

"Guess not" I shrug.

"Think I can get you to tell me with orgasms?"

"You can try."

I know both of us are hitting each other with mental games, which is our strength. But I've had this type of training before. I know it's crotch, eyes, and nose. Problem is, only two of those really work on women, and after Katya, we can't be too careful.

I finally see my chance. Demitri's arms are not as loose as they were. He's plotting his next move. When he blinks, I go for it. I rush him, poking his eye protection, kicking him in his very well-protected junk, and when he folds over, raising my knee to his face. He goes down but takes me with him, rolling until he's on top of me.

"Never lose your focus, *Krasotka*," he whispers, pulling off his face mask and kissing me.

"Alright, practice over. To the gun range!" Aunt Linda calls with an edge of annoyance and laughter in her voice.

"Time to kick your ass again." I grin as Demitri helps me up.

"We'll see."

"How?" Demitri stares at me, his jaw slack, awe all over his face.

"Beginner's luck?" I ask, shrugging my shoulders.

"Fuck that. How?"

"Grew up in Montana."

"But you outshot Aunt Linda," he whispers.

"She knows." I smile.

"Guess we know you can handle yourself if you need to."

"I've been able to handle myself for a while. Now you know it, too."

"I think I'm going to like seeing this side of you, Aunt Mia."

I laugh, shaking my head. "I think Uncle John fits."

"I'd prefer Demitri."

"I know you would. Maybe one day."

He pulls me into his arms, my favorite place to be.

"Think I could talk you into taking me on that date you've been talking about for months?" he asks, kissing my neck in that spot that makes me melt.

"I think we could arrange that. How does Mexican sound?"

"Almost as good as waffles from Sandy's."

"Demitri, are you craving Sandy's?"

"When am I not?"

"Children, we've got more training to get through before you start talking about food," Aunt Linda interrupts.

"God, she's a hard-ass," Demitri grumbles.

"I heard that! And I'm proud to say my ass is still quite hard."

"Aunt Linda!" we both groan.

"I have another question for you."

I look at Demitri, raising my brows. "What's that?"

"What are your thoughts about kids?"

"I don't know."

"You don't want any? You want twenty?"

"Dem. This is where you want to have this conversation?"

He shrugs. "Yeah. Why not?"

"Because your aunt and uncle are standing ten feet away from us, and I don't know if they should be privy to that?"

"Honey, who do you think asked him to ask you?" Aunt Linda laughs.

"This is a trap, isn't it?" I look at the three of them, Demitri genuinely curious, Aunt Linda suspicious, and Sasha expectant.

"Let me get this straight. You want to know after I spend two hours taking a self-defense refresher and then another hour at a gun range because this job might be dangerous if I want kids?"

"Umm-hmm," all three of them reply.

"The short answer is, I don't know. I never thought I'd have someone I trusted enough to even think about it. And I didn't want to do the 'pick a daddy from a book' and get inseminated. And now I'm *Aunt* Mia."

"I know taking up this mantle is important. People need you. But that doesn't mean you have to put your life on the line for it. You have options I didn't have when I started doing this, and then it was too late. I was and am happy with my life and what I chose. That doesn't mean you have to choose the same life."

"What options do I have?"

"You have people you can trust and rely on. You aren't

doing this alone. You have your girls that have the same spark you do, theirs are just hiding a little. You are the one in charge of your own destiny now, Mia. You've made it through hell and have surrounded yourself with the best. Choose your life knowing that."

"That's why you gave me so many keys?"

"Maybe."

Aunt Linda and her evasive answers.

"You haven't answered my question," Demitri whispers, pulling my attention back to him.

I take a deep breath and blow it out before answering him. "I'm not ready. I might be one day, but today isn't that day. I think we have this new adventure we need to try out before we decide sleepless nights and poop are in our future. Is that something you can live with?"

"It's absolutely something I can live with. But I'm open to it if it's something you want."

"You won't hate me if it never happens?"

"Not even a chance. I love you. Right now. I don't need anything more than that to make me a happy man."

"You're saying you want to spend the next couple of years practicing?"

"Oh, we're practicing. As much as possible. We're going to be pros when and if you decide it's what you want."

"I love you."

"Together." He smiles.

"Forever."

The End

Wondering where to go next? Meet Mia and the girls in Knowing Heart and Demitri in Victorious Heart—Daniel and Vic's story. Davis and crew can be found in the Boulder Canyon series.

Find them all with the QR code below!

BONUS BONUS EPILOGUE
MIA

SIX MONTHS AFTER THE SHELBY

"ARE YOU ALRIGHT?" Demitri asks from the other side of the closed bathroom door.

"Yeah, I think so. Just a stomach bug or something."

"A stomach bug that's only hit you once or twice a day and has lasted a week? Mia—"

"Nope. Don't say it."

"*Krasotka*, I think I have to."

"It's too soon. We didn't plan this."

"Baby, the best things happen when you aren't planning for them."

"Says you, who never plans for anything," I weakly argue. I turn on the sink and brush my teeth. When I open the door, Demitri is there waiting, and I fall into his arms.

"This wasn't on the agenda, Demitri. Ever."

"Are you that upset about it or just that it isn't when you wanted it?"

"I don't know."

He smiles. A soft smile that melts me a little. "It's okay to not know. But we should probably get a test on the way home today and confirm? And maybe avoid eating raw oysters and sushi?"

I gag. "Not gonna be a problem."

"Do you feel better now? Want some crackers?"

"Maybe physically, but I'm nowhere near ready for this, Dem."

"I know. But we'll figure it out together."

I follow him to the kitchen where he makes me sit down and eat some toast with butter and drink some ginger tea. I hate ginger tea. I'm a nervous wreck, but I know he's even more nervous. Today is a big day, regardless of what any test can tell us. Today, we meet the half-siblings Demitri has been keeping tabs on. I dutifully eat my toast and choke down the tea, feeling irrationally angry that it made me feel better.

For Demitri, I put a smile on my face. "Let's do this."

He grips my hand, and I realize he needs me today, and I won't let him down.

DEMITRI

We meet Sasha and Linda outside City Brews. It's closed for today's festivities. He's here to help answer any questions the people in the room might have. The family. I still have a hard time thinking of them as my siblings, but according to blood work, that's exactly what they are. We aren't going to talk about how we were able to get their blood to test their DNA. Joker would say it's 'mostly legal' and that's all I'm ever going to ask about it.

"You've got this." Linda smiles. "But would it be too much to introduce me as Aunt Linda?"

"Do I have to introduce Sasha as Uncle Sasha?"

"No!" he barks, laughing. "Just Sasha."

"Only for you, Linda."

"That's Aunt—"

"I know," I interrupt her. "You'll always be Aunt Linda to me. Promise. I just won't say aunt as often."

"Fine."

Sasha and Mia are still laughing at us and our never-ending picking. I only dropped the Aunt because I knew it annoyed the hell out of her, and if we're really related, that's my job, right?

I stop short when we enter the room. I was prepared for the eight siblings I know about, but the room is full. There are kids of various ages running around, and some older people who couldn't possibly be my siblings.

"What the fuck is this?" I turn to Linda, my body tensing up.

"It's family, Demitri. I think if you look at the older women, you might recognize them."

I turn back to the group, and she's right. All of them were in my house while I was growing up. Maids, nannies, assistants. Some of them look at me warily, others with a fondness I'm not sure my own mother was capable of.

"How do I start this?" I quietly ask Mia.

"Want me to do it for you?" she offers.

"Just be with me," I reply.

We walk to the front of the room as others attempt to wrangle the kids. When it's quiet, I wave. "Hi. So, there's a lot of you here." The group laughs. "I guess I should explain some things, huh?"

More laughter from the crowd, but no one is shooting daggers at me anymore.

"First, and most importantly, this is my wife, Mia."

Mia rolls her eyes at me and waves to the group.

"My name is Demitri Pavlov. In the real world, I go by John Smith. All of you are here because we're related."

The room erupts, some looking surprised and staring at their older counterparts. Others talk with the people with them. A few start edging toward the door, but Sasha stops them.

"Please, can you give me a few minutes to explain myself?" I ask. When everyone has settled down again, I begin. "I am the son of Ivan Pavlov. As are some of you. Where we differ in our lives is that you got out and survived. The day Ivan died, my life began without the influence of 'the family'. I'm not asking you for anything. I'm not requesting that we have a relationship and get together for holidays, but I would be open to it. I'm only asking that we talk. Officially meet. Tell you that you have someone out there who has your back if you need it. That's all."

Slowly, the people in the room start moving. Coming up and talking to me, introducing themselves. I don't tell them I already know who they are, but they also introduce their families. The mothers who are there all pull me in for a hug, crying about being so happy to see me. It's a surreal moment. Sasha talks to some of them, and people start eating the food we had brought in for today.

At some point Mia slips away, muttering something about needing the bathroom. I excuse myself and go looking for her when it's been a while, and find her in the corner by the bathrooms, wiping her eyes.

"*Krasotka*. What's wrong?"

"It's not time." She gives me a watery smile.

I know immediately what she's talking about, and I don't hessite to pull her into my arms. "It's not time."

"But I think maybe we talk about when the right time is?"

"Tomorrow, Mia. We'll talk tomorrow. After all, we have forever."

"Together."

THE END

MIA'S DRINK RECIPES

HANKY PANKY

A SWEET GIN martini

- 1 1/2 ounces gin
- 1 1/2 ounces sweet vermouth
- 2 dashes Fernet-Branca
- 1 dash orange juice
- Orange peel, for garnish

In a mixing glass filled with ice, pour the gin, sweet vermouth, and Fernet-Branca. Add a dash of orange juice if you like. Stir well, for at least 30 seconds. Twist an orange peel over the drink to express its oils, then lay it over the rim as a garnish. Serve and enjoy.

WET PUSSY

A concoction of deliciousness

- 1-part Vodka of your choice
- 1-Part Gin
- 1-Part Coconut Rum
- 1-part Peach Schnapps
- A splash of pineapple juice
- A splash of cranberry juice

In a shaker glass with ice, mix up the vodka, gin, coconut rum, peach schnapps, pineapple juice, and cranberry juice. Shake that bad boy up well! Pour into shot glasses. To make a larger batch for a drink, mix in a pitcher and pour over ice.

KERMIT THE FROG PISS

It's a shot. And it's green. A little sweet, a little sour.

- Midori melon liqueur: 1 oz
- Vodka: 1 oz (optionally, you can use rum or schnapps)
- Sour mix: 1 oz

Fill shaker with ice. Add Midori and other liquor of choice, and sour mix. Shake well. Strain into a chilled cocktail or shot glass. Serve and enjoy!

AIDEN
ROCK HILL BOOK TWO

My name is Aiden O'Connor. I'm a partner in ANON Security. I'm former military. I am the oldest son and one of the heirs to the Irish Mob in Boston. The Army is how I got out. They have tried to bring me back, but I keep fighting it. Now, I might not have a choice.

Nola Garcia is the quiet proofreader. She's smart, beautiful, and off limits for so many reasons. She's forbidden, and some people will stop at nothing to make sure it never happens.

My cousin has called me home, separating me from the life I've built and the woman I can't get out of my head. Only for him would I make that trip.

When her life is put in danger, it's up to me and those I trust to put an end to the violence and save her.

I walked away from my family, but I can't walk away from her. I'll fight to be with her—and I don't care if it's against my family or her demons.

My name is Aiden O'Connor. And I'm a man willing to destroy everything for her.

Available on Amazon

ALSO BY CM SMITH

BRIAR MOUNTAIN

Victoria Thorpe is back in Briar Mountain. And she's bringing trouble with her.

As the Thorpe sisters close ranks to protect their own, one by one they find themselves tested by new loves and old enemies.

And each of them will have a choice to make: Keep their hearts locked away and safe...or risk everything for love.

Trusting Heart

Courageous Heart

Knowing Heart

Victorious Heart

Briar Mountain Box Set—Complete Series with Bonus Material including Falling Heart Novella—Available in eBook only

BOULDER CANYON

Boulder Canyon is a town split between those that have everything and those that have nothing by a literal set of train tracks.

For those that have everything, life isn't always what it seems. For those that appear to have nothing, looks can be deceiving.

What happens when paths begin to cross, and secrets are revealed? Because not everything is as it appears in this small town.

Love Comes Home

Love Saves Home

Love Finds Home

Love Takes Home

ROCK HILL

**When the past comes for revenge, what will you do to save the
ones you love?**

Rock Hill is a small-town with big secrets. The mountain range is the
perfect place for notorious families to merge, for histories to come
out, and for love to find a way.

Past traumas, new realities, and the lengths one will go to in order to
protect those they love will be tested.

Welcome to Rock Hill

Demitri

Aiden

For Up-To-Date information on all things CM Smith, please scan the
QR code below for direct access to her website, Amazon Author
page, and Bonus Material.

You can find me on Facebook and IG
as cm_smith_writer_chick, email me
at cmsmith@cmsmithauthor.com, or
visit my website and online store at
www.cmsmithauthor.com

Hope to see you around!

ACKNOWLEDGMENTS

Welcome to the start of a new series! Seriously, how? I hope you found some joy in reading about Mia's journey to healing and Demitri's realization that family is what you make it.

There are always so many people to thank and I never know where to start. For this one, I'm going to start in a different order. I'm going to thank Dr. Jen Greenberg. When I started writing this one, I knew Mia was going to have problems with intimacy. Who better to talk through things with than a sex therapist? She put my mind at ease that I was on the right path and helped me flesh out some things. Plus, she's awesome as fuck.

Which means I need to thank Michelle Fewer. I met Dr. Jen because of her, and what she's created on the beach in the middle of winter is amazing. She brought a group of women together at all stages of their writing journey and created something magical. I can't think of it without tearing up, and I hope I never do.

Speaking of what Michelle created, she gave me the best roomies two years in a row. Golden Angel and Stella Moore the first year—yes! Stella is real, and she has some amazing books! You should check out her and Golden both! This year, I was assigned Jackie Walker. Insomniacs unite! We laughed, we wrote, we stayed up all damn night! It was awesome! I got to hug my Meg Fitz and share a plane ride with Margaret Kay. AJ Ranney was there, too, and I left with new friends, lots of laughs, and almost a whole book written.

Linda! You are my person. I joke that you're the boss of

this whole thing, but the reality is, I couldn't do this without you.

Quinn, this will be you one day, sitting here, trying to figure out all the people you want to thank and blanking on all the names lol. Love you, and can't wait to see what you can do!

Brandi, I love you! I also love that you were fine seeing me tear up by putting me on FaceTime with Carrie Ann.

To my readers, you are amazing humans. The future is uncertain, but I'm glad you're here!

To the Mr. I love you, always. Next week we celebrate nineteen years of being Mr. and Mrs. Smith, and I love you more every year.

To my boys, who are all home with me right now. The future is bright, and I can't wait to see what you all do with the opportunities you have!

To my third shift crew—thank you for putting up with me and my plot bunnies and final edits frenzy. Liz, you are wonderful. Kyle, you da man. LaMichael, you'll never know your name is in here. Jeremiah, I'm proud to call you my adopted son. Now leave LaMichael alone. Nate and Nick—thanks for letting me off the hook with the PSB every once in a while. And Shena, thanks for talking narrators and books with me.

Finally, to all the women out there who have been through their own traumas. For those who are still healing, and those who have managed to come out stronger on the other side. For those who still wonder if it's worth it every day—know that it is always worth it. You are worth it.

This whole series will show the highs and lows of healing from trauma. It might be a little dark at times, but I will always try to show the light. To show that it's worth it.

ABOUT THE AUTHOR

CM Smith lives in a world where small-town romances all have family, love, and steam. And of course, her small towns wouldn't be complete without some suspense. She loves giving the bad guys what they have coming.

CM Smith is a mom of three boys, two boy dogs, and one husband. Most days, she's wondering if the dogs are plotting to replace her in the bed and if the kids are planning a revolt. When she told her Mr. that she wanted to write romance books, he shrugged and said have fun. And she's enjoyed every minute of the process since.

CM is a lifelong reader. She loves all books, but found her passion in romance books. Happy reading!